Castaways

of the

FLYING
DUTCHMAN

OTHER BOOKS BY BRIAN JACQUES

Redwall

Mossflower

Mattimeo

Mariel of Redwall

Salamandastron

Martin the Warrior

The Bellmaker

Outcast of Redwall

Pearls of Lutra

The Long Patrol

Marlfox

The Legend of Luke

Lord Brocktree

The Great Redwall Feast

The Redwall Map and Riddler

Redwall Friend and Foe

Build Your Own Redwall Abbey

Seven Strange and Ghostly Tales

BRIAN JACQUES

Castaways

of the

FLYING DUTCHMAN

Illustrated by Ian Schoenherr

PUFFIN BOOKS

PUFFIN BOOKS

Published by the Penguin Group
Penguin Books Ltd, 27 Wrights Lane, London W8 5TZ, England
Penguin Books USA Inc., 375 Hudson Street, New York, New York 10014, USA
Penguin Books Australia Ltd, Ringwood, Victoria, Australia
Penguin Books Canada Ltd, 10 Alcorn Avenue, Toronto, Ontario, Canada M4V 3B2
Penguin Books India (P) Ltd, 11 Community Centre, Panchsheel Park, New Delhi –
110 017, India
Penguin Books (NZ) Ltd, Cnr Rosedale and Airborne Roads, Albany, Auckland, New Zealand
Penguin Books (South Africa) (Pty) Ltd, 5 Watkins Street, Denver Ext 4, Johannesburg 2094,
South Africa

On the World Wide Web at: www.penguin.com

Penguin Books Ltd, Registered Offices: Harmondsworth, Middlesex, England

First published in the USA by Philomel Books a division of Penguin Putnam Books for Young
Readers 2001
First published in Great Britain by Viking 2001
Published in Puffin Books 2001

2

Made and printed in England by Clays Ltd, St Ives plc

British Library Cataloguing in Publication Data
A CIP catalogue record for this book is available from the British Library

ISBN 0–141–31284–X

HE LEGEND OF THE *FLYING DUTCHMAN*. Who knows how it all began: Throughout the centuries many a seaman could swear an oath that he had seen the phantom ship. Ploughing an endless course over storm-tossed seas and the deeps of mighty oceans. Many a night, mariners have sat together in lantern-lit fo'c'sle heads, speaking in hushed tones of the vessel, and its master, Captain Vanderdecken. What awful curse sent the *Flying Dutchman* bound on an eternal voyage, across the trackless watery wastes, from the Marquesas to the Arctic Circle, from the Coral Seas to the Yucatán Straits, forever roaming alone? Whenever the ghostly craft is sighted, death is near. Bad fortune hovers about those poor sailors, who see by chance what they wish their eyes had never witnessed.

The *Flying Dutchman*!

Salt-stiff rigging and gale-torn sails flapping eerily, a barnacle-crusted prow, down by the bow in soughing troughs of blue-green waves. Crewed by silent wraiths of humanity to whom time and the elements have no end. Vanderdecken paces the quarterdeck, his face like ancient yellow parchment, hair laced by flying spume, wild, hopeless eyes searching the horizons of the world. Bound to the sea for eternity. For what dread crime? Which unspoken law of man, nature, or God, did he break? What dread nemesis doomed him, his crew, and their ship?

Who knows how it all began?

Only two living beings!

I take up my pen to tell you the tale.

THE SHIP

COPENHAGEN. 1620.

THEY SAT FACING ONE ANOTHER ACROSS A table in the upper room of a drinking den known as the Barbary Shark. Two men. One a Dutch sea captain, the other a Chinese gem dealer. Muffled sounds of foghorns from the night-time harbour, mingling with the raucous seaport din outside, passed unheeded. A flagon of fine gin and a pitcher of water, close to hand, also stood ignored. In the dim, smoke-filtered atmosphere, both men's eyes were riveted upon a small, blue velvet packet, which the gem dealer had placed upon the table.

Slowly he unwrapped the cloth, allowing a large emerald to catch facets of the golden lantern light. It shimmered like the eye of some fabled dragon. Noting the reflected glint in the Dutchman's avaricious stare, the Chinaman placed his long-nailed hand over the jewel and spoke softly. "My agent waits in Valparaiso for the arrival of a certain man—somebody who can bring home to me a package. It contains the brothers and sisters of this green stone, many of them! Some larger, others smaller, but any one of them worth a fortune.

Riches to fire a man beyond his wildest dreams. He who brings the green stones to me must be a strong man, commanding and powerful, able to keep my treasure from the hands of others. My friend, I have eyes and ears everywhere on the waterfront. I chose you because I know you to be such a man!"

The captain's eyes, bleak and grey as winter seas, held the merchant's gaze. "You have not told me what my reward for this task will be."

The gem dealer averted his eyes from the captain's fearsome stare. He lifted his hand, exposing the emerald's green fire. "This beautiful one, and two more like it upon delivery."

The Dutchman's hand closed over the stone as he uttered a single word. "Done!"

The boy ran, mouth wide open, gasping to draw in the fog-laden air. His broken shoes slapped wetly over the harbour cobblestones. Behind him the heavy, well-shod feet of his pursuers pounded, drawing closer all the time. He staggered, forcing himself to keep going, stumbling through pools of yellow tavern lights, on into the milky, muffling darkness. Never would he go back, never again would the family of his stepfather treat him like an animal, a drudge, a slave! Cold sweat streamed down into his eyes as he forced his leaden legs onward. Life? No sane being could call that life: a mute, dumb from birth, with no real father to care for him. His mother, frail creature, did not live long after her marriage to Bjornsen, the herring merchant. After her death the boy was forced to live in a cellar. Bjornsen and his three hulking sons treated their captive no better than a dog. The boy ran with the resounding clatter of Bjornsen's sons close behind him. His one aim was to escape them and their miserable existence. Never would he go back. Never!

A scarfaced Burmese seaman crept swiftly downstairs, where he joined four others at a darkened corner of the Barbary Shark tavern. He nodded to his cohorts, whispering, "Kapitan come now!"

They were all sailors of varied nationalities, as villainous a bunch of wharf rats as ever to put foot on shipboard. Drawing further back into the shadows, they watched the staircase, which led from the upper room. The long blue scar on the face of the Burmese twitched as he winked at the others.

"I 'ear all, Kapitan goes for the green stones!"

A heavily bearded Englishman smiled thinly. "So, we ain't just takin' a cargo of ironware out to Valparaiso. Who does Vanderdecken think he's foolin', eh? He's only goin' out there to pick up a king's ransom of precious stones!"

A hawkfaced Arab drew a dagger from his belt. "Then we collect our wages, yes?"

The Englander, who was the ringleader, seized the Arab's wrist. "Aye, we'll live like lords for the rest of our lives, mate. But you stow that blade, an' wait 'til I gives the word."

They took another drink before leaving the Barbary Shark.

The boy stood facing his pursuers—he was trapped, with no place to run, his back to the sea. Bjornsen's three big sons closed in on the edge of the wharf, where their victim stood gasping for air and trembling in the fogbound night. Reaching out, the tallest of the trio grabbed the lad's shirtfront.

With a muted animal-like grunt, the boy sank his teeth into his captor's hand. Bjornsen's son roared in pain, releasing his quarry and instinctively lashing out with his good hand. He cuffed the boy a heavy blow to his jaw. Stunned, the youngster reeled backwards, missed his footing, and fell from the top of the wharf pylons, splashing into the sea. He went straight down and under the surface.

Kneeling on the edge, the three brothers stared into the dim, greasy depths. A slim stream of bubbles broke the surface. Then nothing. Fear registered on the brutish face of the one who had done the deed, but he recovered his composure quickly, warning the other two.

"We could not find him, nobody will know. He had no relatives in the world. What's another dumb fool more or less? Come on!"

Checking about to see that they had not been noticed in the dark and fog, the trio scurried off home.

Standing at the gangplank, the Dutch captain watched the last of his crew emerge from the misty swaths which wreathed the harbour. He gestured them aboard.

"Drinking again, *jah*? Well, there be little enough to get drunk on 'tween here and the Pacific side of the Americas. Come, get aboard now, make ready to sail!"

The blue scar contracted as the Burmese smiled. "Aye, aye, Kapitan, we make sail!"

With floodtide swirling about her hull and the stern fenders scraping against the wharf timbers, the vessel came about facing seaward. Staring ahead into the fog, the captain brought the wheel about half a point and called, "Let go aft!"

A Finnish sailor standing astern flicked the rope expertly, jerking the noosed end off the bollard which held it. The rope splashed into the water. Shivering in the cold night air, he left it to trail along, not wanting to get his hands wet and frozen by hauling the backstay rope aboard. He ran quickly into the galley and held his hands out over the warm stove.

The boy was half in and half out of consciousness, numbed to his bones in the cold sea. He felt the rough manila rope brush against his cheek and seized it. Painfully, hand over hand, he hauled himself upward. When his feet touched ship's timber, the boy pulled his body clear of the icy sea and found a ledge. He huddled on it, looking up at the name painted on the vessel's stern in faded, gold-embellished red. *Fleiger Hollander.*

He had never learned to read, so the letters meant nothing to him. Fleiger Hollander in Dutch, or had the lad been able to understand English, Flying Dutchman.

MORNING LIGHT FOUND THE FOG HAD lifted, revealing a clear blue icy day. The *Flying Dutchman* ploughed past Goteborg under full sail, ready to round the  Skagen point and sail down the Skagerrak out into the wide North Sea. Philip Vanderdecken, captain of the vessel, braced himself on the small fo'c'sle deck, feeling the buck and swell of his ship. Light spray from the bow wave touched his face, ropes and canvas thrummed to the breeze overhead.

Valparaiso bound, where his share of the green stones would make him a rich man for life, he was never a man to smile, but he allowed himself a single bleak nod of satisfaction. Let the shipowners find another fool to sail this slop-bucket around the high seas. Leave this crew of wharfscum to pit their wits against another captain. He strode from one end of the vessel to the other, snapping curt commands at the surly bunch that manned the craft. Often he would wheel suddenly about—Vanderdecken neither liked nor trusted his crew. Judging by the glances he received and the muttered conversations that ceased at his approach, he knew they were speculating about the trip, plotting against him in some way probably.

His solution to this was simple: keep the hands busy night and day, show them who was master. Vanderdecken's quick eye missed nothing; he glanced past the steersman to the ice-crusted rope left trailing astern. Signalling the Finnish deckhand with a nod, he pointed. "Stow that line and coil it, or the seawater will ruin it!"

The deckhand was about to make some remark; when he noted the challenging look in the captain's eye, he touched his cap. "Aye aye, Kapitan!"

Vanderdecken was making his way amidships when the Finn leaned over the stern rail, shouting. "Come look here— a boy, I think he's dead!"

All hands hurried to the stern, crowding the rail to see. Pushing his way roughly through, the captain stared down at the crumpled figure on the moulding below his cabin gallery. Crouched there was a boy, stiff with seawater and frost.

Vanderdecken turned to the men, his voice harsh and flat. "Leave him there or push him into the sea, I don't care."

The ship's cook was a fat, bearded Greek, who had left his galley to see what all the excitement was about. He spoke up.

"I don't have galley boy. If he's alive, I take him!"

The captain gave the cook a scornful glance. "He'd be better off dead than working for you, Petros. Ah, do what you want. The rest of you get back to work!"

Lumbering down to the stern cabin, Petros opened the window and dragged the lad in. To all apparent purposes, the boy looked dead, though when the Greek cook placed a knife blade near his lips, a faint mist clouded it. "By my beard, he breathes!"

He carried the boy to the galley and laid him on some sacking in a corner near the stove. The ship's mate, an Englishman, came into the galley for a drink of water. Placing the toe of his boot against the boy's body, he nudged him. The lad did not respond.

The Englander shrugged. "Looks dead to me, I'd sling him over the side if I was you."

Petros pointed with his keen skinning knife at the Englander. "Well, you not me, see. I say he stays. If he comes around, I need help in this galley, lots of help. He's mine!"

Backing off from the knife, the Englander shook his head. "Huh, yours? Like the cap'n said, that one'd be better dead!"

For almost two days the boy lay there. On the second evening Petros was making a steaming stew of salt cod, turnips, and barley. Blowing on the ladle, he tasted a bit. As he did this, the Greek cast a glance down at the boy. His eyes were wide open, gazing hungrily at the stewpot.

"So, my little fish lives, eh?"

The boy's mouth opened, but no sound came out. Petros took a greasy-looking wooden bowl and ladled some stew into it, then placed it in the boy's open hands. "Eat!" It was bubbling hot, but that did not seem to deter the lad. He bolted it down and held the empty bowl up to the cook. The bowl went spinning from his grasp as Petros hit it with the ladle, narrowing his eyes pitilessly.

"No free trippers aboard this ship, little fish. I caught you, now you belong to me. When I say work, you work. When I say eat, you eat. When I say sleep, you sleep. Got it? But you won't hear me saying eat or sleep much. It will be mostly work, hard work! Or back over the side you go. Do you believe me?"

He wrenched the boy upright and reached for his knife.

The wide-eyed youngster nodded furiously.

Petros filled a pail with water, tossing in a broken holy-stone and a piece of rag, then thrust it at his slave. "You clean this galley out good, deckheads, bulkheads, the lot! Hey, what's your name, you got a name?"

The boy pointed to his mouth and made a small, strained noise.

Petros kicked him. "What's the matter, you got no tongue?"

The Arab had just walked in. He grabbed the boy's jaw and forced his mouth open. "He has a tongue."

Petros turned back to stirring the stew. "Then why doesn't he talk? Are you dumb, boy?"

The lad nodded vigorously. The Arab released him. "You can have a tongue and still not be able to talk. He's dumb."

Petros filled a bowl for the Arab and made a mark by a row of symbols on a wooden board to show the Arab had received his food. "Dumb or not, he can still work. Here, Jamil, take this to the kapitan." He indicated a meal set out on a tray.

The Arab ignored his request. Sitting close to the stove, he started eating. "Take it yourself."

The boy found himself hauled upright again. Petros was acting out a strange pantomime, as many fools do who think somebody is stupid merely because they cannot speak. "You go, take this to Kapitan . . . Kapitan, understand?" Petros stood to attention, mimicked Vanderdecken's stance, then made as if he were a captain dining, tucking an imaginary napkin into his shirtfront. "Kapitan eat, understand. Hey, Jamil, what you call a boy with no name?"

"Nebuchadnezzar."

Petros looked askance at the Arab. "What sort of name that?"

Jamil broke ship's biscuit into his stew and stirred it. "I hear a Christian read it once, from a Bible book. Good, eh, Nebuchadnezzar—I like that name!"

Petros scratched his big, grimy beard. "Nebu . . . Nebu. Is too hard to say. I call you Neb, that'll do!" He presented the boy with the tray, then poked his finger several times into the lad's narrow chest.

"Neb, Neb, you called Neb now. Take this to Kapitan, Neb. Go careful—spill any and I skin you with my knife, yes?"

Neb nodded solemnly and left the galley as if he were walking on eggs.

Jamil slurped stew noisily. "Hah, he understand, all right. He'll learn."

Petros stroked his knife edge against a greased stone. "Neb better learn . . . or else!"

A timid knock sounded on the captain's cabin door. Somehow or other Neb had found his way there. Vanderdecken looked up from the single emerald he had been given as part payment. Stuffing it swiftly into his vest pocket, he called out, "Come!"

As the door opened, the Dutchman had his hand on a sword set on a ledge under the table edge. None of the crew would ever catch him napping; that would be a fatal error. A look of mild surprise passed across his hardened features as the boy entered with a tray of food. Vanderdecken indicated the table with a glance. Neb set the tray there.

"So, you never died after all. Do you know who I am, boy?"

Neb nodded twice, watching for the next question.

"Can you not speak?"

Neb shook his head twice. He stood looking at the deck, aware of the captain's piercing stare, waiting to be dismissed.

"Maybe 'tis no bad thing, I've heard it said that silence is golden. Are you golden, boy? Are you lucky, or are you a Jonah, an unlucky one, eh?"

Neb shrugged expressively. The captain's hand strayed to his vest pocket, and he patted it.

"Luck is for fools who believe that sort of thing. I make my own luck. I, Vanderdecken, master of the *Flying Dutchman*!"

Immediately he applied himself to the food. Wrinkling his nose in distaste, he looked up at Neb. "Are you still here? Off with you—begone, boy!"

Bobbing his head respectfully, Neb retreated from the cabin.

Next day and every day after that was much the same for Neb, punctuated with oaths, kicks, and smarting blows from the knotted rope that the fat, greasy sea cook Petros had taken to carrying. The lad was used to this kind of treatment, having suffered much of it at the hands of the Bjornsen family. Aboard the *Flying Dutchman* the only difference was that there was nowhere to run and fewer places to hide.

However, Neb bore the ill usage. Being mute and not able to complain had made him, above all, a survivor. He had grown to possess a quiet, resolute strength. Neb hatred Petros, along with the rest of the crew, who showed him neither pity nor friendliness. The captain was a different matter. The boy knew that Vanderdecken was feared by every soul aboard. He had a ruthless air of power about him that scared Neb, though he was not needlessly cruel, providing his orders were obeyed swiftly and without question. The boy's survival instincts told him that he was safer with the captain than the others, a fact he accepted stoically.

ESBJERG WAS THE LAST PLACE IN DENMARK the *Flying Dutchman* would touch before sailing out into the North Sea and down through the English Channel. Beyond  that she was bound into the great Atlantic Ocean. Some of the crew were ordered ashore to bring back final provisions. Petros and the Englander mate headed the party. Captain Vanderdecken stayed in his cabin, poring over charts. Before he departed, the Greek cook grabbed Neb and shackled him by the ankle to the foot of the iron galley stove.

"No good giving you the chance to run off just when I'm training you right. Slaves are scarce in Denmark. You can reach the table. There's salt pork and cabbage to chop for the pot, keep you busy. I'm taking my knife with me, use that old one. You know what will happen if the work's not done by the time I get back, eh?"

He waved the knotted rope at the boy, then waddled out to join the others who were off to the ship's chandlery.

Neb could move only a short distance either way because of the iron slave shackle—escape was out of the question. Through the open door he could see the jetty the ship was moored to. Freedom, so near, yet so far away. He applied himself to the task of chopping the pork and cabbage. It was hard work. The knife had a broken handle and a dull blade. In his frustration, he vented his feelings upon the meat and vegetable, chopping furiously. At least it was warm inside the galley. Outside it was a cold, grey afternoon, with rain drizzling steadily down. He sat on the floor by the stove, watching the jetty for the crew returning. They had been gone for some hours.

A half-starved dog wandered furtively along the jetty, sniffing for scraps. Neb watched the wretched creature. Despite his own plight, the boy's heart went out to it. The dog was barely identifiable as a black labrador, half grown, but emaciated. Ribs showed through its mud-caked and scarred fur. One of its eyes was closed over and running. It sniffed up and down the timbers, getting closer to the ship. Poor creature, it seemed ready to take off and bolt at the slightest noise. It had been badly served by some master—that is, if it had ever known an owner.

Pursing his lips together, the boy made encouraging sounds. The dog stopped sniffing and looked up at him. He held out his open palms to it and smiled. It put its head on one side, regarding him through its one great, sad, dark eye. Neb took a piece of salt-pork rind and tossed it to the dog. Gratefully it golloped the scrap down, wagging its tail. He made the noise again and took more rind, holding it out to the dog. Without hesitation it came straight up the gangplank and boarded the ship. Within seconds the boy was stroking the labrador's wasted body while it devoured the food. There was plenty of tough rind left from the salt pork, sometimes the hands used it for bait to fish over the side at sea.

While the dog ate, Neb took a rag and some warm water with salt in it. The dog allowed him to bathe its eye. Freed from the crust and debris of some old infection, its eye grad-ually opened—it was clear and undamaged. Neb was pleased and hugged his newfound friend. He was rewarded by several huge, sloppy licks from the dog's tongue. Knowing the effects of salt-pork rind, he gave it a pannikin of fresh water. As the dog curled up by the galley stove, a fierce affection for the ownerless creature burned within Neb. He decided there and then that he was going to keep it.

Spreading some old sacks under the far corner of the table, he pushed the dog onto them, all the time petting and stroking it. His new friend made no fuss, but went quietly and willingly into the hiding place, staring at him with great trust-ing eyes as he covered it with more sacks. Neb peeped into the secret den. He looked warningly at the dog and held a finger to his tight-shut lips. It licked his hand, as if it understood to remain silent.

A sound from behind caused Neb to scuttle out from be-neath the table. Captain Vanderdecken stood framed in the galley doorway, his teeth grinding as his jaw worked back and forth. Neb cowered, expecting to be kicked. Normally he slept beneath the galley table, but only when told to go to bed. The captain's voice had the ring of steel in it.

"Where's Petros and the rest, not back yet?"

Wide-eyed with fear, the boy shook his head.

Vanderdecken's fists clenched and unclenched, and he spat out the words viciously. "Drinking! That's where the use-less swine will be, pouring gin and ale down their slobbering faces in some drinking den!" He stamped off, raving through clenched teeth, "If I miss the floodtide because of a bunch of drunken animals, I'll take a swordblade to them!"

Neb knew by the captain's frightening eyes that there was

going to be trouble, no matter whether the crew arrived back early or late. For refuge he crawled back under the table and hid with his dog. A warm tongue licked his cheek as he huddled close to the black labrador, staring into its soft, dark eyes and stroking its thin neck. Neb wished fervently that he could talk, to speak gently and reassure the dog. All that came from his mouth was a hoarse little sound. It was enough. The dog whimpered quietly, laying its head on his lap, reinforcing the growing bond between them.

Less than an hour later, hurried and stumbling footsteps rang out on the jetty. Neb peered out. The five men who had been sent for provisions came tumbling aboard, followed by Vanderdecken like an avenging angel. He laid about them with the knotted rope end that he had snatched from Petros, thrashing them indiscriminately, his voice thundering out with righteous wrath.

"Brainless gin-sodden morons. Half a day lost because of your stupidity! Can't you keep your snouts out of flagons long enough to do a simple task? Worthless scum!"

The Dutchman showed no mercy. He flogged the five hands with furious energy, savagely booting flat any man who tried to rise or crawl away. Neb could not tear his eyes from the fearful scene. The captain's coattails whirled about him as he flogged the miscreants. Knotted rope striking flesh and bone sounded like chestnuts cracking on a hearth amid the sobs and screams of his victims.

When Vanderdecken had exhausted his energy, he flung some coins at the chandler's assistant, waiting by the jetty with a loaded cart. "You, get those supplies aboard before we lose the tide!"

Whilst the materials were being transferred, Petros raised

his bruised and tearstained face. He had spotted something none of the others had noticed. The emerald glinted on the deck where it had fallen from the captain's pocket when he was beating the crewmen.

Slowly, carefully, the fat cook stretched out his grimy hand to retrieve the gemstone.

"Eeeeyaaaargh!" he screeched as the Dutchman's boot heel smashed down on the back of his hand. Vanderdecken snatched the emerald, continuing to grind Petros's hand against the deck, thrusting all his weight onto the iron-tipped heel.

"Thief! Drunkard! Pirate! No man steals from me! There, now we have a one-handed cook. Back to work, all of you, cast off for'ard, aft and midships! Make sail, leave no lines drifting, coil them shipshape. Seamen? I'll make seamen of you before this voyage is out!"

He stormed off to take the steersman's place at the wheel.

Whimpering and moaning piteously, Petros crawled into the galley, falling flat on Neb's outstretched leg, which was still chained to the stove. Raising his tearstained face to the boy, he sobbed piteously. "He broke my hand, see. Petros's hand smashed, an' what for? Nothing, that's what for. Nothing!"

Neb felt sick just looking at the hand. It was wretched beyond healing, a horrific sight. Blubbering into his greasy beard, the cook looked to Neb for help. "Fix it for me, boy. Make bandage for poor Petros's hand."

Neb felt no pity for the fat, wicked cook. He was secretly glad that the hand that had often beaten him was now useless, but he had to get the man upright before he looked under the table. The boy made his muted noise and pointed at the chain, indicating he could do nothing until he was freed.

Amid much groaning and wincing, Petros found the key with his good hand and unlocked the shackle. Neb helped him up onto a bench, where he sat weeping and nursing his hand.

Drizzling rain gave way to a clear evening. Ropes and lines thrummed as the vessel's sail bellied tautly, backed by a stiffening breeze. The wheel spun under Vanderdecken's experienced hands as he guided the *Flying Dutchman* out into deeper waters. It was well out to sea by the time Neb was done with his ministrations. Medical supplies were virtually nil aboard the vessel, but the boy used some relatively clean strips of coarse linen from a palliasse cover. Tearing the cloth into strips, he soaked them in clean, salted water and bound the hand and arm from fingertips to elbow. Petros howled as the salt stung broken bone and torn, swollen flesh, but he knew the salt would clear up any infection.

All the time Neb's dog stayed silent in his hiding place.

The Englander and Jamil came furtively into the galley. Petros kept up his whining, glad he had more of an audience to listen to his complaints. "See, the poor hand of Petros. What use is a man at sea with only one good hand? I ask you, my friends, was there any need for that devil to do this to me?"

The Englander ignored the cook's misfortune. "What did you try to pick up off the deck, something that belonged to the cap'n, eh?"

Petros held out his good hand to the pair. "Help me to my cabin, Scraggs. You, too, Jamil. The boy is too small for me to lean on. Help me."

Scraggs, the Englander, grabbed the bandaged hand from

its sling. "What did you pick up off the deck? Tell us."

"Nothing, my friend. It was nothing, I swear!"

Jamil's curved dagger was at Petros's throat. "You lie. Tell us what it was or I'll give you another mouth, right across your filthy neck. Speak!"

Petros knew they meant business, so he spoke rapidly. "It was the green stone, the dragon's eye. A man could have bought three tavernas with it!"

Scraggs shook his head knowingly and smiled at Jamil. "See, I told you: emeralds. That's what this trip's about." Looking hugely satisfied that his hunch had been confirmed, Scraggs strode from the galley, leaving Jamil to help Petros to his cabin. Scraggs paused in the doorway and pointed his own knife in Neb's direction.

"Not a word of this to anyone, lad. D'ye hear?"

Neb nodded vigorously.

The Englander smiled at his own mistake. "How could you say a word, you're a mute."

THE *FLYING DUTCHMAN* WAS NOW ON course, cutting the coast of Germany and the Netherlands, picking up the English Channel currents. Neb had spent a happy few days. Petros refused to leave his  bunk, and lay in his cabin, moaning night and day. Alone in the galley, Neb cooked for all hands. The menu was not difficult to contend with—salt cod or salt pork, boiled up with whatever came to hand: cabbage, turnips, kale. Neb threw it all in a cooking pot and boiled it with pepper and salt. Now and then, to satisfy his longing for something sweet he would pound up some ship's biscuit, damp it down into a paste, mix in a bit of dried fruit—figs, apricots, and raisins. Baked up in the oven, this made a stodgy pie. There were no complaints, in fact one of the hands remarked that it was an improvement on the Greek's efforts.

Neb decided to call his dog Denmark, that being the country from which they both came. There was a marked change in the black labrador. Overnight under his young master's care he had grown bigger, sleeker, and healthier. A very intelligent dog, quiet and obedient. At a quick nod from the boy, Denmark would immediately go to his place under the table.

Neb worked hard around the galley. As long as the crew got their meals, they seldom came near the place. In the forecastle of the *Flying Dutchman* was a big cabin, where the crew ate and slept; Neb had to go there every day, usually in the evening. He would brew fresh coffee in a large urn—it always had to be on tap for any hands to drink hot, night or day.

They were sailing through the English Channel—the white cliffs of Dover could be glimpsed from the fo'c'sle head. Crewmen coming off watch were bustling in, pale-skinned from the cold. At the urn, they guzzled down earthenware mugs of the cheap coffee. It was strong and black. Made from roasted acorns, chicory, and a few coffee beans, it tasted bitter, but it was a hot drink.

Neb was pouring boiling water into the urn, the crew ignoring him completely. Because he could not talk, they treated him as deaf, dumb, and dim-witted, a thing people did to anyone not the same as themselves. Neb could see their faces in the surface of the copper urn, which he had polished earlier. Though they whispered, the boy heard every word of the conversation between Scraggs, Jamil, and the Burmese scarface, whose name was Sindh. They were plotting against the captain.

"You go into his cabin with a blade while he sleeps."

"Oh no, not Jamil. They say the Dutchman never sleeps."

"Stay out of that cabin, my friend. He keeps a sharp sword there, always near at hand. If we want to finish Vanderdecken, it must be done by us all, swiftly, out on deck. That way he can be thrown right over the side an' we sail off, eh?"

Scraggs sipped his coffee thoughtfully. "Aye, you're right,

Sindh . . . when 'tis good and quiet. When he comes out to check on the night watch before turning in. That's the best time."

The scar on Sindh's face twitched. "Good, me an' Jamil will change watches with the two out there later tonight. You can hide yourself on deck."

A stiletto blade gleamed as Scraggs laid it on the table. "You two grab him, I'll give our cap'n a swift taste of this beauty, then we strip the body and he's ready for the fishes!"

Sindh traced his blue scar with a cracked fingernail. "When the kapitan is gone, what then, Scraggs, my friend? One green stone is hard to split three ways."

Scraggs winked at them both. "Then I take command. We sail her to Valparaiso and I as cap'n pick up the rest of the stones. There should be plenty to go round 'twixt three then."

Sindh thought about this for a moment before replying. "Why can't I be kapitan, or Jamil here?"

"Because I'm an Englander, I look more like a Dutchy than you two ever could, an' I speak the lingo. Any objections?" Scraggs toyed with the dangerous-looking stiletto, watching them. Jamil smiled and patted the mate's hand.

"Of course not, my friend, it is a good plan. But I do have a harmless little question. What happens when we have both the ship and the stones? We cannot sail back to Europe."

"Simple, we follow the coast up north until we sight a place called Costa Rica. Anchor up there to take on fresh water and fruit. While the crew are busy doing that, we jump ship. Other side of the mountain there is the Caribbean Sea, Hispaniola, Cartagena, Maracaibo, beyond the reach of law. Sunny climes, blue seas, golden sands, an' we three, rich as kings. Think of it—we could build our own castles, own ships, employ servants, or buy slaves. That would do me fine, never to feel another cold day for life!"

Petros came stumping through from a cabin that led off the main one. The conspirators nudged one another and fell silent. The Greek cook clipped Neb's ear with his good hand. "You never brought me any coffee. Get on, boy, leave some on the table by my bunk!" Obediently Neb poured a bowl of coffee and hurried through to the other cabin, with Petros following, berating him. "After all I do for you, save your life, feed you, teach you how to be sea cook. This is how you treat Petros. I should have left you for the fishes. Don't spill that coffee, put it down there. Not there . . . there! Get out of here and leave me now. Nobody wants a poor sea cook with one hand. I'm in pain night and day, with not a soul to care. Out, out!"

Neb retired gratefully to his galley.

Sitting beneath the table with his dog, Neb stroked Denmark as he pondered his dilemma. Three crewmen were planning to murder the captain! From what Neb had seen of the Dutchman's crew, he knew they were lawless drunkards and thieves. Vanderdecken was a hard and cruel ship's master, but he was the only one aboard who could keep the vessel running in an orderly and disciplined manner. Without a proper captain the alternatives were bleak. Neb doubted that such a wayward bunch would take orders from Scraggs, nor was he sure the Englander would be able to bring them to their destination safely. Even if he did, what then? How could he warn the captain of the plot on his life? Vanderdecken would take scant notice of his crew's lowliest member, a dumb, mute boy. The dog watched Neb with its soft, dark eyes. As if sensing his dilemma, it licked the boy's hand and gave a single low whine.

Later that evening footsteps sounded out on deck. Neb nodded to Denmark, and the dog vanished beneath the table to its hideout. The boy peered around the galley door. There was Vanderdecken, emerging from his cabin at the stern. Coming toward him from midships were the two hands, Jamil and Sindh. The boy's stomach went into a knot of anxiety. He could feel a pounding in his chest.

Somewhere between the captain and the two crewmen, Scraggs was waiting in hiding, holding the stiletto ready. A thousand things raced through Neb's brain, silly inconsequential ideas. He dismissed them all. What could he do?

The captain halted in front of Jamil and Sindh, eyeing them suspiciously. He knew the watch order. "What are you two doing out here? Ranshoff and Vogel are the late-night watch."

He caught Jamil looking over his shoulder towards the rear of the galley. Vanderdecken turned as Scraggs broke cover and ran towards him. Jamil and Sindh threw themselves upon the captain from behind, grabbing him by his neck and arms. Neb saw the blade flash upward as Scraggs covered the last few strides. He could not see the captain murdered.

Flinging himself out the galley door, Neb collided with Scraggs. Carried forward, they bulled into Vanderdecken, with Scraggs bellowing, "Hold him tight, I'll deal with the lad!" Caught between the captain and the mate, Neb gave out a mute cry as the stiletto blade arched overhead.

There was a deep, mumbling growl as a black shadow flew

through the air. Landing on Scraggs's back, the dog Denmark sank its fangs into the mate's shoulder. As Neb went down, he grabbed for the two crewmen's legs and held on tight.

Vanderdecken was a tall, powerfully built man who could hold his own with any crew member. Shrugging off the two who held him, he grabbed Scraggs's knife arm with both hands. The captain swung hard, whirling the murderous mate around and around. The knife clattered to the deck as Vanderdecken swung the man, both staggering across towards the rail, then he released Scraggs. The mate's startled yell was cut short as he hit the rail and jackknifed over into the sea. His head struck the side and he went under.

The *Flying Dutchman* sailed onward to the vast Atlantic, leaving Scraggs and his dreams of riches in the depths of the English Channel. Vanderdecken smashed Jamil and Sindh to the deck with wild blows and kicks. He grabbed the stiletto and stood over the petrified men, his whole body shaking with wrath, bloodlight in his wild eyes. Neb stood by, holding on to Denmark's neck, terrified at what he thought would happen next.

Suddenly a great sigh shook the captain's shoulders, and he grated harshly at the conspirators. "On your feet, you treacherous rats! Walk in front of me to the fo'c'sle cabin, or I'll cut your throats where you stand! You, boy, follow behind me with that dog. Cover my back!"

The remainder of the *Dutchman*'s crew were sitting around the stove drinking coffee, or lying in their bunks and hammocks. With a loud bang the cabin door burst open. Sindh and Jamil were booted roughly inside, landing flat on their faces. Looking up with a start, the crew beheld Captain Vanderdecken with Neb and Denmark behind him. "Muster all hands now. Jump to it!"

There was an almighty scramble as Petros and others who had side cabins came stumbling in. An awful silence fell on the crew—they quailed under their captain's icy glare. Ramming the stiletto into his belt, he seized Jamil and Sindh, hauling them up by their hair and bellowing at them.

"Who else was in this with you? Tell me or I'll throw you to the fishes, like I did with that villain Scraggs!"

Jamil clasped his hands together and wept openly. "There was only us two, Kapitan. Scraggs made us do it. We were afraid of him. He said he'd kill us if we didn't!"

Sindh joined him, tears running down the blue scar channel in his face, pleading for his life.

"He speaks the truth, Kapitan. We didn't know Scraggs meant to kill you. We thought he was just going to steal the green stone. Spare us, please, we meant you no real harm!"

Ignoring their snivelling pleas, Vanderdecken beckoned to a burly German crewman. "Vogel, you are first mate now aboard my ship and will be paid as such. Make two hanging nooses and throw them over the mid-crosstrees. These criminals must pay for what they did."

Vogel saluted but did not move. He spoke hesitantly. "Kapitan, if you execute them, it will leave us three hands short. No ship of this size could round Cape Horn with three experienced seamen missing."

There was silence, then the captain nodded. "You are right, Mister Vogel. See they only get half-rations of biscuit and water until we make harbour. They will be tried and hanged by a maritime court when we get back to Copenhagen. When they are not on duty, see they are shackled in the chain locker. Is that clear, Mister Vogel?"

The new mate saluted. "Aye, Kapitan!" He turned to Neb. "Half-rations of biscuits and water for the rest of the trip, d'you hear that, cook?"

As Neb nodded obediently, Vanderdecken turned his quizzical gaze on the boy. "This lad is the cook? How so?"

Petros nursed his damaged hand, whimpering. "Kapitan, my hand is bad hurt. I could not cook with one hand."

He tried to shrink away, but Vanderdecken grabbed Petros by the throat. He shook him as a terrier would a rat, the Greek's terror-stricken eyes locked by the Dutchman's icy glare. The captain's voice dropped to a warning rasp. "I signed you aboard as cook, you useless lump of blubber. Now, get to your galley and cook, or I'll roast you over your own stove!"

He hurled the unfortunate Petros bodily from the cabin. There was danger in Vanderdecken's voice as he turned on the rest of his crew. "Every man does as I say on this vessel. Nobody will disobey my orders. Understood?"

Averting their eyes from his piercing stare, they mumbled a cowed reply. "Aye aye, Cap'n."

Neb trembled as the captain's finger singled him out. "You, come here. Bring the dog, stand beside me!"

Neb obeyed with alacrity, Den following dutifully alongside him. There was silence, and Vanderdecken's eyes roamed back and forth beneath hooded brows—each crewman felt their fearful authority. "This boy and his dog, they will watch my back wherever I go. They will stay in my cabin, guarding me from now on.

"Vogel, take the wheel, put out a new watch. When we pass the Land's End light, take her south and one point west, bound for Cape Verde Isles and out into the Atlantic. We'll take this ship round Cape Horn and up to Valparaiso in record time.

"The Horn, Vogel, Tierra del Fuego! The roughest seas on earth! Many a vessel has been smashed to splinters by waves, storm, and rocks there. Seamen's bones litter the coast. But by thunder, I intend to make it in one piece. The rest of you, as master of the *Flying Dutchman,* I'll tolerate no slacking, disobedience, or backsliding. I'll see the white of your rib bones beneath a lash if you even think of crossing me. Now, get about your duties!"

Pushing men contemptuously aside, Vanderdecken strode from the fo'c'sle cabin with Neb and Den close in his wake. The boy was completely baffled by the turn of events—glad not to be under Petros's sadistic rule, yet apprehensive to find himself expected to be in close proximity to the captain all the time. One other thing gnawed at his mind: Cape Horn and the other strange-sounding place, Tierra del Fuego, the roughest seas on earth. What were they really like? A warm nose touching his hand reminded him that whatever the danger, he was no longer alone. He had a true friend, the dog.

AFTER A WHILE NEB LOST
count of time; nights and days came and
went with numbing regularity. It was a world
of water, with no sign of land on any
horizon. Both he and the dog had been sea-
sick. There were moments when the boy
wished himself back on land. Even living in
Bjornsen's herring cellar seemed preferable to
the high seas. As the *Flying Dutchman* sailed
south and a point west, warm waters and fair weather fell behind in the ship's wake. It grew progressively colder, windier,
and harsher. The south Atlantic's vast, heaving ocean wastes
were relentless and hostile, with troughs deep as valleys and
wavecrests like huge hills.

It took a lot of getting used to, one moment being lifted
high with nought but sky around . . . next instant, falling into
perilous troughs, facing a blue-green wall of solid water. Having few duties to keep him busy was very frustrating, and Neb
sat with Denmark just inside the stern cabin doorway, forbid-
den to move until the captain ordered it.

Vanderdecken talked to himself a lot when studying charts
and plotting his vessel's course. The boy could not avoid hearing most of what was said.

"Yesterday we passed the coast of Brazil in the Southern Americas, somewhere 'twixt Recife and Ascension Island. I gave orders to the steersman to take another point sou'west. In three days we should pick up the currents running out from Rio de la Plata, sailing then closer to the coast, but keeping well out at the Gulf of San Jorge towards Tierra del Fuego and Cape Horn, the most godforsaken place on earth."

Neb could not help but shudder at the tone of Vanderdecken's voice. He hugged his dog close, seeking reassurance in the friendly warmth of Denmark's glossy fur. The captain glanced across at him, setting down his quill pen.

"Bring food and drink, boy, and don't waste time dawdling with the hands. I need you back here. Jump to it!"

There were lines strung across the deck. Without these ropes to hold on to, a body could be swept over the side and lost for ever in seconds. Neb came staggering into the galley with his dog in tow, both of them drenched in icy spray. Petros had wedged himself in a corner by the stove. His stomach wobbled as he strove to stand normally on the bucking, swaying craft. The Greek cook glared hatefully at the boy, upon whom he seemed to blame all his misfortunes.

"You creep in here like a wet ghost. What you want, dumb one?"

Neb picked up a tray from the galley table and conveyed by a series of gestures that he had come for food and drink. With bad grace Petros slopped out three bowls of some unnamed stew he had concocted and three thick ship's biscuits that clacked down on the tray like pieces of wood. He waved his knife menacingly in Neb's direction.

"You an' that mangy dog get food for nothing. Get out of Petros's galley before I kick you out!"

He raised a foot, but dropped it quickly. The black labrador was standing between him and the boy, its hackles up, showing tooth and fang, growling dangerously. Petros shrank back.

"Take that wild beast away from me, get your own coffee an' water from the crew's mess. Go on, get the dog out!"

Neb delivered the food to Vanderdecken, then went off to the crew's mess bearing his tray.

Jamil and Sindh had just arrived in the fo'c'sle cabin after checking the rigging. As Neb came through the door, they cast surly glances at him, another case of malcontents blaming him for their bad luck, though with some justification in their case. Vogel, the German mate, was also suspicious of Neb and his dog. Talk among the crew was that the captain used them both to spy on the crew. Not wanting to lose his position as mate, Vogel elbowed Jamil and Sindh aside, allowing the boy to fill two bowls with coffee and one with water for the dog. "When you two have had coffee, I'll chain you back in the anchor locker," he said to the seamen. "Kapitan's orders. Hurry up, boy. There be cold, thirsty men waiting to get a drink!"

The tone of the mate's voice caused Denmark to turn and snarl. Vogel sat quite still, as if he was ignoring the dog, though it was obvious he was scared to move. "Get that hound out of here, back to the kapitan's cabin!"

Neb nodded meekly, not wanting to upset the big German. Sindh took his turn at the coffee urn, commenting, "Bad luck to have dog aboard ship, eh, Jamil?"

The Arab grinned wickedly. "Aye, bad luck. This ship be all bad luck, poor fortune for poor sailors. Wrong time, bad season to be going 'round Cape Horn. You know that, Mister Vogel?"

The mate stared at the hawkfaced Arab. "Never a good time for going 'round Horn, no time. I know of ships that never get 'round. Many try once, twice. For long time. Ugh! They run out of food, starve. You see that bad ocean out there, dumb boy? That is like a smooth lake to the seas 'round Tierra del Fuego and Cape Horn!" Neb placed his drinks on the tray and manoeuvred carefully out of the cabin, with Jamil's parting remarks in his ears.

"Ship won't run out of food if it gets caught in the seas— we got fresh meat on board. Dog! You ever eat dog before, Mister Vogel?"

"No, but I hear from those who have, in Cathay China— they say dog make good meat, taste fine. Hahahaha!"

Neb crossed the spray-washed deck with a set jaw and a grim face, Denmark at his heels.

Winter came howling out of the Antarctic wastes like a pack of ravening wolves. Once the *Flying Dutchman* had passed the Islands of Malvinas the ocean changed totally. It was as if all the waters of the world were met in one place, boiling, foaming, hurling ice and spume high into the air, with no pattern of tide or current, a maelstrom of maddened waves. Beneath a sky hued like lead and basalt, gales shrieked through the ship's rigging, straining every stitch of canvas sail, wailing eerily through the taut ropelines until the vessel thrummed and shuddered to its very keel. Every hatch and doorway was battened tight, every movable piece of gear aboard lashed hard down. Only those needed to sail the ship stayed out on deck, the rest crouched fearfully in the fo'c'sle head cabin, fear stunning them into silence.

Petros tried to make it from the galley to the fo'c'sle cabin. As he opened the galley door, the ship was struck by a giant wave, a great, milky-white comber. It slammed the galley door wide, dragging the cook out like a cork from a bottle, flooding inside and snuffing out the fire in the stove with one vicious hiss. When it was gone, so was the cook, the huge wave carrying his unconscious body with it, out into the fathomless ocean.

Neb and Denmark were in the captain's cabin, viewing the scene through the thick glass port in the cabin door. He had once heard a Reformer in Copenhagen, standing on a platform in the square, warning sinners about a thunderous-sounding thing called Armageddon. Both the boy and the dog leapt backward as a mighty wave struck the door, causing it to shake and judder. Neb clasped the labrador close to him. Had the *Flying Dutchman* sailed into Armageddon?

Vanderdecken was in his element out on the stern deck. None but he had a real steersman's skill in elements such as these—he seemed to revel in it. A line wound and tied about his waist and the wheel held him safe. He fought the wheel like a man possessed, keeping his ship on course, straight west along the rim that bordered the base of the world. Only when the vessel rounded Cape Horn would the course change north, up the backbone of the Americas to Valparaiso. With the fastenings of his cloak ripped apart and the hat ripped from his head by the wind's fury, the captain bared his teeth at the storm, hair streaming out behind him like a tattered pennant, salt water mingling with icy tears the elements squeezed from his eyes. Bow-on into the savage, wind-torn ocean, he drove his craft, roaring aloud. " 'Round the Horn! Lord take us safe to Valparaisooooooo!" He was a skilled shipmaster and had learned all of his lessons of the seas the hard way.

But the maddened seas off Tierra del Fuego washed over the bones of captains far more experienced than Vanderdecken, master of the *Flying Dutchman*.

TWO WEEKS LATER AND HALFWAY BACK TO the Malvinas Islands, the *Flying Dutchman* languished in the swelling roughs with sheet anchors dragging for'ard and stern, beaten backwards from the Horn. The captain paced the decks like a prowling beast, flogging with a rope's end and berating the hands, angered at this defeat by the sea. Men were aloft, chopping at rigging and cutting loose torn sail canvas. A ship's carpenter was up there also, binding cracked and broken spars with tar-coated whipping line.

Neb was back as cook, swabbing out the galley and salvaging what he could from the food lockers. There was precious little, as some of the vegetables in sacks and a cask of salted meat had  been swept away when Petros was lost. One of the clean water barrels had its contents tainted by seawater. The dog dragged saturated empty sacks from beneath the table, his old hiding place. Soon Neb had a fire going in the stove and warmth began returning to the galley. He chopped vegetables and salt cod to make a stew and put coffee on to brew in a big pan.

It was very unusual for the captain, but he came into the galley and sat at the table, eating his meal and drinking coffee there. Denmark stayed between the stove and the far bulkhead. The dog never showed any inclination to be near anyone except Neb. Ignoring the animal's presence, the captain gave orders to the boy.

"Take that food and coffee to the fo'c'sle head cabin, serve it to the hands. Don't hurry, but listen to what they are saying, then come back here. Go on, boy, take your dog, too." Neb did as he was bidden. While he was gone, Vanderdecken sat at the galley table, the door partially open, staring out at the restless waves, thinking his own secret thoughts.

After a while Neb returned, carrying the empty stewpot, with the dog trailing at his heels. Vanderdecken indicated a packing box, which served as a chair at the table.

"Sit there, boy, and tell me what you heard."

Neb looked perplexed. He pointed to his mouth and shrugged.

The captain fixed him with a stern, piercing stare. "I know you are mute. Keep your eyes on me and listen. Now, the crew are not happy, yes? I can tell they're not by the look in your eyes. Keep looking at me. They are talking among themselves. It's mutiny, they want to take over my ship and sail back home. Am I right?"

Neb's eyes widened. He felt like a flightless bird in the presence of a cobra. His gaze riveted on the remorseless palegrey eyes.

The captain nodded. "Of course I'm correct! Who is the one doing the most talking, eh, is it Vogel? No? Then perhaps there's another, Ranshoff the Austrian? No, he's too stupid. Maybe there's two spokesmen, the pair I had put in chains?

I'm right, aren't I! It's Jamil and Sindh. Though I'll wager that Sindh is the one who does most of the talking."

Neb sat fascinated by Vanderdecken's uncanny judgment. He did not move, the icy grey eyes held him pinned, as if they were reading his mind like a book.

The captain laid a short, fat musket on the table. It had six stubby barrels, which could discharge simultaneously at one pull of the trigger. A pepperpot musket of the type often used in riots with devastating effect in enclosed spaces.

"Aye, your eyes are too honest to lie, boy. Stay here, lock the door, and admit nobody but myself." Concealing the weapon beneath his tattered cloak, the Dutchman swept out of the galley.

Locking the door securely, the boy, trembling, was left with his dog. They sat staring at one another, Denmark laying his head upon his young master's lap, gazing up at him with anxious eyes.

Neb had no idea how long he sat thus, awaiting the report of the fearsome musket. But none came. He thought that maybe the crew had overcome their harsh captain and thrown him overboard. The boy's eyes began to close in the galley's warmth, when Denmark stood up, suddenly alert. Somebody banged on the door, and a voice called out.

"Open up, boy, it's your captain!"

Trembling with relief, Neb unbolted the door. Vanderdecken strode in and sat at the table. "Bring my logbook, quill, and ink from my cabin."

Whilst he made more coffee, Neb listened to Vanderdecken intoning as he wrote in the ship's log:

"We sail back to Cape Horn at dawn's first light. This time the *Flying Dutchman* will make it 'round the Horn. Every man will be on deck working. Tonight I quelled a mutiny among the crew; now there are no voices raised against my command. Sindh, a Burmese deckhand, was the ringleader. He no longer has to wait until we get back to Copenhagen for judgment and execution. Using my authority as captain to stem mutiny and preserve good order aboard the vessel, I summarily tried and hanged him myself!"

Vanderdecken glanced up from his writing at Neb's horrified face. For the first time the boy saw what appeared to be a smile on the captain's face. "If ever you command a ship, which isn't very likely, always remember this, boy, should the voyage prove risky and the returns valuable, it is wise to sign up your crew from all nations. That way they lack any common bond. A disunited crew is the easiest one to control. Take my word for it."

Those were the last words Vanderdecken spoke that night. He slept sitting in the chair, the pepperpot musket on the table in front of him.

Neb and Denmark lay down together near the stove by the far bulkhead, watching the strange man. Red reflections from the galley stove fire illuminated his harsh features: they never once relaxed, not even in sleep.

Four days later the *Flying Dutchman* was off the coast of Tierra del Fuego again, with Vanderdecken as steersman and all hands on deck, striving in the depths of midwinter to round the cape once more. It was sheer madness and folly to attempt such an undertaking at that time of year, but none dared say so. Armed with sword and musket, the captain drove his crew like slaves. Sleep was snatched in two-hour shifts, rations were reduced to half fare, men were constantly forced aloft to cut away, repair, or adjust battered rigging.

Neb was kept on his feet night and day, rationing out boiling coffee, cooking the meagre scraps that were the crew's diet and battling constantly to keep the galley dry and the fire going. It was extra difficult, because most hands slept there now—under the table, on empty sacks in all four corners, catching what rest they could until lashed out by the knotted rope end of Mister Vogel, the mate.

Vanderdecken drove himself even harder than his crew, retiring only briefly once a night to his cold, stern cabin and eating both little and infrequently.

Neb had never imagined the sea more wild and cruel. Under the hurricane-force winds, icicles formed sideways, sticking out like daggers astern. There was no lee side to anything on Cape Horn. Now and again, through the sheeting mixture of sleet and rain, the coast could be glimpsed. Gigantic dark rocks, with a nimbus of ice and spray framing them, looked for all the world like prehistoric sea monsters, waiting to devour anything that sailed too close. Cold and wet became a thing that had to be lived with. Some of the crew lost fingers and toes to frostbite, two of them on the same day fell from the rigging to their deaths in the bedlam of freezing waves. Sometimes Neb imagined he could hear thunder in the distance, or was it just the boom of tidal-size waves, crashing upon the coastal rocks?

Driven forward one day, then twice as far back the next, the ship tacked sideways and often turned completely about, sails filling to bursting, then slackening with tremendous slapping sounds. Half the cargo of ironware was jettisoned into the sea to keep the vessel afloat. One morning Neb was recruited to join a party in the midships hold, where groaning timbers were leaking water into the hatch space. All day he spent there, plugging away at the cracks with mallet, flat chisel, and lengths of heavy tarred rope they called oakum.

The boy's hands became so bruised and cracked with the cold that another crewman had to take his place. Neb fought back tears of pain as he thrust both hands into a pail of hot water on the galley stove. Denmark whined and placed his head against the boy's leg. Even over the melee of waves, wind, and creaking timbers, Vanderdecken's voice could be heard cursing the crew, Cape Horn, the weather, and the heaving seas with the most bloodcurdling oaths and imprecations.

Three weeks later the *Flying Dutchman* was in the same position, pushed back again, halfway betwixt Tierra del Fuego and Malvinas Isles. Defeated for the second time by Cape Horn!

Weary, sick, and half starved, the crew lay in their fo'c'sle cabin. There was a terrible atmosphere hanging over the place. No longer did the men speak to one another, they stayed in their bunks or huddled alone in corners. Some had missing finger and toe joints from the frostbite. All of them, to a man, were beginning to suffer with scurvy, owing to the lack of fresh vegetables. Teeth loosened and fell out. Hair, too. Sores formed around cracked lips. The two who had perished were not mourned—their blankets, clothing, and personal effects were immediately stolen by former crewmates. Survival was the order of the day, with each man knowing his chances of staying alive were growing shorter, alone and freezing out on the south Atlantic Ocean within the radius of the great white unknown regions of Antarctica.

Locked in the galley with his dog Denmark, Neb could do nothing but carry out his captain's orders. He smashed up broken rigging to feed the stove fire, supplementing it with tarred rope, barrel staves, and any waste he found. Water was growing short, the coffee supply was almost negligible, food was down to the bare minimum. Still he carried out his duties as best he could, knowing the alternative would be for him and the dog to move into the crew's cabin. He shuddered to think how that would end up. Vanderdecken had told him that was what his fate would be unless he obeyed orders.

The captain kept to his cabin at the stern, showing himself only once every evening when the day's single meal was served. Armed with pepperpot musket and sword, he would arrive at the galley with his tray and command Neb to open up. Having served himself with weakened coffee and a plate of the meagre stew, he would half-fill another bowl with drinking water and give Neb his usual orders.

"Heed me carefully, boy. I will return to my cabin now. Place the pans of stew, coffee, and water for the crew out on the deck and get back inside quickly. I'll ring the ship's bell, they'll come and get their meal then. I'll ring the bell again in the morning when they return the empty pans. Collect them up and lock yourself in again. If they catch you with that galley door open, the scum will slay you, eat your dog, and strip the galley bare. You open this door only to me. Understand?" Neb, his eyes never leaving the captain's, saluted in reply and set about his tasks.

Only once did a crew member venture out on deck for

reasons other than going to the galley door. Mister Vogel, the German mate, driven almost mad with hunger and cold, approached the captain's cabin. He was a big, powerfully built man. Emboldened by the ship's predicament, he banged upon Vanderdecken's door. When the door did not open, he began shouting. "Kapitan, it is I, Vogel. You must turn this ship around. If we stay here longer, all will be lost. Kapitan, I beg you to listen. We are fast running out of food and water, the men are sick and weak, this ship will not stand up to these seas for long. We are going nowhere! Give the order to put about and sail for safety, Kapitan. We can go anywhere, Malvinas, San Marias, Bahia Blanca. The Americas are close. There we could refit the vessel, sell what cargo remains on board, take on another cargo, and sail for Algiers, Morocco, Spain, even home to Copenhagen. Soon you will have mutiny aboard if we sit here, Kapitan. You know what I say makes sense. Do it, now, I implore you in the name of the Lord!"

Vanderdecken cocked the big pepperpot musket. It was a clumsy but awesome weapon—one pull of the trigger could send out a fusillade of leaden shot, six heavy musket balls. Without opening the cabin door he fired, the blast killing Vogel instantly. Neb and his dog jumped with shock at the sound of the explosion. Reloading swiftly, the captain marched from the cabin with sword and pistol, a maniacal light in his eyes, calling out in a voice like thunder. Neb and the crew could not help but hear him.

"I am Vanderdecken, master of the *Flying Dutchman*! I take orders from neither God nor man! Nothing can stop me, nothing in this world or the heavens above. Cower in your cabins or throw yourselves into the waters, what need have I of worthless wharf dregs who call themselves sailors. Sailors. I will show you a sailor, a captain! As soon as I have this ship rigged and ready, I set course again for Tierra del Fuego! I will take my vessel 'round the Horn single-handed. Do you hear, single-handed. Stand in my path and I will slay you all!"

NOT ONE SOUL ABOARD THOUGHT THAT
he could ready the ship for sail alone. But Vanderdecken did
it. All night and half a day he could be heard, banging, clat-
tering, scaling the masts, dragging sailcloth
from lockers, reeving lines, and lashing yards.

His final mad act was to slash the sheet anchors
free, fore and aft, then he dashed to the steering
wheel and bound himself to it. The *Flying
Dutchman* took the swell of the gale as it struck
her stern. Off into the seas the battered craft sped, like a fleeing stag pursued by the hounds of hell into the midwinter
wastes of the ocean, headed again for Cape Horn and destiny.

One week later the food and water ran out. Without the
captain's protection now, Neb was left to fend
for himself. The boy had never been
so frightened before. Now, bolting
the galley door, he fortified it by
jamming the table and empty
barrels against it. Whenever a
crewman hauled himself
across the swaying, rolling
decks to bang upon the galley
door, Denmark's hackles rose and

he barked and snarled like a wild beast until the crewman went away.

Each time the ship lost way and was driven back in the pounding melee of blue-green waves, Vanderdecken screeched and raved, his sanity completely gone, tearing at his hair and shaking a bloodless fist at the seas and sky, sometimes laughing, other times weeping openly in his delirium.

On the first day following that dreadful week, the *Flying Dutchman* was driven backwards for the third time by a howling hurricane of wind, snow, and rain. But straight to the east the vessel careered this time, sails torn, masts cracked, shipping water that sloshed about in empty holds from which the last scraps of cargo had been jettisoned to save the ship.

Then by some perverse freak of nature the weather suddenly calmed itself! An olive-hued stillness hung upon the Atlantic; rain, snow, and wind ceased. Startled by the sudden change, Neb and his dog came out on deck. The crew deserted their accommodation, creeping out furtively into the dull afternoon. It was as if heaven and all the elements were conspiring to play some pitiless joke on the *Flying Dutchman*.

"Eeeeaaaarrrggghhh!" All hands turned to watch Vanderdecken, for it was he who had roared like a condemned man being dragged to execution. With his sword he was feverishly hacking at the ropes that bound him to the ship's wheel. Tearing himself loose, oblivious to the onlookers, he jabbed the blade skyward and began hurling abuse, at the weather, at the failure . . . At the Lord!

Even though the crew were men hardened to the vilest of oaths, they were riveted speechless by their captain's blasphemy. Neb fell on his knees and hugged the dog that stood guarding him. Across on the eastern horizon, bruised dull skies gave way to immense banks of jet-black thunderclouds, building up out of nowhere. With fearsome speed they boiled and rumbled until they darkened the daylight overhead.

Simultaneously, a bang of thunder shook the very ocean and a colossal chain of crackling lightning ripped the clouds apart. Men covered their eyes at the unearthly scene. The green lights of Saint Elmo's fire caught every spar, mast, and timber of the vessel, illuminating the *Flying Dutchman* in an eerie green glow. Vanderdecken fell back against the wheel, eyes staring, mouth gaping as the green-flamed swordblade fell from his nerveless grasp. Neb had buried his face in the dog's coat, but as Denmark crouched flat, he unwittingly allowed his master this view.

A being, not of this earth, was hovering just above the deck. It was neither man nor woman, tall and shining white, bearing a great sword. It turned and pointed the sword at Vanderdecken. Its voice, when it spoke, was like a thousand harps strummed by winds, ranging out over the sea, beautiful yet terrifying. "Mortal man, you are but a grain of sand in the mighty ocean. Your greed and your cruelty and your arrogance turned your tongue against your Maker. Henceforth, and for all the days of time, this ship, with you and all upon it, are lost to the sight of heaven. You will sail the waters of the world for eternity!"

Neb saw Scraggs then, and Sindh, Petros, Vogel, and the two hands who had been swept from the rigging and drowned. All of them, pale, silent, and dripping seawater, stood by the crew, staring with dead eyes at their captain. It was a sight to haunt the boy's dreams for centuries to come. A sea-scarred ship, crewed by the dead and those who would never know the release of death, standing in the fiery green light, silently accusing the captain who had brought the curse of the Lord upon them and the *Flying Dutchman.*

Without warning the elements returned. At the sound of a second thunderbolt the waves sprang up. Icy sleet carried sideways on the wailing wind drove a huge roller, smashing into the vessel's port side. Neb and Denmark were washed from the deck straight into the Atlantic Ocean. Clinging to the dog's collar with both hands, the boy did not see the wooden spar that struck him, nor did he know that his good and faithful dog pulled him up onto that same spar, saving them both. The last thing he remembered was a cold abyss of darkness. The *Flying Dutchman* receded into storm-torn darkness, leaving astern a dog clinging to a spar, with an unconscious boy draped across it, cast away upon the deeps.

Vanderdecken and his crew
sailed cursed into eternity,
leaving in the *Dutchman*'s wake
two castaways upon the sea.
A struggling dog, a helpless boy
pounded by storm and wave,
victims of the dread Cape Horn,
that deep and watery grave.
But lo! The angel returned to them,
commanding, serene, and calm,
bringing a message unto their minds,
preserving the friends from harm.
"You are saved by innocence of heart
and granted your lives anew,
the gift of heaven's mercy
bestowed in faith, on you!
I am sent to bless you both
with that which you shall need:
boundless youth, understanding,
and speech to succeed.
Throughout the ages, roam this world,
and wherever need is great,
bring confidence and sympathy,
help others to change their fate.
Fear not the tyrant's bitter frown,
but aid the poor in their woe,
make truth and hope bring evil down,
spread peace and joy where you go!"

THE
SHEPHERD

THE NIGHT WIND KEENED OUT ITS LONELY
dirge across the barren coast of Tierra del Fuego. Ragged
drifts of cloud shadowed the moon, casting weird patterns of

silver and black over the land below. Mountain-
ous dark green waves, topped by stark white
crests and flying spume, thundered madly,
smashing against the rocks, failing in their
quest to conquer the shore, hissing vengefully
through the small, pebbled strand, retreating to
the seas for a renewed assault on Cape Horn, where two
mighty oceans meet.

Neb regained his senses gradually. He was being dragged
around the rocks and shallows of a little cove; the dog had its
teeth sunk into his collar, trying to pull him clear of the water.
An incoming roller knocked them both flat, but the labrador
clung stubbornly to him. Painfully the boy staggered to his
hands and knees. Shuffling, crawling, he assisted the faithful
creature attempting to tug him beyond the tideline. He
lay there a moment, dazed, then he retched, shivering and vomiting seawater among a debris of sea-
weed, driftwood, and pale sand scattered with
pebbles, his whole body shuddering with the effort.

"Gurround! Gurr Neb grrr!"

The sound came from nearby. Neb got to his knees, wiping his mouth with a sand-crusted forearm, and looked around. There was no sign of any living being, except for the dog. A thought flashed through his mind that somebody was trying to talk to him. Yet it was not an actual sound, just a feeling.

The rough voice came again. He realized it was like a thought, something invading his mind.

"Gurround Neb, wurrrr safe, grrr!"

The dog's paw was worrying at his leg, as Neb stared up at the cliffs above, searching in case someone was hiding there. All this time his mind was in a jumble of speculation: What could it be? A voice, not aloud, but like a spirit inside his head. Was it the angel, haunting his imagination? No, angels didn't growl! Neb flinched as the dog's blunt claw scraped his leg. Turning, he took the dog's face in both hands, staring deep into its warm brown eyes. He thought as they gazed at one another, What is it, Denmark, can you feel something, too?

The reply hit him like a bolt as he heard the dog's thought.

"Denmurrk, gurr . . . I Denmurrk, grr, Neb 'live!"

Then Neb heard his own voice, but not from within his head as a thought. It was from his mouth! A shout, echoing from the cliffs, above the sea and wind.

"You Den! You Dennnnnnn!" Immediately Neb's hand shot to his throat, and he spoke, halting, but quite clear. "I . . . talk!"

Denmark bowled him over, covering his face with a warm, slobbery tongue, both paws on his shoulders. "Gurrrrr! We t . . . talk, Neb, Denmurrrk . . . gurr . . . talk!"

Overcome by the sudden miracle, Neb and Den suddenly found themselves expressing their joy in the way any boy and

his dog would, rolling over, wrestling in the sand, tears streaming from their eyes as Neb roared with laughter and Den
barked aloud.

Old Luis the Shepherd heard the noise. He had climbed
down a wide rift in the cliffs, descending to the shore. There
were always bits of interesting flotsam to be found, besides
driftwood and sea coal for his fire. But this was a sound he had
never heard on the hostile coast of the Tierra, the strains of
happiness. Shouldering his bundle of wood, Luis picked up
the small sack of sea coal he had garnered and waded into the
shallows, where a rocky point divided the shore. Gathering
his woolen blanket cloak about him, and holding on to a rock
to steady his balance against the sucking tidewater, he narrowed his eyes against the flying spray. Then, still peering up
the beach, he sloshed through the shallows, crow's-feet
crinkling around his eyes. Luis could not help smiling at the
odd sight.

A gaunt boy, ragged and rake-thin, his hair matted with
sand and seawater, was screeching and laughing wildly as he
danced around and capered like a mad thing. With the lad was
a big, emaciated black dog, its ribs showing through the sheen
of its saturated coat. It stood on hind legs, both forepaws on
the boy's shoulders, as it leaped about with him, barking and
howling at the moon.

Luis walked towards the pair, waving the bundle of firewood, calling out in his native Spanish tongue. "*Hola!* Are you
stricken by the dance of Saint Vitus? Why do you celebrate on
these Tierra shores in such weather? My friends, what brings
you here?"

Neb and Den halted, staring at the old fellow, unsure of
what to do next. Thoughts raced between them. "Stay, Den,

he is friend, I understand how he speaks."

Denmark licked his young master's hand. "Grr, old one good, gurr. Den not know his speak. You do, Neb?"

Luis put down the wood and the coal and held out his open palms to them in a gesture of peace. "Friend, you must have come here from a ship, maybe it was wrecked. Are there no others left alive?"

Neb shook his head dumbly, not trusting his newfound voice.

The old shepherd merely nodded. "May the Señor God give their poor souls rest. So there are only two left alive, you and the dog, eh. My name is Luis the Shepherd—how are you called?"

Slowly the boy pointed to the dog. "Den!" Then he pressed a finger to his own chest. "Neb!"

Luis repeated his former question. "How did you come here?"

The strange boy did not reply, but the old man watched as tears flowed silently down Neb's cheeks.

Carefully the old man approached Neb. He touched the youngster's cold, damp arm, then placed a palm on his hot, dry forehead, murmuring gently, "Young one, you are starving, soaked, and fevered. You will not have much to give thanks for if you perish out here in the open. Your dog needs rest and food, too. My hut has food and fire—you will both be warm and dry. Come with me, I won't harm you. Come!"

Luis took off his cloak and draped it about the boy's trembling shoulders.

Neb and Den exchanged thoughts. "This is a good old man, we will go with him, Den."

"Gurr, I go with you."

• • •

Luis had quite a big hut, which of necessity suited the lay of the windswept clifftops. It was dug into the lee of a slanting rock, which formed one wall and part of the roof. The rest of its construction was mainly of ship's beams, planking, and tree boughs, chinked together with stones and earth sodding. The whole thing had a lining of ship's-sail canvas, of which Luis seemed to possess a fair amount. It had a rough door, which had once belonged to the cabin of some sailing vessel, with a canvas curtain draped across to keep out draughts. There were no windows, so all in all it was fairly weathertight. Luis seated them in a peculiar construction made from a wrecked lifeboat, padded out with dry grass and sacking. It was very comfortable. He fed wood and coal to the fire, which was held in a deep brazier of strap iron. On a tripod over the flames was an upturned ship's bell, with the name *Paloma Verde* engraved into its soot-blackened metal. Luis struck it with a ladle; it clanked dully.

"Sometimes the sea is kind to a poor man. It washes up gifts for him. See, a cooking pot, a lifeboat couch, and many other things I have taken from the shores. Señor Neptune can be a good friend. Look at tonight—he sent a lonely old shepherd two guests to share his fire and food. Wait!" He rummaged in a corner, bringing forth a thick sheepskin poncho and some soft, clean flour sacks, which he gave to Neb. "Give me your wet clothes, dry yourself and that good dog with the sacks, then put on the sheepskin. It is a fine warm one. Do not fall asleep yet, young one. You must both eat first."

Neither the boy nor the dog had ever known such kindness in their short, hard lives. Luis handed them each a bowl of hot mutton and barley soup, which they ate in silence. He watched them both, refilling the bowls twice. The old shepherd then brewed a hot, dark, fragrant drink from cut and dried leaves, to which he added sugar that he broke from a big cone and creamy ewe's milk.

Luis sipped his own, noting their grateful reaction. "That is called tea. It comes from the east, where it grows in far Cathay. Some years ago a merchant vessel was wrecked off the coast. My friend the sea provided me with four barrels of tea. It is rare and valuable. Do you like it, Neb?"

Sniffing at the fine aroma, Neb replied, "It is good!"

The meal finished, Luis watched with eyes that were grey and watered from years in the hostile climate. As his guests' heads began to droop with weariness, he mused quietly. "You are the strangest pair ever to come my way, but the Tierra has taught me to ask no questions. If one day you wish to tell me about yourself, boy, I will listen. If you should choose to keep your secret, well, who am I but a poor old shepherd who takes bad and good fortune alike. Life is but part of the Lord's great mystery. He did not put me on this earth to interrogate others. Sleep now, you are tired, sleep."

A final thought communicated itself from boy to dog. "Luis is a good man, we are safe here, Den."

"Gurrrr, no more Dutch . . . man, grrrr!"

TIERRA DEL FUEGO. 1623. THREE YEARS LATER.

DAWN CAME, AS HEAVY AND GREY AS THE
headland rocks, with pale light piercing forbidding cloud
banks on the far horizon. Aided by Neb and Den, Luis
 herded his small flock back from the clifftops.
Hooking a half-grown ewe with his crooked
staff, the old shepherd turned her back inland.

"Come away from the cliff edge, little one,
or you will never grow to be a mother. Go, join
your family."

He waved to the boy, who was some distance away.
"That's the last one, my son. Take them to the pen. It is not
good for sheep to roam loose on a day like this."

Cupping both hands around his mouth, Neb called back.
"Aye, winter played a trick on us, hanging about and not letting
spring arrive yet. Don't stay out too long, Luis. We'll see you
back at the hut!"

The shepherd's leathery face wrinkled into a smile. He
stood with his back to the cliffs, watching his two friends moving the flock along, as though they were born to the task.

Before the dog arrived, Luis had only a bellwether to lead
his animals, a crusty old ram with a clanking iron bell tied

about his neck, a flock patriarch who bullied and jostled his charges into submission. Sheep would always follow a bell-wether, often into dangerous areas, much to the shepherd's dismay. However, with the arrival of the dog, all that changed. Luis was astounded at how quickly Den learned to take commands; the black labrador immediately took issue with the lead ram and gave the bellwether more than one severe lesson.

Den became the flock leader. Though he graciously allowed the bellwether his customary position in front of the sheep, it was the dog who circled them, giving directions and keeping the creatures together and safe. Den had grown stronger. In the course of three years he was bigger and healthier with a coat that shone like black silk. A far cry from the half-starved bonebag Luis had first discovered at the sea's edge with Neb. The old shepherd turned to stare out at the restless face of the deeps, his thoughts turning to dwell on the boy.

Neb! That strange boy, the gift Luis had received from these same stormy seas. The boy who had only a few words and some odd sounds upon arrival at Tierra, yet within an amazingly short time was speaking fluent Spanish. But he was not a Spaniard. Luis knew this because in odd moments he had heard Neb singing snatches of sea shanties in several languages, mainly some Scandinavian tongue, Danish perhaps. The boy had been a mystery and a wonder to Luis in these years. He was highly intelligent, and after a month or so of his coming, very strong and agile. The shepherd put down the boy's physical fitness to his own good cooking.

Neb took to sheep herding like a duck to water, and he and the dog were a superb team. They had but to look at one another and any problem with the flock was solved. The boy never spoke of his past life, seeming only to live for the moment. Sometimes Luis would sit by the fire late at night, staring at his sleeping face, trying to fathom the enigma of this sea child. Always Neb would open his eyes and smile disarmingly. He would question the old man on many things. What was the best way to shear a sheep, which grasses and herbs could cure various forms of lamb ailments, which plant should the flock avoid eating? Luis would forget his original thoughts about Neb's clouded past and would converse animatedly with the lad, speaking to him as the son he never had.

Yet, before Luis turned to sleep, his mind would stray back to the question of his young friend. Who were his parents? How did he come to be living here, in a shepherd's hut at Tierra del Fuego, the place some called the Tip of the World? Where was he bound, how were he and Den able to comprehend one another with such surety, and, more important, why had neither the boy nor the dog grown taller or seemed to age by a single day since they had arrived? Granted, they had both filled out and grown quite healthy, but not older.

Then a feeling would steal over the old shepherd. He had grown very fond of his two friends, never wanting to see either of them unhappy, for he knew with a rock-sure certainty they had lived through much misery and pain, both of the body and spirit. He would be antagonizing Neb by ceaseless interrogation. If the lad wanted to remain silent about his former life, then so be it.

Expelling a small cloud of white mist with a perplexed sigh, one night the old man stared out at the sea when suddenly the breath froze on his lips. Luis saw the ship, not half a league from land, bathed in the weird green light of Saint Elmo's fire. Even from that distance he could see the sails, gale-torn and tattered, with ice shrouding spars and rigging from stem to stern. No wake followed the vessel, no seabird flew near to it. The ship was not sailing on the waves, but slightly above them. Fear gripped the very heart of Luis. He felt the presence of evil, mingled with despair for the souls aboard that spectral ship. Making a hurried Sign of the Cross, he kissed his thumbnail and turned to hurry away from the clifftop. In all his years on the coast of Cape Horn, Luis had seen many things. But none like the sight of Vanderdecken's ship. The *Flying Dutchman*!

WINTER FINALLY GAVE WAY TO SPRING.
Late-afternoon breezes soughed over the short headland
grass as Den drove the flock towards the penned area. Lean-
ing on the open gate, Neb watched his dog's
progress. The boy chuckled aloud, communi-
cating his thoughts to Den. Rain began to
spatter the back of his hand on the gatepost.
Once the mental telepathy between them both
had been firmly established, Neb soon learned
that his dog had a wit and sense of humour that any intelligent
being would envy. He laughed aloud at Den haranguing the
sheep, listening to the dog's mental grumbling.

"Grrr move, you useless lumps of wool and mutton, move!
Ahoy there, Bellface, grrr stir your stumps and lead 'em into
the pen. Not that way, you blathering bonebag, over there!
Can't y'see Neb holding the gate open? Grrrr, leave it to you
and the whole flock would end up going over the cliff!"

The bellwether turned and stared resentfully at Den.
"Baaah!" Den returned the stare with interest, baring his
teeth. "Baaah to you, too, sir! Now get 'em in that pen or I'll
give that baggy tail of yours such a nip that I'll bite it off!" Finally getting things right, the bellwether led the flock past
Neb into the pen. Neb closed the gate and looped a securing

rope noose around the gatepost.

Den joined him, standing on hind legs, forepaws perched on the gate. Neb patted the labrador's head, passing him a thought. "Haven't you taught these sheep to speak yet?"

Den shook his head in disgust. "All they know is to eat, sleep, and look stupid. 'Baaah' is about all I can get out of them!"

Rain was starting in earnest. Neb hunched his shoulders against the onslaught, hiding a smile. "I remember when every second thought from you was either a wuff or a gurrr."

Den kept his gaze on the sheep milling about in the pen. "'Wuff' and 'gurrr' are important expressions to dogs. But 'baaaah' or 'maaahah'—sheep don't even know what that means."

Neb pulled up the hood on his poncho. "Just thank the Lord that sheep weren't born intelligent, or they'd be twice as hard to control. If I thought somebody was keeping me only for wool and meat, I'd be off like a shot and away!"

Den bounded off in the direction of the hut, leaving a thought to Neb. "Well, I'm off like a shot for the hut. You can stay here and exchange baaahs with them if you like."

Neb stayed awhile, making sure the sheep settled down. It was close to lambing time, and some of the ewes were slow and heavy with their unborn burdens. A sheet of lightning lit the horizon far off, accompanied by the rumble of thunder from the ponderous, dark cloud masses. The boy shuddered. Closing his eyes, he gripped the rail once again. In his mind's eye he saw the ship's deck peopled by the living and the ghastly dead, felt the *Flying Dutchman* roll to the storm's swell beneath his feet, envisaged Vanderdecken, wild-eyed, lashed to the ship's wheel. Neb shook himself. Tearing his cold hands from the gate rail, he dashed off to the hut, forcing his mind to blank out the terrifying scene.

Luis was waiting by the fire with hot tea, mutton stew, and bread made from wild maize. He smiled up at the boy as Neb cast off his wet poncho and sat down next to Den. Luis listened to the thunder rumbling far off. "The Drums of Heaven. It will be a bad storm tonight, my son." He peered across the fire at the silent boy. "My son, are you ill? You look pale, what is it?"

Applying himself busily to the meal at hand, Neb shook his tousled hair and flashed Luis a quick smile.

"It's nothing, I'm all right, old man. You should be concerned about the flock and that storm brewing outside. I think it will be a hard one."

Luis crossed himself again. "I pray the Lord it will not be so. With eight ewes ready for lambing, what shepherd wants a storm to upset them? We'd best keep an eye on the weather tonight."

Den nuzzled his head under Neb's hand, sharing a thought. "It was the Dutchman, wasn't it. I felt him, too, when I heard the thunder, as if he were reaching for us."

Neb scratched behind his dog's ear. "Aye, I felt the ship was close somewhere—it's a hard thing to drive from your mind. But we're safe, and we have our angel to thank for it."

Den replied with his usual dry wit. "We have a lot to thank that angel for. I'll bet it was the angel who taught Luis to make mutton stew taste so heavenly."

The shepherd had been watching them both closely. Handing Neb a bowl of tea, he chuckled. "Talking to Señor Den again, eh, boy? What did he say to you?"

Neb winked secretively at Luis. "He says your mutton

stew tastes heavenly."

The shepherd rocked back and forth as he laughed. "What a good dog he is. Truthful, too!"

Neb took his tea to the door and opened it halfway. "Just look at that rain coming down. I'll sit here and take first watch on the pen."

Shortly after midnight the storm's intensity doubled. Thunder boomed overhead like a cannon, lightning sheeted and crackled over the headlands, and the rain drove sideways on the wind, spattering heavily on the hut's outer rock wall. Neb and Den lay asleep in the old lifeboat. Luis kept watch by the door, holding it half open against the elements with one foot. Bleating piteously, the sheep flattened themselves against the ground. A hard gust of wind slammed the door shut. Luis winced, rubbing his foot where the door timbers had cracked against his ankle. He leaned forward, thrusting the door open again.

The wind had torn the pen down. The flock were loose. Den's bark, close to Neb's ear, roused him into wakefulness. Luis was grabbing his crookstaff from its hanger, pulling his coat about him and shouting.

"Hurry, friend. The pen is destroyed, our sheep are running. I'll turn them from the cliffs. You save the ewes and get them inside the hut here. *Vamos!*"

The old shepherd ran out and was soon lost to sight in the rainswept darkness. Den was ahead of Neb as he struggled into his poncho and dashed outside. The next hour was an onslaught of furious activity. A stray ewe charged right into Neb, knocking him flat and winding him. The boy hung grimly on

to the bleating creature and dragged it by one ear and its tail
across the pasture and into the hut. Den was already back with
two ewes he had driven before him. One was already giving
birth at the back of the hut; the other lay against the keel of the
lifeboat maaahing for all it was worth. Shaking rainwater from
his coat, Den trotted past Neb, communicating a hasty
thought.

"Stay here with them, help them as Luis showed you. I'll
find Luis and bring him back here with the other ewes!" The
boy set about putting water to heat on the fire; he gathered as
many clean flour sacks as he could find. Turning his attention
to the ewe in the far corner, Neb found she had already delivered herself of a lamb and was licking the little creature. Both
mother and babe appeared to be getting along quite well, so he
went after the ewe he had brought in. It panicked, staggering
upright and leading him on a chase around the hut. He
tripped over the third ewe as it came from beneath the
lifeboat. The one he was chasing butted the door and fled outside. The boy dashed out, stopped momentarily, then, ignoring the ewe, ran for the cliffs with his dog's urgent call ringing
through his brain!

"Neb, Neb, Luis has fallen over the cliff!"

The labrador was barking aloud, looking over the cliff
edge as Neb hurried up and threw himself flat at the rim of
the plateau. About twenty feet below him, he could barely
make out Luis, lying on a ledge. The old shepherd had a ewe
in his arms; both were lying still. Neb sent Den back to the hut
for a rope, then he climbed down the slippery rock, clawing at
any niche he could get his freezing fingers into. Sliding and
stumbling, he reached the ledge. Lifting the old man's head
carefully, he laid it in his lap and murmured anxiously. "Luis,

old friend, are you hurt? Speak to me, Luis!"

Slowly opening one eye, the shepherd looked from the ewe he was clutching to the boy. He spoke barely above a whisper. "Ah, my son from the sea, look at this poor little one. She will never become a mother, or see another dawn." Leaning over Luis, the boy broke his grasp upon the dead sheep. It rolled to one side on the ledge.

Neb rubbed the old man's hands, trying to get some circulation going in them. "Forget the ewe, Luis. Are you hurt? Tell me!"

The old shepherd sighed. "I cannot move my legs, and it pains me to breathe. No, please, keep your poncho on, son. You need it." Then he lost consciousness.

The rope snaked down, striking Neb's shoulder. Den stood on the cliff edge with the other end clenched in his jaws. Wrapping Luis in the thick sheepskin poncho, Neb fashioned around him a cradle of rope, making sure it was firm and secure. He climbed back up to the plateau, using both handholds in the rock and the rope. Between them, Neb and Den hauled the old shepherd's still form back up to the clifftop. How Neb found the strength and endurance to get his injured friend back to the hut, he did not know, but he accomplished the task. With Luis draped about his shoulders and his own legs quivering furiously, Neb staggered through the doorway and collapsed inside.

After a while he was wakened by Den licking his face. Neb stood up slowly, but found that his head remained bowed from the strain that had been put upon him. He no longer had the strength to lift Luis, so he dragged him across to the lifeboat and rolled him in onto the soft grass and sack padding. Luis gave out a long, high-pitched moan, like that of a wounded animal. Neb made tea, cooling it by pouring in lots of milk. He managed to get a drop between the cold, parched lips of his friend, but Luis coughed it back up, pleading feebly.

"No more, I cannot swallow. I'm cold . . . so cold!"

Neb piled wood and sea coal on the fire brazier. He stroked the old man's forehead, murmuring to him. "Is that better? You lie still, I'll take care of you."

The shepherd's eyes beckoned him to lean in closer. When he spoke, Luis's voice was barely discernible. "Let me sleep . . . so tired . . . tired."

Outside the storm had abated, the wind had died down to a mere whisper of breeze, and the rain had ceased. A calm, starlit sky was visible through the partially open door. Two lambs had been born, and the ewes wandered out into the quiet pastures with their wobbly-legged babes. Neb made Luis as comfortable as he possibly could. The old man slept with his two friends close by, watching the gentle rise and fall of the coverlet as he breathed.

Dawn was but a few hours away when Neb and Den fell into a slumber. All the earth seemed very quiet; even the seas off the Cape stilled their wrath to a placid murmur. Then the angel spoke to the boy. "You made his last years the happiest he ever knew. Your time here is over. Both of you must travel on when you hear the sound of a bell. The world is wide and has other needs of your gifts. Once the bell sounds you cannot linger in this place."

Morning sunlight shafting through the doorway, coupled with the labrador baying aloud, aroused Neb from his short but deep sleep. He could not piece together a coherent thought from the dog, only a feeling of immense grief. The boy knew what it was all about when he looked upon the old shepherd's face. There in the lifeboat Luis lay, forever still, his features peaceful as he slept the eternal sleep of death.

The weather that sad day continued fine, the sunniest day Neb and Den had ever seen since their arrival upon Tierra del Fuego. The flock had dispersed, with nobody to tend to their movements. Only one ewe could be seen in the pasture, with its lamb revelling in the joy of newfound movement, skipping and leaping awkwardly about. Hardly a thought had passed between the boy and his dog. They sat outside the whole morning, heavy-hearted, gazing at the hut where the old shepherd lay. Neb finally rose at midday.

He went inside the hut and gathered together a sack of provisions, his sheepskin poncho, and the crooked staff that had belonged to Luis. Lighting a tallow candle, he touched the flame to the interior sailcloth lining of the hut in several places. Dry-eyed, the boy placed his hand upon the shepherd's cold brow and said slowly, "Good-bye, old friend. Thank you for the happiness you brought into our lives. Rest in peace."

Neb left the hut without looking back.

He sat outside with Den, both of them watching the smoke curling up from the roof and wafting away on the breeze in silence. An hour passed; they moved back from the heat. The hut was now well ablaze. With a crash of burning timber the roof collapsed inwards. It was then that the old bellwether ram plodded up from wherever he had been grazing. Ding! Clank! Ding! Clank! Ding!

Neb had not seen the bellwether since the previous morning. He thought the old ram had probably been killed in the storm, maybe fallen over the cliff, or succumbed before the onslaught because of its great age. The boy smiled sadly as the old creature approached him, its primitive iron bell clanking mournfully. A pang of realization suddenly pierced him like a sword.

"It's the angel's message, the tolling bell!"

The dog turned its sorrowful brown eyes up to him. "I dreamed about the angel, too, but I never thought our ram's bell would carry the message. What do we do now?"

Tears flowed unchecked from Neb's clouded blue eyes. He slowly picked up the old man's crooked staff, watching the bellwether back away from the glowing embers of the shepherd's dwelling, its simple iron neckbell still dinging and clanking hollowly. "We must follow the angel's command. It is time to go!"

Up the valley they went together, north to Punta Arenas and the plateau land of Patagonia, leaving behind Tierra del Fuego, where great oceans meet at the bottom of the world.

Away o'er wild and watery wastes
Vanderdecken sails his ship,
restless phantom, cursed by heaven
to that doomed eternal trip.
While decades turn to centuries,
as down throughout the ages
a boy and dog, forever young,
tread history's vast pages.
Sharing times, both bad and good,
a friendship formed in smiles and tears,
guided by their angel's hand,
two innocents roam the years.
O'er hill and mountain, land and sea,
'cross desert dry and pasture green,
mystic countries, towns, and cities,
what strange sights those two have seen.
Gaining wisdom, wit, and knowledge,
in joy, and sorrow, peace, and war,
helping, caring, bringing comfort,
always travelling, learning more.
Is it not surprising, then,
each of them has changed his name,
Den is Ned, and Neb is Ben,
the two who from the *Dutchman* came?
Where are they now, our dog and boy,
where heaven commands they go,
beyond the echo of some far bell?
Read on and you shall know!

THE
VILLAGE

ENGLAND. 1896.

THE RAILWAY HAD FINALLY COME TO
Chapelvale. Obadiah Smithers drew a turnip-shaped gold
watch from the pocket of his brocade waistcoat and consulted
 it. "Hmph! Eighteen minutes past two, a quar-
ter hour late. I'd liven 'em up if it were me running this railway, by thunder I would. Time's
money, and I can't afford to waste either, that's
what I always say!"

The young lady sitting opposite him clung
to the velvet strap as the train jerked noisily to a halt. She adjusted her bonnet, agreeing with the older man.

"That's what my papa always says, too, sir."

Obadiah plastered a few strands of hair into position on
his red, perspiring brow. Standing, he adjusted his black-
tailed frock coat and donned a silk top hat.

"Sensible man, your father, 'twas him and I who persuaded
the powers that be to install this branch line to
Chapelvale. Progress, y'know, this town needs
t'be dragged into modern times, been a
backwater too long. Can't stop
progress, m'dear."

Maud Bowe hated being referred to as "m'dear," or "young lady." However, she smiled sweetly at Mr. Smithers. "Indeed, sir, progress and modernity go hand in hand."

But Obadiah was not paying much attention to her observation. He was struggling to get the door of the private compartment open, without much success. Lowering the window, he bellowed officiously at a porter, "You there! Get this confounded door open this instant!"

Both engine and leading carriages had overshot the platform by twenty feet or more. Recognizing Chapelvale's most prominent citizen, the porter came running and snapped the door open with alacrity. Obadiah fumed as he allowed himself and Maud to be helped down onto the sleepers and rough limestone pebble. "What's the matter with you people, eh? Can't you stop the train in its correct position?"

Bridling at the unjust accusation, the porter complained. "Ain't my fault, sir, I don't drive the engine, y'know!"

Obadiah Smithers's face went brick red in its frame of muttonchop whiskers. He shook his silver-mounted walking cane at the man and almost tripped over a sleeper. "Damn your impudence! Get along to the guard's van an' pick up this young lady's luggage before the train goes an' it ends up who knows where. Go on, get along with you!"

A towheaded lad aged somewhere between thirteen and fourteen years, accompanied by a big, black labrador dog, emerged from the guard's van. Over one shoulder the boy toted a canvas bag with a drawcord neck. He dug into his pocket and passed a silver sixpence to the guard, winking. "Thanks for the ride, Bill!"

The guard, a cheery-looking young man, grinned as he returned the wink and patted the dog's head. "Now, don't go shoutin' to everyone that I let you 'n' Ned ride without a ticket. You'll get me in trouble, Ben. 'Bye, you two!"

The porter came scurrying up. "Baggage for the girl in the private compartment, you got it there, Bill?"

A lady's travelling valise and a fancy carpetbag were slung out onto the platform by the guard. "There y'are, two pieces!"

Black smoke wreathed up from the engine into the hot blue summer sky. All along the platform train doors were slamming shut. The dog Ned stood patiently at Ben's side as they took stock of their surroundings. A uniformed station-master waved them away from the train with his folded flag as, whistle in mouth, he checked the length of the platform. Hissing noises emanated from the engine as it dripped water on the track. Suddenly, it emitted a rushing cloud of steam. Maud screamed shrilly, hobbling up onto the platform in her long, fashionably narrow skirt.

Whooshing steam enveloped Obadiah Smithers as he stamped onto the platform, roaring, "Engine driver, what's your name, man? Near scalded us both t'death, you idiot. I'll report this to your superiors!"

His speech was drowned by a long blast from the train whistle combined with the noise of the stationmaster's whistle and a grinding of wheels and gears. Chuffing noisily, the train rumbled away up the branch line. Whilst Smithers harangued the stationmaster, a local carrier bore Maud's luggage to a horse-drawn cart outside the station fence.

With the train's departure, Chapelvale resumed its customary calm. Ben communicated a thought to his black Lab. "Come on, let's take a look at the village."

Ben was opening the white picket gate of the station when he found himself in competition to get out of the gate with the impatient Smithers. "Out o' me way, silly young ass!"

Ben was trapped in the gateway by the man's bulk as he tried to push past, brandishing a silver-mounted stick angrily and shouting, "Make way for your elders an' betters, or I'll . . ."

"Grrrrrrrrr!"

Ned was beside Smithers's leg, the labrador's hackles bristling as it bared its teeth. Obadiah Smithers froze in his tracks. The dog took a step aside, allowing the man an escape route, but Smithers stepped back a pace, too, allowing both boy and dog to pass through the gate. His confidence returned once he was clear of the pair, Obadiah closed the gate and ranted at them in high bad humour. "That beast should be destroyed—it nearly attacked me! I'll call a constable if you set it on me again!"

The boy turned to face him, smiling at first. Then the smile went from his face. With eyes like two chips of blue ice, he stared at the big, stout man. Smithers was lost for words. Those eyes. He shuddered, transfixed by the strange lad. There was neither fear nor respect in the boy's silent gaze, only contempt. Dismissing him, the boy turned away and walked off with the dog loping alongside him.

Snorting indignantly, Smithers turned to the girl. "Did y'see that? Impudent young blaggard. If he crosses my path again I'll lay this stick about him, and that growlin' cur, too, see if I don't!"

Ignoring his bluster, Maud went to stand by the cart, and Smithers turned his wrath upon the driver. "What're you standing there gawking at? Let's get going!"

Outside the station, Ben and Ned stood at the top of the lane looking down towards the village, which nestled snugly in a valley between two hills. Roads leading in and out were little better than broad tracks of well-trodden, hard-packed earth, old and dusty. None of them straight paths, they meandered and rambled quaintly. Some were skirted by hedges of privet and hawthorn, overhung by elm, beech, and holm oak trees. Others had dry stone wall edgings, the soft greystone chinked with moss and bordered by hogweed, dandelion, and yarrow. The far hill had a spired church on its brow. Cottages and small landholdings dotted patchwork fields where sheep, cows, and horses grazed. Ben stared at the not-too-distant village square with its black-and-white Tudor shops and buildings, none over two storeys high. He passed a thought to his friend.

"There's the chapel on the hill and the village in the valley. Chapelvale. What do you think, Ned?"

The labrador's tail wagged idly. "Sleepy little place. I hope the people are nicer than that big, blathering lard barrel we met at the station. I like it, Ben, but what are we supposed to be doing here?"

Ben scratched behind the dog's ear. "It's got me stumped. We both had the same feeling—this was the place to get off the train. Let's go and take a look at the village. If nothing comes up, we might just move on to somewhere else."

A boy and girl, obviously brother and sister, were walking up the lane towards the greystone station. The girl was about Ben's age, the boy slightly younger.

Ben waved cheerily at them. "Hello there, wonder could you help us?"

They immediately warmed to Ben's friendly manner. He looked a carefree type, with his unruly blond hair and blue eyes, long white canvas pants and a crewneck cream sweater, and a coat that appeared slightly large. There was an air about him, as if he had some sort of seafaring experience. The big, black labrador with him was wagging its tail, a nice, companionable dog. The boy stroked it.

"We haven't seen you two around Chapelvale before, are you new here? How can we help you? This is a fine dog you've got!"

"What an intelligent boy, he recognized quality right off!"

Ben cut across the Lab's thoughtful remark. "We're straight off the train, never been here before. I'm Ben, which is Neb backwards, short for Nebuchadnezzar. This fellow is Ned, which is Den backwards, short for Denmark. Bit of an odd name for a dog, ain't it?"

The girl, who had dark hair and brown eyes, was very pretty, even prettier when she smiled. "Nebuchad . . . what? Sorry, my name's Amy, Amy Somers. This is my brother Alex. I'm quite nice, but he's fairly dreadful sometimes. What is it you want, Ben?"

"Er, someplace we can get something to eat. We're absolutely famished, aren't we, Ned?"

The dog nodded. Alex looked startled.

"Ned, your dog . . . he just nodded his head?"

Ben scratched Ned's neck roughly. "It's just his collar, it bothers him on warm summer days. Now, is there anywhere we can buy some food?"

Alex thought a moment, frowning. "I think you'll be out of luck, Ben, shops are closed today, but take a stroll around the village square. Maybe you'll find something, though I doubt it. Good luck anyway."

Ben and Ned moved off.

Amy called after them hopefully. "Will you be staying in Chapelvale, Ben?"

He winked at her and smiled secretively. "Who knows, maybe."

Alex called out rather anxiously. "Be careful, Ben, watch out for the Grange Gang!"

The strange boy shrugged carelessly. "Who are the Grange Gang?"

"A gang of rotten bullies who go about trying to make people's life a misery. Particularly strangers and old people."

Amy warned, "I'd steer clear of them if I were you."

Ben turned to look at Amy. She felt her skin prickle at the sudden iciness in his strange blue eyes. Then it was gone, and he chuckled quietly.

"Don't worry about us, pals. We've met gangs before!"

Amy watched Ben and his dog wander off down the lane. "I'll bet they have, too. He's the oddest boy I've ever seen, but I like him."

Alex found himself agreeing with his older sister. "I do, too, I don't know why. And that black labrador . . . I wish we had a dog like it. I hope they stay. D'you think they will, Amy?"

His sister repeated the strange boy's words. "Who knows, maybe."

Alex had been right—all the shops in the market square were closed for the afternoon. It was as if Chapelvale was taking a long siesta in the summer heat. The worn cobblestone paving, whitewashed walls, and heavy black beams, combined with blue-grey slate roofing and dark green roller blinds in shop windows, accentuated the lazy noontide stillness and the absence of folk out shopping.

The boy and his dog crossed the square together and made their way up the big, sloping hill behind the village. Shops thinned out, and so did the houses after a while. Ned gave Ben a sad look. "Please tell me we're not looking for another barn to spend the night in."

Ben passed his thoughts back to the labrador. "We never asked to turn up in this village. I'm sure the angel has guided us here. Just thank your lucky stars it's a peaceful little country place."

The dog raised his eyes mournfully. "Oh, it's peaceful enough."

Ben tickled his ear fondly. "Stop grumbling, a barn is better than a dry ditch beneath a hedge. We'll get a good breakfast tomorrow morning, as soon as everywhere is open. Bacon, sausage, toast, eggs . . ."

Ned let his tail droop. "D'you mind, my tummy's rumbling!"

A FAT PEAR, BROWN WITH ROT, SPLATTERED against the parlour window, causing the black cat inside to leap down from the sill, where it had been sunning itself. Old

Mrs. Winn watched the overripe pulp slide down the glass, then heard the chanting begin. It came from behind the thick fringe of purple-and-white rhododendron bushes growing at the bottom of her sloping lawn.

"Winn Winn, Winnie the Witch! Winnie the Witch and her big black cat! Winn Winn, Winnie the Witch!"

This was followed by barely stifled giggling and the hollow boom of a wet earth clod striking the old lady's front door.

She spoke to the cat, who was her only companion. "Those children are back again, Horatio. Why do they persecute us? We've never harmed them, have we?"

Horatio jumped lightly into her lap, staring at his mistress with magnificent amber eyes, meowing faintly as he stroked his head against her open palm. Mrs. Winn sighed.

"If Captain Winn were still alive, they wouldn't be so quick to bother us then, eh, Horatio?"

She stared sadly at the oval framed portrait hanging above

the fireplace mantelpiece. Captain Rodney Winn, R.N., stood frozen in time there, dapper as a new pin in his number-one dress uniform, complete with medals, braid, and bars. His peaked cap was tucked under one arm, a strong right hand resting on a table that contained a potted aspidistra and a Moroccan leather-bound Bible. Not a hair of his white goatee was out of place. Square-jawed and resolute, the captain had steady blue eyes that commanded all he surveyed, a man among men. Hero of the Sevastopol blockade and many other naval encounters in the Crimean War of the 1850s. Now sadly deceased.

The parlour window shuddered under the impact of a bloated dead toad, which fell onto the outside sill. Chanting broke out anew as Mrs. Winn rose stiffly from her chair and made for the door.

"Winnie the Witch with the wrinkly face, come on out and give us a chase!"

She collected her cleaning equipment and opened the door slowly. Horatio slid by her, his tail curling sleekly. He watched as the old lady placed mop and bucket to one side. Taking a straw-fringed brush, she began sweeping the broken soil clod from her porch onto the flower bed below.

"Look, Winnie the Witch is going to chase us on her broom. See, I told you she was a real witch!"

Shaking her broom at the rhododendrons, Mrs. Winn called out, "Don't be so silly, go away and leave us alone, you naughty children. Have you nothing better to do?"

Derisive laughter hooted out from behind the bushes. "There's her black cat, all witches have got a black cat!"

Dipping her mop in the bucket of soapy water, Mrs. Winn began cleaning mud smears from her neat green door with its polished brass knocker and letter box, crying out as she did, "If you don't go away, I'll fetch a policeman!"

"Haha, fetch the bobbies. We don't care, old pruneface!"

Wearily the old woman carried her cleaning stuff down to the front lawn. Flicking the bloated toad carcass from the sill, she started in mopping the filth from the parlour window-panes. Again a voice challenged her.

"Hurry up, Winnie, fly off and bring the bobby, hah. Fat lot of good that'll do you!"

She knew they were right. Her tormentors would leave the moment she made a move for the police, but once the constable had come and gone, they would return to renew the persecution. It was an all-too-familiar pattern during the last months. Her house was isolated, standing alone on the far hill slope outside the village. She had no neighbours to call upon for help. Clamping her jaw resolutely, she grabbed her pail of soapy water and hurled it at the bushes. It fell short, splashing on the lawn. This caused great hilarity from the gang in hiding. They rattled the bushes until several clumps of rhododendron blossoms fell to the ground.

"Hahaha! Silly old witch, you missed! Witchie, witchie!"

Horatio's tail swirled around the doorjamb. He stalked smoothly back into the house. Mrs. Winn watched him go. She swayed slightly in the hot afternoon sun, wiping a bent wrist across her forehead, then, gathering up her cleaning implements, she trekked wearily in after the cat. As she closed the front door, a fresh battery of rubbish rattled against the panels outside.

"Winn, Winn, Winnie the Witch! Hahahahaha!"

Striving to ignore the children, she boiled a kettle and made tea, pouring some into a saucer and adding extra milk for the cat. Horatio liked the drink of milky tea. She stroked the back of his head as he bent to lap it up.

"They won't leave us alone, Horatio. If it's not those youngsters, then it's Obadiah Smithers with his legal notices, trying to get me out. Oh dear, Horatio, only one week left after today. Those lawyers from London will be here to enforce the clearance notices—I could lose my house! Unbelievable! And the village, oh, Horatio, the poor village."

Horatio licked a paw and wiped it carefully over one ear, staring solemnly at her, as if expecting an answer to the problem. However, it never came. Mrs. Winn sat looking at her work-worn hands, a tidy, plump little old lady, with silver hair swept into a bun, her slippered feet scarcely touching the rustic, tiled floor from the chair she sat in.

Outside the golden afternoon rolled by, punctuated by the guffaws and mocking comments from behind the rhododendrons. Mrs. Winn toyed absently with her thin, gold wedding band, turning it upon her finger. From out in the mosaic-tiled hallway, flat chimes from a walnut-cased grandfather clock announced the arrival of half past three. A shaft of sunlight from the kitchen window, which illuminated the old woman's chair, had shifted slightly, leaving her face in the shade. Her half-filled teacup stood on the table in its Crown Derby saucer, a wedding present from her favourite aunt. The tea had grown cold.

She closed her eyes, trying to shut out the din from outside. It was no use, an afternoon nap was out of the question. Horatio prowled about for a while, choosing finally to settle at her feet. Mrs. Winn was seldom prone to feeling sorry for herself, but now she dabbed away a threatening tear with her apron corner. Clenching a fist in a sudden show of temper, she spoke to her cat. "Ooh! If only somebody would happen along and teach those wretches outside a lesson! . . . If only . . ."

Then she sat staring at the white-and-blue flower-patterned tiles around her kitchen sink. Some summer afternoons could be very lonely for an old widow and her cat.

BEN AND NED WERE WALKING ALONG TO-
gether, still discussing the merits and drawbacks of barns. In
the absence of anything better, the dog was warming to the
idea. "I like lots of nice deep straw in a barn.

Good fun, straw is. You can roll about in it and
jump off bales."

Ben smiled mischievously as he answered
his dog's thought. "Huh, you can brush your
own self off tomorrow if you're planning on
rolling about in straw all night. I'm not your kennel maid."

The labrador looked indignant. "Never said y'were, and by
the way, when did I last roll about in a barnful of straw, eh?"

Ben mused a moment before answering. "Er, April the
ninth, 1865, if I remember rightly. The day Robert E. Lee sur-
rendered to Grant. We were in a barn somewhere outside
Kansas City."

"Oh yes, you jumped on my head, I remember that
much!"

"Had to jump on your fat head. Otherwise you'd have
kicked off doing your barking exercises and betrayed us to
those renegades. Don't forget, Ned, I saved you from becoming a dogskin saddlebag."

The labrador sniffed airily. "Thank you kindly, young sir,

but this isn't the American Civil War. 'Tis nought but a sleepy English backwater village. I'll bark to my heart's content. Got to exercise the old bark now and again, y'know. Never can tell when it'll come in useful!"

Ben halted. "Quiet, Ned, d'you hear that? Sounds like shouting?"

The dog's keen ears rose. "It is shouting. 'Winnie the Witch with the crinkly face, come on out and give us a chase.' Might be some type of quaint local custom, eh, Ben?"

As they rounded a tree-fringed bend, Ben caught sight of the big, old, redbrick house, standing alone on the hillside.

"What did Alex say that gang's name was, Ned?"

"Er, the Grange Gang, I think. Why?"

"I think we may have found them. Come on, let's go and take a quiet peep at what's going on."

There were ten of them altogether, led by Wilf Smithers and his cousin Regina Woodworthy. Wilf kept the others busy searching for more ammunition to throw, whilst he and Regina stood by, shaking the rhododendron bushes. A fat boy with piggy eyes, who had been searching the garden, came creeping back through the shrubbery. He was carrying a double handful of rotten vegetation.

Wilf pulled a face, turning away from the stench that emanated from the mess. "Phwaw! That doesn't half stink. Where'd you get it, Tommo?"

The fat boy threw the stuff awkwardly. It landed short of the house, splattering on the front steps. He sniggered with glee, wiping his hands upon the grass. " 'Round the back there, Wilf. Winnie the Witch has a big compost heap piled up against the wall!" He watched Wilf's tough, sun-reddened face for signs of approval.

The leader of the Grange Gang ignored his minion and gave orders to the others. "You lot get 'round to that compost heap and fetch a load back here. We'll make the witch's house smell like a sewer before we're finished. Bring as much as you can!"

Ben and his dog had been eavesdropping from the other side of the garden wall. Ned's hackles rose. "Witch hunters persecuting some poor old lady! Grr, stupid ignorant louts, I can't abide them!"

Ben was of the same mind. "There's always bullies to pick on somebody who can't defend themselves, Ned. Let's go and upset them a bit."

The labrador shook his head. "If we're staying 'round here awhile, it won't do for you to invite trouble right off. Leave this to me, pal!"

Ben cautioned his friend. "Don't go causing them any real damage, Ned. This isn't the Battle of Trafalgar, you know."

Ned's face was the picture of injured doggy innocence. "Who, me? What possible harm could a gentle, ancient pooch do to a gang of great, tough teenagers?"

Thinking back to past adventures, Ben was about to remind Ned of several incidents. But when he looked around, the labrador had vanished like a black shadow.

The gang were taking their time gathering garbage from the compost pile—rotting apples, carrot tops, withered cabbages. Wilf's deputy, Regina, crouched impatiently behind the bushes. "What's the matter with 'em, Wilf, have they gone asleep 'round there?"

Wilf was facing away from her, peering across the garden. "I'll kick that Tommo's behind if he doesn't move himself!"

Something heavy hit Regina's back and knocked her flat.

She turned over and found herself facing a giant mad dog! It was black as night, showing gleaming white fangs as its lips twitched hungrily. Dark eyes glittering, fur standing up on its spine, it stood, snarling, ready to attack.

Regina managed to stammer. "W-W-Wilf, there's a d-d-dog!"

She need not have spoken, the beast already had Wilf's undivided attention. The boy took one pace back and fell flat on his behind. The dog turned to face him, froth showing in its jaws.

"Grrrrr gurrrr, wooooof!"

The thunderous bark galvanized them both into instant motion. Scrambling upright, Regina ran for it, banging into Wilf and smacking his head against the sandstone garden wall. "Owwooof! Yaaaaagh!"

Ned had the way out blocked. Wilf and Regina both fled towards the compost heap, which, being piled high against the wall, offered the only quick way out of the garden. The big black labrador pursued them, snarling and growling viciously. The rest of the gang took one look at the savage hound and tried to make good their escape. However, the soft, ripe compost couldn't bear their joint weight, and Wilf, Regina, and their cohorts found themselves sinking into the odious squelching mire, shrieking and grabbing at one another. As he barked and bayed like a mad wolf, Ned allowed a little slather of froth to wreathe his jaws, though inside he was giggling like a puppy. The fleeing Grange members fell over one another, kicking and fighting to be first over the wall, faces, hands, elbows, and legs covered with the stinking mass of decayed vegetation.

Standing outside, Ben saw the first few fling themselves from the walltop, thudding painfully onto the dusty path.

Before they could rise, more yowling muddy apparitions landed on them. It was utter bedlam! Ben pulled a disgusted face at the smell hanging on the air, then he turned away, carelessly whistling an old sea shanty, his untidy blond shock of hair bobbing as he entered the garden jauntily.

Ned came bounding up, his teeth bared in a huge doggy grin. "Now you know why my barking practice is important. Did you hear me, Ben, I made more din than a pack of beagles. Pretty good going, I'd say!"

"Excellent! You did very well for an ancient hound. Bet they cover a mile or two before they stop running. What's this? Look, Ned, there's an old lady coming out of the house."

Mrs. Winn had a walking stick in her hand in case of trouble, and she stopped several yards from them. Her voice had a sharp note to it as she looked them over. "You don't look like one of those hooligans. What are you doing here? Is that dog yours?"

Ned sat still and did some friendly dog-panting exercises, which he rated as important as barking practice.

Ben flicked the hair from his eyes with a swift nod and smiled disarmingly. "Afternoon, marm. We didn't mean to trespass, but we thought that gang was annoying you. Not nice that, annoying folk."

Mrs. Winn peered closer at the strange, polite boy. His white canvas pants and crewneck sweater, together with what appeared to be a cut-down naval jacket, gave him the look of a seaman, freshly arrived ashore.

Behind his smile she could sense calm; however, it was mainly the boy's blue eyes that caught her attention—they seemed ageless, misty blue, like the summer horizon of a far sea.

She blinked, beckoning the two forward with her stick. "Does that dog attack cats?"

The labrador shot out an indignant thought. "Attack cats, me? Is the old dear mad? I love the furry little things, as long as they keep their claws to themselves. Huh, attack cats!"

Ben patted his dog fondly. "Ned's just fine with cats, marm. He's friendly, too. Give the lady your paw, Ned!"

Mrs. Winn held out her hand, and Ned dutifully presented a paw.

Obviously impressed, the old lady stroked Ned's sleek coat. "Oh, you're a good dog, Ned, good dog!"

Ned gave her the benefit of his soulful gaze. "Thank you, marm, and you're a nice lady, nice lady!"

She turned to the strange boy. "So, what's your name?"

"Ben, marm, just call me Ben."

She offered her hand. Ben shook it gently, and she winked at him. "My name's Winifred Winn, but you can call me Winnie, and stop 'marming' me. You sound like my husband used to. 'Marm' this and 'marm' that. Well, Ben, I suppose you like apple pie and lemonade, and I'll bet Ned wouldn't mind a dish of water and a beef bone with lots of marrow and fat to it."

"Ooh, ooh! I could grow to love this old lady dearly!"

Ben bypassed the dog's compliment. "That'd be very nice, ma . . . er, Winnie, thank you."

She ushered them both inside. "It's the least I can do to thank you for driving those wretches away from the house. The trouble they've caused me! And the whole village. But enough of that, you've probably got troubles of your own. Come on, you two, we'll use the parlour. It's not often I have visitors."

BEN SAT AT A SPINDLE-LEGGED COFFEE
table in the parlour, tucking into a sizeable wedge of Mrs.
Winn's apple pie, with fresh cream poured over it. There was

a tall glass of homemade lemonade with it.
Ned had retired to the kitchen for his beef
bone and water, where Mrs. Winn also gave
him a piece of shortbread pastry. Horatio
arched his back and leapt onto a table, until
the big dog passed him reassuring thoughts.
The cat did not reply, but after a while began purring and
came down to rub itself against Ned's leg.

Mrs. Winn smiled approvingly as she came
out to fetch the rest of her apple pie and cream.
Returning to the parlour, she set it down in front
of her guest.

"Boys always like apple pie; help yourself,
son, you look as if you could use some more. Go
on, don't be shy!"

Ben took another generous slice. "Thanks . . .
Winnie, we haven't had much to eat since yesterday morning."

As he ate, the blue-eyed boy studied the portrait over the mantelpiece. "Is that your hus-

band's picture? Anchor Line cap'n, eh?"

Mrs. Winn stared curiously at him. "Not many lads your age would know that the Royal Navy is called the Anchor Line. Are you a seafarer, Ben?"

The boy took a thoughtful sip of lemonade. "Not really. I've knocked about on barges and coasters as a galley lad. You hear things about the sea . . . it's always interested me. I've read quite a lot of sea stories, too."

The boy did not like lying to the old woman, but he knew he could not tell her the truth. Who would believe that he and Ned had sailed on the *Flying Dutchman* in the year 1620! It would strain any credibility to believe that boy and dog were still alive and well, ageless, in the year 1896.

He caught Mrs. Winn staring at him intensely and turned away as she asked, "I won't tell anyone, Ben, where are you really from?"

He shrugged. "I think I was born in Denmark, Copenhagen, but I'm not sure. Ned's from there, we've always been together. We've lived in quite a few places . . . here and there."

Mrs. Winn shook her head, perplexed. "I'll bet you have. Any parents, brothers or sisters?"

"Not that I know of, ma . . . Winnie. I was planning on staying in Chapelvale for a while, as soon as I can find somewhere that allows dogs. I don't suppose you'd know of a place?"

Mrs. Winn suddenly felt sorry for her strange visitor. He looked so young, so alone. Concern showed in her voice. "You mean that you haven't anywhere to stay?"

Ben nodded. "I've got money. I could pay for lodgings, and I'd see Ned didn't bother anybody."

The old lady sat watching the boy. The flat grandfather

clock chimes rang out four-thirty. Ben had finished the last morsel of apple pie when his dog came from the kitchen and lay down contentedly, his head resting on the boy's scuffed boot. Fidgeting and fussing with her apron corner, Winnie looked up to the ornate moulded ceiling, then down to her husband's portrait, finally settling on Ben.

Something in her eyes told him she had reached a decision. Tapping her worn gold wedding ring against the chair arm, Mrs. Winn pursed her lips. "You aren't in any kind of trouble, are you, my boy?"

Ben sat up straight. "Certainly not, Miz Winn!"

She touched his hand reassuringly. "I believe you. You said you were thinking of staying in Chapelvale for a while. I suppose that means you'll be moving on one day. Hmm, you're a puzzle, Ben. There's more to you and your dog than meets the eye, a lot more."

She cleared away the plates and glasses, watching the crestfallen lad out of the corner of her eye. "Shall we say that you can stay here for a few days, then? I don't think those bullies will bother coming 'round to harass me if they see Ned wandering in the garden."

Ben brightened up immediately. "Oh, thank you, marm! Ned'll keep them away and I'll help you 'round the house and do your shopping for you, and I can pay for lodgings, too. I have money, you know. . . ."

Mrs. Winn held up her hand, cutting Ben off frostily. "Please, I'm not rich, but I have enough to get by on with Captain Winn's pension. I'm not beholden to anybody, and I don't need you to pay me—I'm allowing you to stay here as a friend."

Ned passed a thought to his master. "What a nice old lady

Winnie is. This place feels just like home, whatever home's supposed to feel like. Don't forget to thank her for me. I've been trying to talk with that cat, Horatio, but he's not got much to say for himself. It must be with his having no other creatures to speak to that he's lost the art of conversation, poor fellow."

Ben answered the dog's thoughts. "Well, when you do finally get chatting together, see what you can find out from him. It might give us a clue as to why we've been sent here."

Mrs. Winn tapped Ben's shoulder. "Are you listening to what I'm saying, young man?"

"What, oh, er, sorry, Miz Winn. I must have dozed off!"

The old lady chuckled. "Hmm, you looked as if you were ready to drop off there, sitting and staring at the dog. I was just saying that you and Ned could take the rear upstairs bedroom. I sleep down here in the small sitting room nowadays. My left leg's not too good, I need help getting upstairs. Perhaps you'd best go and take a nap. There's a nice bathroom up there, too."

Ben rose gratefully. "Thank you, Miz Winn. Thanks for everything from both of us. I think I will take a bath and a nap."

The old lady took Ben's hand. "Help me upstairs and I'll show you your room. I'll have dinner ready for you both at seven. Come on, Ned, good boy!"

The labrador looked questioningly at Ben. "I don't mind the nap, but a bath's out of the question. It's not half an hour since I had a good scratch and lick!"

Ben tugged at the black Lab's tail as they went upstairs. "Miz Winn means me, not you!"

• • •

It was a comfortable room with a soft, old-fashioned bed. Ben picked up a framed sepia photograph from the bedside table. A young man and woman with two small boys stood on a palm-fronded verandah. The boy studied it. "Hmm, looks like India or Ceylon, some sort of plantation."

Mrs. Winn was mildly surprised at her strange guest's knowledge, yet looking at his wise blue eyes, it seemed right somehow that he should know about the photograph. "Your second guess was correct, Ben. It's Ceylon. That's my son Jim with his family—he manages a tea plantation for a British company out there. I've not yet seen his wife Lilian, or the children. That photograph is all I have of them. Maybe some-day they'll come over for a visit. . . ."

Mrs. Winn suddenly looked very sad, and she sighed. "Still, maybe it would be better for me if they stayed in Ceylon."

Ben became curious. "Why do you say that, Winnie?"

She shuffled slowly out of the room as she replied. "I'll tell you at dinner. Stay where you are, lad, I can manage going downstairs on my own quite well."

After a good hot bath, Ben dressed in a clean change of clothing from his canvas bag and lay on the bed, watching a shaft of late day sunlight on the floral wallpaper. Birdsong from the garden and the distant rumble of a train sounded pleasant and comforting. He drifted off into a slumber, happy that Ned and he had found somewhere to stay.

The dream stole unbidden into his sleep. Gale-force winds sweeping over a heaving deck, tattered sails framed against a storm-ripped sky, great grey-green waves rushing across the raging main. He was clinging to the dog as they were washed overboard through the shattered midship rails.

Water, water, the earth was awash in wild seawater, pounding in his ears, filling his nostrils, that odd faraway sound of muffled breath escaping beneath the ocean's surface. Then spray churning white as he and the dog surfaced in the vessel's wake. He tried to swim with one hand, whilst clinging to the dog's collar with the other, when he was struck by a spar and his dream became cascades of coloured lights, exploding from the darkness. A velvety calm enveloped Ben as he floated off someplace in time and space. A gentle golden radiance filled his spirit when the angel's voice called, soft as noon breeze in summer meadows.

"Rest here, stay awhile, help those in need of your gifts. Even in a place such as Chapelvale there are petty tyrants and those whose hearts are ruled by greed. You and your dog must come to the aid of the good folk here. But, hearken, at the sound of a single toll from a church bell, you must leave!"

The message of the bell—a church bell this time—remained clear in Ben's mind, even as his dreams raced on, over centuries, across seas, over mountains, through distant lands, wherever he and Ned had been sent to assist the oppressed in their struggle against villainy. He saw faces from the past, friends and enemies alike, felt the apprehension of arrival, the joy of being part of so many communities and the sorrow of having to depart and leave them behind. Always onward to fresh adventures, with his faithful, unchanging friend Ned. The last thing that trailed through his dream was a vision of the *Flying Dutchman,* with Vanderdecken wild-eyed at the ship's wheel. Away, away across the dark waters it fled, until it, too, was lost to sight. Ben's slumber drifted with him off in the opposite direction, to calm, untroubled sleep.

● ● ●

Mrs. Winn's cottage pie was as mouthwatering as the dessert of jam roly-poly pudding and custard. She certainly knew how to cook for a hungry lad and his dog.

Ben brought up Mrs. Winn's remark from the afternoon. "Winnie, I hope you don't mind me asking, but why did you say that it would be better if your son and his family stayed in Ceylon? Don't you want them to visit you?" As if she had been waiting for a sympathetic ear, the old lady poured forth her tale of woe.

"A man from up north has come to live just outside of Chapelvale. His name is Obadiah Smithers, and he is in the business of industrial speculation. Do you know what that means? Small villages and hamlets right across Britain are being destroyed by men like Smithers. They build their mills and factories with chimneys belching black smoke, sink mines with slag heaps defacing the countryside, hack out quarries, scarring the fields and destroying the woodlands— all in the name of progress, which they say nothing can stop! Yet all they bring, the Smitherses of this world, is misery, for money. Temporary hovels for their workers, low wages, and folk working right 'round the clock to make vast profits for their masters."

Ben could see by Mrs. Winn's clenched fists and quivering voice that she was defiant, yet frightened. He spoke soothingly. "So, what is it that Smithers wants with Chapelvale? It's just a little village."

With an effort she steadied her voice. "He wants limestone, would you believe. It appears Chapelvale is sitting on top of huge limestone deposits! As you know, limestone is the basis of cement, and what with all the building going on all over England, cement is in great demand. Progress means

more buildings: more buildings, more cement! Obadiah
Smithers, together with Jackman Donning and Bowe, a
London firm, did a survey of the land and made the discovery.
They plan to have a limestone quarry and a cement
factory, right here in Chapelvale. They even had the railway
branch line built so they can deliver cement anywhere.
By next Thursday, when the demolition order is made
official, the shops, houses, school, the entire village will be no
more!"

"Couldn't you move to another village?"

Ben's remark was quite innocent. He was taken aback at
the vehemence of the old lady's reaction—she virtually ex-
ploded.

"Move? Certainly not, young man! Chapelvale and the
surrounding lands first belonged to the Winn family. I con-
sider it my village!"

The boy shrugged. "Has nobody tried to stop all of this?"

Mrs. Winn banged the table with frustration. "I tried, the
day that Smithers posted his first notice in the square. I went
straight to my lawyer, Mr. Mackay, and stated my claim as a
member of the Winn family. But the only deeds of ownership
I have are for this house. I haven't any other written proof—I
don't even have the deeds to the village almshouse in the
square, though Captain Winn said it still belongs to his family and it is our inheritance."

"A village almshouse?"

The old lady poured tea as she explained. "Long ago an
almshouse was a place where poor people could find free
food and lodging. They were generally owned by rich
families, or the Church. Poor friars, brothers of begging
orders, mendicant monks, often stayed at them. Nobody really

knows how old our almshouse is, but it's very ancient. Unfortunately, it's in a dreadful state of repair. An old friend of Captain Winn's has taken to living there. His name is Jon Preston—the villagers think that he's quite mad."

Ben replenished the old lady's teacup. "I'd like to meet him."

She shook her head with a quick, severe, bird-like movement. "I'd advise you to steer clear of him, lad. That old hermit doesn't take kindly to strangers or young people!"

She sniffed, wiping her eyes with her apron hem. "He'll have to find somewhere else to live after next Thursday. The deadline comes in force then and there's little I, or anyone else, can do about it."

The strange boy's blue eyes softened. He felt sad for the old lady. "Only one week, but why?"

Mrs. Winn gave a hopeless little shrug. "Smithers and his London investors are powerful people. I can't prove the Winn title to Chapelvale land, and I haven't the money to fight them. Jon Preston said he'd look for evidence, and Mr. Mackay has done his best to help, but it's no use.

"A month ago Smithers and his friends took out a Court Order. They posted a notice in the village square. It says that any person—but it really means me—must prove ownership of the land. In the event of no legal claims turning up, Smithers and the Londoners intend to purchase the village, shops, houses, almshouse, farms, everything. Then they can demolish Chapelvale to make way for their quarry and cement factory.

"That was a month ago—there's only seven days left now. Not only that. I know Smithers allows that boy of his to run loose with his gang. They harass me, the shopkeepers, and village folk. Some folk are so tormented by them that they'll be glad to move away in the end!"

Ned and Horatio had wandered into the parlour. They both lay stretched on the hearthrug when the hall clock chimed nine. Other than that the room lay silent in the gathering dusk of a late-summer evening. Mrs. Winn sat staring out of the window at her garden with its high redbrick wall, rhododendrons and roses, the neat square lawn separated by a gently curving path with borders of pansies, gypsy grass, and busy lizzie. Ben resisted the urge to comfort her. Instead he passed a thought to his dog.

"Did you hear all that?"

The big black animal opened one eye. "Well, almost, I've got the general idea of what's going on. Though I don't see how we can help."

Ben's fists clenched involuntarily. "But we've got to help. Now I know why the angel steered us to Chapelvale, Ned: We must help these people to help themselves in some way or other! Ned, you've closed that eye—are you going to sleep?"

The labrador's eye flicked lazily open. "No, I'm giving it some thought. The best way to solve a problem is to sleep on it. Not a lot we can start doing until tomorrow, is there, Ben?"

The boy watched Mrs. Winn rise and start clearing away the dinner things. He helped her to carry the dishes out to the kitchen, then took up a dishcloth. "You wash and I'll wipe, Winnie. We'll soon get these dishes cleared away, and please stop worrying, everything will turn out all right, you've got me and Ned to help you now."

She shook her head and smiled. "Ned can't help with

the dishes." Turning away from the sink, Mrs. Winn found herself staring into the boy's wise blue eyes.

"You'd be surprised how me and Ned can help you!" he said.

AS SUNLIGHT STREAMED THROUGH THE window onto the counterpane, a dairy cart clattered by in the lane. Ben wakened gradually, taking stock of his new

 surroundings. The house was quiet, which gave him the feeling it was quite early. He let his gaze wander from the lace curtains and the warm July day outside. Stretching lazily, he lay back, studying the flowered wallpaper and the small iron-and-tile fireplace with a lacquered screen standing on its hearth. He heard the hall clock chime faintly from downstairs and counted each chime. . . . Ten!

Leaping out of bed, he dressed hastily, rushed to the bathroom, splashed water on his face, and dashed downstairs, having to leap the last three to avoid tripping over Horatio.

Ned was sitting in the kitchen beside an empty bowl. He nodded at Ben. "Morning. Sleep well?"

The boy answered the thought as he picked up a note from the table. "Why didn't you come up and wake me earlier?"

The dog put his front paws up on the table alongside his mate. "Didn't want to disturb any plans you were sleeping on, you know, to help Mrs. Winn. What does her note say?"

Ben scanned the scrap of paper. " 'Gone to village to do some shopping, porridge in pot on range, make tea for yourself. See you later. Winnie.' "

He felt the pot, it was still hot. So was the tea in the teapot. The boy served himself and sat at the table, thinking. "She can't have gone too long ago."

The big black labrador blinked patiently. "Not more than ten minutes or so. Well, what's the plan, O wise master?"

Over the centuries, Ben had come to appreciate the dog's banter. Dishing himself a large bowl of porridge, he conversed as he ate.

"A library, that's it, Ned. If Chapelvale has a library, that'd be a good place for us to start. It would probably have local history and reference books concerning this area. Might give us a lead or two."

The labrador snorted. "A lead: was that meant to be a joke? Libraries aren't fond of dogs roaming 'round loose among the books. Not great readers, us dogs."

Ben poured tea, stirring in lots of sugar. "Right, Ned, so what are your plans for the day?"

The dog trotted out of the kitchen, passing on his thoughts. "Open the front door, mate, I think I'll take a stroll 'round the village. Keep the old ears open, y'know. Might hear some information to pass on to the young master, eh?"

Ben grinned. "I'm older than you. Let me see, I was born in sixteen hundred and seven, that makes me two hundred and eighty-nine years old. You were only four when I met you. That makes you, er, two hundred and eighty. So be more respectful to your elders, pup!"

Ned turned and poked his head around the doorway. "Pup

indeed! Listen, laddie, one human year is equal to eight dog years. So that makes me . . . er, hmmm . . . a lot older than you by far, so show a little respect and mind your manners!"

The boy, his hair an unruly thatch, watched his friend trot off down the path. "Go easy now, old fellow, it'll soon be time for your nap. Hahaha!"

The dog turned and wrinkled his nose. "Silence, insolent child!"

After breakfast Ben saw Alex and Amy Somers in the lane, and nodded back at the house. "D'you like my new place?"

Amy giggled. "That's Miz Winn's house, she's nice. We went there with Dad when he treated her cat. Are you staying there, Ben?"

The boy flicked the hair from his eyes. "For a while. Listen, you two, I need your help again. You know Chapelvale, is there a local library hereabouts?"

The girl pointed. "Over by the school, actually it's attached to our village school. The librarian is Mr. Braithwaite. He works in the library right through the summer holidays. You'll like him, he's funny."

Alex led the way. "Come on, we'll take you there. What do you want, some kind of special book? Where's your dog today?"

Ben strolled along with the friendly pair. "Oh, he's around somewhere. He often goes off on lone rambles. I was wondering if I might get hold of a book about the local history of Chapelvale. I'm trying to help Mrs. Winn prove her claim to the land hereabout."

Amy pulled a face. "Oh that, you should hear the names our dad calls Mr. Smithers. If Smithers has his way, it looks like we will be moving to Hadford soon."

Ben noticed the angry look on the girl's pretty face.

"Hadford, where's that?"

Alex explained. "It's the nearest big town, all factories and streets full of chimney smoke. Dad won't lose his job, he's the veterinary surgeon for most of the county, but if Smithers buys every shop in the village and sets up his quarry and cement works, everyone will have to move. I'd hate to live in Hadford! Chapelvale's a good little village. We like it here."

Ben nodded. "Good! Then let's see what we can do to save the old place. Will you help me?"

His new friends' eyes shone with excitement. "I'll say we will!"

Mr. Braithwaite had a slight stoop, and small spectacles balanced on the end of his nose. He also had a huge cloud of frizzy grey hair, which he constantly scratched at absentmindedly. As Ben and his friends entered the library, Mr. Braithwaite glanced up over his glasses at them. "Hmm, er, Alexander and Amelia, er, er, Somers, isn't it, hmm yes, right, er. Not like you two t'be in the er, library when the hmm, school's finished for summer, er, er, no indeed!"

Amy introduced their new friend. "Sir, this is Ben, he wants to look at local history books. We're trying to save the village, you see."

The librarian-cum-schoolmaster came out from behind his counter. Scratching his head with one hand, whilst brushing dandruff from his collar with the other, he peered at the strange boy with blue eyes.

"Hmm, ah yes, very good! Is there, er, any specific reference you wanted to er, see, young, er . . . man?"

Ben tried his best to look intelligent and polite. "Yes sir,

I'd like to look at anything in connection with Chapelvale and the Winn family, please."

Mr. Braithwaite nodded furiously, a pencil falling from behind his ear as he warmed to his favourite subject. "Hmm, mm, mm, yes, Chapelvale, Winn family, very good! I'm er, actually er, quite a noted, er, devotee of hmm, local history. Now, if I'm, er, correct, the volume you want is called, er, *Village Chronicles of the British Isles,* part, er, four! Yes, very good, very good, by Roger, let me see, Russell Hope. By Roger Hope Russell, er, pardon me!"

They followed him as he scurried animatedly to a back shelf and knelt on the floor, his head to one side, muttering. "Domesday Commentary, Anglo-Saxon Settlements . . . Aha! Here 'tis, the very volume, er, er, indeed!"

The huge, dusty, leather-bound volume made an echoing thud when Mr. Braithwaite slammed it on the table. With the enthusiasm of an amateur historian, he scoured the index. "Chapelmount, Chapel Norton, Chapelton . . . Yes, yes, got it! Page 986, appendix B."

Leafing through the yellowed pages, Mr. Braithwaite found the relevant item. He stood scratching his frizzy mop in a shaft of sunlight, until he was surrounded by a halo of dandruff. He nodded approvingly as Ben read aloud from the page.

" 'Chapelvale (circa 1340), medieval village land. Granted to a Sea Captain (origin and name unknown) by the Black Prince, Edward III. Church built there, later to become an almshouse. Used by wayfaring poor and mendicant monks. Second church building (circa 1673) following Test Act and persecution of Catholics under Charles II. Mainly pasture and some agriculture. Middle England village with square. Nearby town Hadford.' "

Ben scanned the page in silence awhile before looking up. "Nothing more of any real interest here. Thank you, sir. Is there anything else about Chapelvale in your library?"

Mr. Braithwaite rocked back and forth on his heels. "Any what? Oh, er, hmmm. No no, nothing, er, I'm afraid!"

Ben signalled his friends with a nod. "Many thanks for your help, sir. We've got to go now. Good-bye!"

The stooped librarian stood watching them leave, searching for the pencil behind his ear, which had fallen earlier. "Quite, er, yes. Good-bye, er, er. . . . Call again if there's anything you should, er, need, very good, very good, yes!"

They emerged from the library into the sunlit late morning. Ben chuckled. "What an odd old fogey."

Without warning Alex went pale. He turned to go back into the library. Ben checked him, noting his frightened look.

"Steady on, there. What's the matter with you, pal?"

Staring straight ahead, Amy answered for her brother. "It's the Grange Gang!"

Wilf Smithers, Regina Woodworthy, and the gang had formed a semicircle about the library steps, blocking the way.

Ben threw an arm around the younger boy. "Stick with me, they won't bother us, pal!"

As they started down the steps, Wilf and Regina circled either side of them, their aim to get behind the trio and cut off any retreat. Wilf pinched Alex's cheek and smiled maliciously.

"Hello, it's little Alexandra!"

Clearly terrified, the boy turned beetroot red and kept silent.

This encouraged the bully, who sniggered. "Alexandra's gone all shy. Blushing, are we, Alexandra?"

Amy came fearlessly to her brother's defence. Whirling on Wilf, she shouted at him defiantly, "He's not Alexandra, his name is Alexander! You big bully, why don't you go away and leave us alone?"

Wilf pretended he had not heard her, but Regina positioned herself in front of the smaller girl. She stood blocking Amy's path, arms folded and a sneer on her face, which was red and bruised from her fall off the garden wall a day earlier.

"Are you going to make us go away, eh?"

Smiling at the results of his dog's chase, Ben addressed the Grange Gang girl in a friendly tone. "That's a nasty bruise on your face, what happened to you?"

Wilf was two steps above Ben. He turned on the newcomer. "It's none of your business. Anyhow, who are you? An' what do you want around here?"

Smiling even wider, the boy shrugged. "Oh, I'm nobody really, just been to the library to catch up on a bit of reading. But I don't imagine reading interests you. No, you look more like the type who likes to colour in the pictures."

The rest of the gang looked at one another, shocked. You didn't talk to Wilf Smithers like that. The village bully was the biggest, strongest boy in Chapelvale, and he had a reputation for being quick-tempered and extremely violent. Wilf's face turned brick red at the stranger's insult. Clenching both fists, he snarled dangerously. "I'll colour your face in for you, smart mouth!"

Amy shook with fright as Wilf launched himself down the steps, fists swinging. Ben was bound to get hurt.

However, the smaller, towheaded lad stood there, still smiling, as if unaware of the danger. Moving a swift half-pace to one side, he turned to face Alex. "D'you think he's upset?"

Ben ducked his head slightly.

It was a perfectly timed move. Wilf's fist actually brushed the back of Ben's hair, then he went sailing past his victim, carried by his own impetus. Stumbling awkwardly, he fell down the last four steps onto the gravel path. Before anyone could react, the boy skipped nimbly down and began hauling Wilf upright, helpfully brushing the bully's clothing off.

"What a dreadful fall. Are you all right? Easy now, friend. Hope you haven't broken anything!" Wilf's nose had scraped the gravel, and a swelling was starting to show on his forehead. He shoved free of Ben's hands.

"Leggo of me, I'm no friend of yours!"

The smile had never left Ben's face for a moment. "Oh, what a shame, I hoped we would be pals. I was looking to make new friends in Chapelvale."

The bullying girl grabbed Amy's arm, digging her nails in cruelly. "I'll be seeing you around!"

But she instantly released her hold, wincing painfully. Ben had her other hand in a curious grip and was shaking it heartily.

"Any friend of Amy's is a pal of mine. Hope I'll see you around, too. Look, Alex, I'm making new friends already!"

He released Regina's hand. She shot a furious glance at Wilf, who called to the rest of the gang, "Let's get them!"

Ben placed himself in front of Alex and Amy, backing slowly up the steps as the gang members began closing in. He whispered to his friends. "Get out of here, make a run for it. It's me they want!"

Alex was about to dash off, but his sister caught his arm. "We're not going without you, Ben!"

Before she could say any more they were surrounded.

There was a panicked squeak from Tommo, the fat boy, followed by a deep, rumbling snarl. The gang froze!

The black labrador had come up behind them like a phantom. Hair bristling, muscles bunched, he stood panther-like, ready to spring to the attack, quivering lips pulled back to reveal his powerful canine fangs.

Ben's hand went up. "Stay, boy. . . . Stay!"

Regina pulled a small gang member in front of her for safety. "It's the dog! Do you own it?"

Seating himself on the steps, Ben shook his head. "Who, me? No, I don't own him, he just follows me about. Haha! He must like me, 'cos he's not too friendly with anyone who tries to harm me or my friends. Ned, come on, boy, good dog!"

Stiff-legged and growling with menace, the big, black dog stalked up to stand beside his mate, throwing out a thought. "Let me chase 'em, just for exercise. That big one, Wilf, I'll rip the seat out of his pants! I don't like him one bit!"

Ben took hold of Ned's collar. "Thanks anyway, but you stay put for the moment. Carry on with your fierce dog act."

Ned strained against Ben's hold on his collar, rearing up on his hind legs as if trying to get at the gang. Ben did his part by showing difficulty holding the dog back and calling, "You'd best get going, pals, but walk, don't run, whatever you do. Go on, I'll keep him here until you're well out of the way!"

Amy had never seen the Grange Gang go so carefully. They retreated as if they were walking on eggs. From a distance, Wilf turned and pointed a finger at Ben.

"I'll see you again, when you haven't got that dog with you!"

The blue-eyed boy waved cheerily. "That'll be nice, Wilf,

take care of those scratches on your nose. It's red enough as it is!"

Mr. Braithwaite emerged from the library, scratching his head. "Er, could you stop your dog barking, please? Hmm, I can, er, hear it, y'know, in the, er, er, library. Oh, it's stopped, hmm, very good, very good. Nice doggie, er, run along now."

Ned sent Ben a thought. "Huh, if I scratched as much as he does, you'd prob'ly say I had fleas and make me take a bath!" The towheaded lad could not help laughing aloud.

Amy stared at him. "What's the matter, Ben?"

He flicked the hair from his eyes. "Oh, nothing really. You were right, Amy, Mr. Braithwaite is funny. I like him."

OVER BREAKFAST ON SATURDAY MORNING, Ben had a request to ask of Mrs. Winn.

"Miz Winn, that room across the landing from my room upstairs, the one with the thick door and brass lock. What do you use it for?"

She looked at him over the rim of her teacup. "I don't use it for anything, that was Captain Winn's study. He called it his den. All his stuff is in there. I only go in once every couple of months to dust around."

Ben had made an educated guess that the room would be the captain's private sanctum. Apart from one or two souvenirs he had brought home for his wife and some photographs that decorated the mantel, there was not much evidence of a Royal Navy ship's commander about the rest of the house. Evidently Mrs. Winn kept the room as some sort of shrine to her husband's memory. She watched Ben's eyes carefully.

Knowing what he was going to say next, he hesitated a moment before speaking. "Miz Winn, would it be all right if I took a look in there?"

The black dog had wandered up to the table. She patted his head, feeding him buttered toast crusts, and kept Ben waiting on her answer, which she gave after a lengthy interval. "Is it important that you look in the captain's room, Ben?"

The boy nodded earnestly. "Time's running short for your village. We might find something up there that could help."

She took a final sip of tea. "Right, then, you may take a look this afternoon, when we get back from shopping in the village. I'll need your help to carry things, I'm not just shopping for myself any more. Come on, then, let's make an early start!"

Hiding his frustration at not being able to search immediately, Ben thanked her and passed a thought to Ned. "Never mind hiding under the table, you're coming, too!"

Morning sun dappled through the trees growing behind the village square. The place hummed gently with that Saturday morning sound of folk doing their weekend shopping. Ben carried Mrs. Winn's basket dutifully, wondering when she was going to finish getting her supplies. They had gone from shop to shop, the old lady bustling about, dropping items into the basket, talking aloud to herself. "There, sugar and rice and some nutmegs for my Sunday rice pudding. Come on, young man, keep up!"

At last they emerged from the shop. Mrs. Winn pursed her lips, mentally itemizing the grocery list. "Oh dear, I forgot the tea! Maybe I'll get some cocoa, too, a mug of cocoa's nice at bedtime. Do you like cocoa, Ben? You stay here, I'll go and get it." She vanished inside the shop again.

Ben changed hands, swapping the basket from right to left and tightening his hold on a package beneath his arm. He caught a thoughtwave from Ned. "Good boy, don't let that basket drop now. Over here, Ben, look who's with me."

The Somerses were sitting on the post office steps, stroking Ned, who was enjoying the attention immensely. Ben spoke aloud to the dog as he approached.

"You great lazy lump, you should be carrying this. Whew! Miz Winn certainly takes some keeping up with for an old lady. Hello there, you two!"

Amy pointed to the package beneath his arm. "What's in the parcel, Ben?"

To her surprise he looked faintly embarrassed. "Some new clothes. Miz Winn bought them. I didn't want her to, but she thinks I need to look respectable for Sunday church service tomorrow. Move over there, pals."

Ben sat with them on the post office steps, watching folk following their weekend shopping routines as always. Shop doorbells tinkled as people came and went, standing beneath the canvas awnings, gossiping and viewing the goods behind the bull's-eye-paned windows of drapers, chandlers, butchers, and dairy produce merchants. Housewives with heavily laden shopping bags hanging from the handles of baby perambulators, calling to husbands who were chatting to other menfolk outside the newsagent and tobacconists. Children with coned paper bags, emerging from the sweetshop, sucking on treacle toffees, aniseed balls, and nut brittle, gazing absently about to locate their parents. Ben could not help commenting.

"Odd, isn't it. You wouldn't think that the place has less than a week left as a village. Don't they care, what's the matter with them?"

The girl watched Ben's intense blue eyes studying the scene. "My mum says it's because they're village folk, with a village mentality. She says they won't accept it could happen to them. These village families go back centuries. They just don't know what progress and change mean. If anything frightens them, they push it to the back of their minds and get on with their lives. Hoping it'll go away, I suppose."

Alex's face reddened, and he stared down at the step. "Like me. I try to ignore Wilf Smithers and his gang. I wasn't much use to you yesterday, never said a word, just stood there like a lump."

Ben patted his friend's arm reassuringly. "But you did do something, pal, you stood alongside Amy and me. It was Ned who saved the day. I was as scared as you or your sister—there was a whole gang of them. No shame in being afraid when you're outnumbered more than three to one, right, Amy?"

The girl could see their new friend was being kind to her brother, and she nodded. "That's right, Ben. There's better ways of being brave than letting yourself get beaten up by Smithers's gang."

Ben rose as he saw Mrs. Winn approaching. "Your sister's right, Alex. Courage shows itself in different ways—chin up, pal, you'll see."

Mrs. Winn loaded more purchases into the basket and greeted the two young people.

"Well, good morning, do you remember me? You came with your father when my cat was sick last year. Now let me see, you both had names beginning with A . . . Amelia and Alexander!"

Alex had cheered up a bit, and he corrected her. "Amy and Alex, Miz Winn. I remember you gave us apple pie and lemonade. How is your cat now?"

Mrs. Winn rummaged through her purse as she replied.

"Horatio's fine, thank you, fine. Ben, how would you like to take your friends for some ice-cream? Evans Tea Shoppe makes their own, you'll enjoy it. I'll come over later for tea and a scone. Here, Amy, you can be in charge of the ice-cream money. Don't forget to buy one for Ned, too. He's a good dog."

Ben picked up the basket. "Where are you going, Miz Winn?"

Setting her lips tightly, she pointed at two figures entering a building on the square's east side. "Right where those two are going, to my lawyer's office. I've been hoping to see Mackay. Time's of the essence, isn't it." She had said nothing about an appointment. "I'll see you later."

As they watched Mrs. Winn walking swiftly across to the lawyer's office, Amy nodded to the man who was ushering a young lady into the building ahead of him. "That's Obadiah Smithers, Wilf's dad. He's the one who's buying the village to turn it into a cement factory. I don't know who the lady is, though."

Ben glanced at the pair. "Neither do I, but I saw them get off the train together when I arrived here. Maybe she's from London, part of that firm Smithers has dealings with—"

Alex interrupted. "Jackman Donning and Bowe, that's who my dad said they were. Wonder which one she is?"

EVANS TEA SHOPPE DID SERVE GOOD ICE-
CREAM. It came in a long dish, pink and white with rasp-
berry sauce and chocolate crumbs sprinkled on top. Mr. Evans
 worked in the back of the shop, baking and
making ice-cream. Blodwen, his wife, an im-
mense jolly woman with a strong Welsh accent,
served them. Though animals were not usually allowed inside, she was charmed by the big
black labrador, who looked very meek and offered his paw. Mrs. Evans lifted the edge of the tablecloth.
"Ooh look you now, there's a lovely dog, he is. Sit him under
the table now. Indeed to goodness, who'd be keepin' a fine
dog like him outside with no ice-cream!"

As Ned tucked into his ice-cream, which came on a tin
plate, Ben tuned in to the dog's thoughts. "Delicious, wonderful stuff. Just the thing after a hard morning's shopping!"

Ben put his feet on the dog's back as he answered. "You
great furry fraud!"

Ben pulled aside the lace curtain. From where he was
sitting he could see an ancient, rambling, one-storey building
at the square's northwest corner. It was a jumble of wattle
and daub, stonewalling and patches of worn brick, with
crumbling mortar, makeshift repairs against the ravages

of time. The faded roof of thatch sat on it like a badly fitted wig with a raggedy fringe. A large bump sticking up in the centre of the roof gave it an odd, rather comical aspect. The whole thing was fronted by an overgrown patch of greenery and a rickety fence, partially broken by bushes growing through it. Sunlight shading through high hawthorns lent it an air of picturesque dilapidation. He pointed with his spoon.

"Is that the place they call the almshouse?"

Alex looked up from his ice-cream. "Yes, but you'd best stay away from it, Ben. The mad professor lives there!"

Ben laughed, as if the other boy was joking. "Haha, mad professor?"

Amy backed her brother's statement up. She whispered, "It's true, Ben, a mad professor does live in the almshouse. He doesn't like people and he seldom comes out—even Wilf Smithers and the Grange Gang don't go near there. They say he has a double-barrelled shotgun and he's not afraid to use it. Alex is right, keep away from the almshouse!"

From her side of the table Amy could see Mr. Mackay's office. "Look, Ben." She pointed. "There's Miz Winn coming out of the lawyer's office. I wonder what she was doing in there?"

Even from a distance it was plain to see that the old lady's dander was up. Mr. Mackay, a small, dapper lawyer, was standing between Mrs. Winn, Obadiah Smithers, and Maud Bowe, anxiously trying to prevent trouble. He was not having much success. The old lady, her chin thrust forward pugnaciously, was wagging a finger at Smithers and Bowe, evidently giving them a piece of her mind. Several times the pair tried to walk away, but she confronted them, not giving up until she had said what she wanted. It was Mrs. Winn who finished the argument as well. She stamped her foot and marched off, leaving her foes dumbfounded. Mr. Mackay scuttled back into his office, glad to have all three away from his premises before they attracted too much notice.

Amy nodded admiringly. "Here she comes, good old Winnie. Oh, Ben. I wish there were more folk in Chapelvale like her. She won't give up without a fight!"

The blue-eyed lad licked the last of his ice-cream from the spoon. "Who knows, maybe there are, once they get stirred up enough to do something about their problems."

Mrs. Winn's black-button boots clicked sharply on the floor as she marched into Evans Tea Shoppe. Her cheeks were quite pink and she was obviously irate. She rapped twice on the counter. "A pot of Ceylon tea and a hot buttered scone, if you please, Blodwen!"

Blodwen gave her a cheery nod. "Indeed to goodness, Winnie Winn, there's bothered you look. Sit you down, dearie, I'll bring them right to you!"

Amy moved swiftly to make room as Mrs. Winn came to sit at the table. She blew out a long breath, took a small mirror from her bag, and began primping the hair that wisped out on either side of her navy blue straw boater hat. Her order arrived swiftly; she poured a cup of tea, took three good sips, and tried to compose herself. Then she spoke.

"Well! The very nerve of that Smithers and that young snippet with the dreadful London accent!"

Ben felt like smiling at her indignation, but he put on a serious face. "Did they upset you, Miz Winn?"

She drew herself up and took another sip of tea. "Upset me? Certainly not! I wouldn't lower my standards and allow myself to be upset by the likes of them. Do you know, they made me a cash offer for my home and the almshouse? A piffling sum! When they saw I was not impressed, they doubled the offer. Hmph! I told them they could quadruple their paltry money, it still wouldn't budge me an inch!

"Then Smithers said he had taken legal advice, he said that if I still refused their offer after his scheme was under way, he could have me forcibly put out of my home and he could take possession of the almshouse without further permission!"

Blodwen Evans had been lingering nearby, eavesdropping, as she usually did on any good village gossip. She moved in to collect the empty ice-cream dishes. "And what did Mackay have to say about that, Winnie?"

The old lady seemed to deflate, her voice dropped to a murmur. "He said Smithers and his friends had the law on their side. That unless I can prove valid ownership and proper legal documents I haven't a leg to stand on."

Blodwen Evans gestured with a thumb to where her husband was at work in the back of the shop. "Aye, Smithers made my Dai a miserable offer as well, but what can we do, we ain't got the money to fight him. My Dai says we'll prob'ly have to take the offer for the teashop an' move back to Wales. Still, that may not be. I've talked to a lot of folk. There's Pettigrew the newsagent, Riley the ironmonger, Mrs. White from the sweetshop, and Mr. Stansfield the butcher. They say it can't happen, you know. Look you, even Smithers can't demolish a whole village just for some old limestone!"

Ben interrupted her. "He can, Mrs. Evans, and he will, unless something is done to stop him."

Any further conversation was cut short by loud banging on the wall from the alley outside. A row of willow-pattern plates standing on edge upon a shelf began to tremble and clatter under the pounding vibration from the outside of the wall. Mr. Dai Evans came running out into the shop, wiping flour from his hands and untying his baking apron.

As his wife hurried to steady the plates, she called to him. "It's that young Smithers an' his gang again, Dai!"

He dashed outside. Amy was about to rise when Ben stopped her. "Wait a moment, let's listen."

From outside Dai Evans could be heard shouting. "I know it's you, Wilf Smithers, no use leanin' against that wall, lookin' as if butter wouldn't melt in your mouth. Go on, be off with the lot of you!"

Wilf Smithers's voice sounded out impudently. "It wasn't us! We've got as much right to lean against this wall as anyone. Why blame us?"

Mr. Evans's voice shook with temper. "I know it was you lot. If you're not gone from here in two ticks, I'll call the constable!" Dai walked back into the shop, his fists clenching and unclenching at his sides, shaking his head and muttering. "I tell you, Blodwen, they'll have us out of here one way or the other. I'll be glad to get back to Wales, look you!"

Blodwen set the last plate straight and was just moving back to the counter when the wall shook in time with the chanting of the Grange Gang outside.

"Dai diddly eye dai . . . Dai Dai!"

She had to hurry to get back to her plates. Dai Evans grabbed a metal hooked pole he kept for pulling down the shade blinds. "Right, that's it, boyo, I've 'ad enough!"

Ben was on his feet, with Ned beside him. He stood in front of Dai, his voice calm. "You'll end up in trouble yourself if you go 'round breaking heads with that thing, Mr. Evans. Leave this to me."

Dai stared at the lad's steady blue eyes, unsure of what to do, until Mrs. Winn stood up. "Do as he says, Mr. Evans, you can trust the boy."

As Ben walked from the Tea Shoppe, Dai Evans stood to one side, avoiding Ned, whose hackles had risen. The big, black labrador was growling, low and ominous.

There was a moment's silence, followed by screams, yells, and barking, then the pounding of feet. Ben strolled back into the shop and sat down. He winked at Blodwen Evans. "More ice-cream, please, marm, and a pot of fresh tea for Miz Winn. My turn to pay for this one, pals."

Five minutes later the dog returned and flopped down beneath the table, passing Ben a thought. "I chased 'em up as far as the station, where they ran into the waiting room. Stationmaster didn't like it much, he was chasing them out as I left. Wilf tried arguing with him, said he'd tell his dad that the stationmaster was driving them out into the teeth of a wild dog. Stationmaster didn't seem bothered, said he didn't care if there was a pack of wolves outside, they weren't allowed on railway property without a valid ticket for a train journey. Told them to go and play their silly games elsewhere. Any ice-cream left?"

Ned was the hero of the hour. Dai and Blodwen Evans refused to take any money for tea or ice-cream. Dai knelt by the table, feeding the labrador a plateful of vanilla ice-cream with fresh milk poured over it. Ned lapped away happily as Dai ruffled his ears.

"There's a good dog, you are, wish I 'ad one like you, boyo. How did you get him to do it, Ben?"

It was Amy who answered for Ben. "It was nothing really, Mr. Evans, it's just that Ned can't stand noise or bad manners."

Ben grinned at her over his plate of ice-cream. "Well said, Amy, you're getting to know Ned rather well!"

MAUD BOWE SAT PRIMLY AT THE SMITHERSES'
table with Obadiah and his wife Clarissa. They waited in silence as the maid served a gammon ham salad. Obadiah
 poured himself a glass of claret, ignoring his
wife and Maud, who preferred barley cordial in
the afternoon. When the maid had retired, shutting the door behind her, Maud continued her
one-sided argument. Mr. Smithers dismissed
her every point, overriding everything she said.
Though in the light of what had taken place with Mrs. Winn,
it was Maud who was winning the debate.

She tapped the spotless white damask tablecloth with a
dainty finger. "As I've said, sir, this is going to cost us quite a
bit!"

Smithers took a large swig of wine and stifled a belch.
"Nonsense, m'girl, everything's well in order, take it from
me."

Mrs. Smithers gazed at her salad, slightly shocked that a
young girl would argue with her husband, a thing she never
dared do. But Maud persisted. "Everything may well be in
order with the rest of the villagers, sir. But Mrs. Winn is the
one who is digging her heels in, she's going to be trouble. If
she refuses our offer, we'll have to wait seven clear days just

for a possession warrant. That's what my father says, and he knows the law, believe me!"

Smithers poured himself more claret, stuffing a piece of gammon in his mouth with his fingers. Table manners were not his strong point. He pointed a greasy finger at Maud. "Good man, your father, nice fellow. But he doesn't know everything. Not by a long chalk, missie!"

Maud hid her revulsion of the ill-bred northerner, but spoke out pertly in her father's defence. "My father knows his business, sir! He has made contracts with building firms that will not wait seven extra days. If Mrs. Winn is not out of her house on the deadline stated in the clearance notice, it will cost our scheme dearly with penalties for broken agreements. I hope you are aware of the position that delays can put us in!"

Mrs. Smithers flinched as her husband's temper broke. He sprayed ham and claret into the air as he shouted, "Don't you dare to tell me my business, girl! I know these villagers better than you or your father. Hah! What has that old Winn biddy got to prove her claims, eh? Nothing! We'll be saving ourselves money by clapping a compulsory court order on her. A mere pittance set by the county developer, that's all she'll get for her house! As for the almshouse, it belongs to nobody, we'll get that free! The rest of the villagers are too disorganized to resist us. They know virtually nothing about the law, we'll pay 'em the set rate for their properties. Little enough that'll be, I can tell you!"

He sat back, digging a scrap of ham from his teeth with a fingernail. But Maud would not be browbeaten. Wiping her lips daintily on a damask table napkin, she pushed aside her plate and rose from the table. "I'm going to my room, sir. Nothing has changed, we need to get the old lady out of her house by the appointed time. Whilst I'm upstairs, I'll give some thought to the problem. Perhaps you would do well to follow my example!"

She swept out of the dining room without another word, leaving Obadiah Smithers spluttering to his wife. "Cheeky little snip, who does she think she's talking to, eh? She's not twelve months out of some fancy finishing school. Hah! I was building my fortune the hard way, long before she was born. Right?"

Mrs. Smithers poured herself a glass of barley water as she replied dutifully to her irate husband. "Yes, dear, would you like some barley water? It's nice and cool."

Claret slopped onto the tablecloth as he poured more from the decanter. "Barley water, bah! Can't abide the filthy stuff. Look out, here's that harum-scarum of mine."

Wilf entered from the lawn by the French windows, red-faced and breathing heavily. He plonked himself down in the chair Maud had vacated. Taking the gammon ham slices from her plate, he lathered them with mustard and crammed them between two pieces of bread. His mother lectured him as he tore at the sandwich.

"Oh, Wilfred, you haven't washed your hands and you're late for lunch again. Leave that salad alone, it was Miss Bowe's. I'll tell Hetty to bring you a fresh plate. Dearie me, just look at you—"

Smithers interrupted his wife brusquely. "Oh, leave the lad alone, Clarissa. Stop fussin' an' faffin' about him! Now then, you young rip, got enough to eat there, eh?"

Wilf grumbled through a mouthful of ham sandwich, "Could do with some lemonade an' a piece of cake."

Mrs. Smithers got up from the table. "I'll go and fetch

them."

Her husband called out as she left the room. "No need for you to go, what'm I payin' servants for?"

She paid him no heed and made her way to the pantry.

Smithers poured himself more claret. "Huh, women!"

He leaned close to his son and nudged him, lowering his voice confidentially.

"So then, what've you been up to, you and that gang of yours?"

Wilf wiped mustard from his mouth with the back of a grimy hand. He knew it was better to speak of victories than defeats to his father. "Just livening things up in the village. Gave old Evans a bad time. I heard him say he'd be glad to get back to Wales."

Mrs. Smithers came in bearing a glass of lemonade and a plate of sliced sultana cake and was making as if to sit down when Obadiah stared pointedly at her.

"Finished your lunch, m'dear?"

She understood immediately that he wanted to be alone with Wilf. "Yes, dear, I'll go along and give Cook the menu for dinner this evening. Do you think Miss Bowe likes roast beef?"

Obadiah snorted. "Who gives a fig what she likes. She'll get what she's given in my house, and be thankful for it!"

Mrs. Smithers nodded and left the room.

Obadiah watched his son swigging lemonade and stuffing cake. "Never mind Evans and the rest. I've got them well under control. Mrs. Winn's the fly in the ointment—have you and your friends been 'round to her house lately? I need her out of there."

Wilf stopped eating and gnawed at a hangnail. "There's a

lad always hanging 'round with her. He's got a black dog with
him, big, vicious thing. Makes it hard to do anything with them
around, but I'll try."

His father's face hardened, he grabbed Wilf's arm tight.
"I've seen them. Listen, don't let the dog bother you. The
moment it bites you or your pals, let me know. I'll get the constable to round it up and have it destroyed. I'm surprised at
you, though, Wilf. That boy is half a head shorter than you
and a lot lighter. Big fellow like you should be able to whale the
livin' daylights out of him, that'd teach him a lesson. You're
not scared of him, are you, son?"

Wilf's face grew even redder. "Me, scared of that shrimp?
Huh!"

His father smiled. "Good boy, just like me when I was
your age. You find a way to get him on his own and give him a
good thrashin'. Don't let up if he cries, show him who's boss.
Will y'do that for me, eh?"

Fired by his father's words, Wilf nodded vigorously. "I'll do
it, all right. I owe that one a few good punches!"

Obadiah released his son's arm. Digging into his vest
pocket, he produced an assortment of silver coins and gave
them to him. "Here, buy your friends some toffee and tell
them to keep old Ma Winn on her toes."

Wilf jammed two slices of sultana cake together and took
a bite. He ruled the Grange Gang with an iron fist, not toffee,
and he would keep the money. "Thanks, Dad, I will," he lied.

MRS. WINN TOOK A KEY FROM A JUG ON THE kitchen shelf. "Let's take a look at the captain's room, Ben."

Ned's ears rose slightly. "I'd better come with you, a good bloodhound may be required to search the room."

Ben tugged his dog's ear lightly. "You're no bloodhound, Ned."

The labrador sniffed airily. "I should hope not—great, mournful-looking lollopers, that lot. But you know I'm pretty good at sniffing things out, so come on, my old shipmate!"

Ben helped Mrs. Winn to negotiate the stairs, trying not to show his impatience at her lack of speed. He told himself that he, too, would be old one day, then caught Ned's thoughtful observation. "Will you? When'll that be?"

The door was a heavy mahogany one, shining from layers of dark varnish, with brass trimmings.

Mrs. Winn gave the key to Ben. As he fitted it into the lock, he gave an involuntary shiver. Images of the sea welled up in his mind, ships, waves, wind, thrumming sails. He pictured himself and Ned long, long ago, locked in the galley of the *Flying Dutchman,* whilst outside, Vanderdecken murdered the seaman Vogel by shooting him. Then Mrs. Winn's hand was on his arm, breaking the spell.

"Ben, are you all right, boy?"

Reality flooded back, and he straightened up, turning the key. "I'm fine, Miz Winn. It was the lock, bit stiff I think. There, that's got it. Ladies first!"

It was a proper old seafarer's room, all shipshape and Bristol fashion, as the saying goes. Captain Winn had been a meticulous man, always storing things tidily. Framed certificates and merit awards, alongside pictures of various ships, carefully posed crews, and the captain himself depicted with groups of his numerous friends, hung in even lines on the walls. There was a brass-railed table, which had once graced a ship's cabin. On it stood a sextant and a globe.

In a corner a polished shell case stood, serving as a receptacle for some rolled-up charts and a couple of walking canes with carved heads. A rolltop desk took up most of another corner. Beside it were two sea chests. One was a beautiful example of carved Burmese teak, inlaid with mother-of-pearl and custard-coloured ebony. The other was a plain, black, naval-issue, officer's steamer case, with the name "Captain Rodney Winn. R.N." neatly painted on it in white enamel.

Mrs. Winn had to remove some interesting specimens of conch and nautilus shells from the top of the desk before she could open it. From a tiny drawer she took two keys, one plain and serviceable, the other very ornate, with a red silk tassel hanging from it. She unlocked the two chests, handing over the keys to Ben.

"All the captain's personal papers are in the desk and these two boxes. When you finish up here, make sure you lock everything up and put the keys back, Ben. I don't want to rummage through all this. Too many memories. Far too many ghosts for someone of my age. Hmm, I'll have to come up here tomorrow and have a good dust around. Captain Winn couldn't abide dust, hated it! Oh, would you like to see something, lad? Take a look at this."

She opened a wall cupboard, which was actually a built-in wardrobe. All the captain's uniforms, from ceremonial dress to everyday duty, were hung from a rail. Below, on shelves, his accoutrements were displayed—white gloves, cotton and wool for different climates, leather ones for formal occasions. Various ties, cravats and bows, medals bars, ribbons, stars, and other decorations were placed with care alongside gold-braid sleeve bands. Most of all, Ben admired a magnificent Royal Navy captain's sword and sheath, complete with gold tassels. He turned to comment on it to Mrs. Winn, but she had gone.

Ned's thought confirmed this. "She's gone downstairs, looking rather sad, too. What a good woman. Wouldn't it be nice if we could stay here for good, Ben. You remember that saying, there's no place like home. I'm beginning to realize what it means. I really like it here."

The lad sat down on the carpet, next to his friend, and stroked beneath his chin as he passed back a wistful thought. "I know what you mean, pal, but you know as well as I do, when the time comes to move on we've no option but to go."

They sat in silence for a moment, imagining what it would be like if they were ordinary mortals, growing older, growing up, staying in one place, living a normal life.

The big labrador broke the spell by butting Ben in the stomach and playfully knocking him flat on his back. "Come on, shipmate, aren't we supposed to be helping Miz Winn save her home and land by searching the room for clues?"

Ben opened the captain's chest. "This looks as good a place to start as any."

The Royal Navy chest was literally crammed with old dispatches, charts, and long out of date yellowed newspapers, all in careful order.

Ben flipped through them, Ned watching him rather impatiently. "Anything of value there, Ben?"

The boy looked up from his task. "Not really, it's all like a record of Captain Winn's career, admiralty orders, sea blockade plans, and these newspapers. Look, 1854, war declared against Russia by Britain and France. September fourteenth, the Allied armies landing in the Crimea, the siege of Sevastopol. It goes on and on, British history, right through the Indian Mutiny, up to Africa and the Zulu wars in the late 1870s. No family history here that would help us. Let's have a look at this fancy trunk."

He opened the carved chest. This looked more interesting at first glance. It had a fragrance of flowers, rose and lilac. Fine, dark red tissue paper separated the contents. Ben unpacked it and found a Chinese dragon-embroidered gown, bundles of letters tied with blue silk ribbon, a huge family Bible, a child's crayon drawings of landscapes and people, signed laboriously with the name James Winn, and photographs, some in cardboard frames bordered by hearts and doves.

Ben spread these on the carpet and studied them. "Hmm, what a handsome couple. Young Lieutenant Winn and his fiancée, Winifred, taken on the seafront at Brighton. Some wedding photographs, a picture of this house with Miz Winn standing in the garden. Here's another of them both with a baby carriage that must have been taken when their son Jim was born. Winnie wasn't joking when she said there were lots of memories here. What d'you think, Ned?"

The labrador turned over a packet of letters with his nose. "Shall we take a look at these? There's lots of 'em."

Ben shook his head. "No, they're love letters from when the captain and Winnie were courting. We don't want to pry into personal things like that. They're far too private." He set the letters to one side. "Well, I think we'd better take a look in the desk. There doesn't seem to be anything that can help us here."

Ned gazed reprovingly at his friend. "Except the Bible!"

Ben did not catch his dog's drift for a moment. "The Bible?"

The labrador placed his paw on the volume. "Aye, Ben, the good book—every family should have one. Good for the spirit, a great source of scripture, and usually a book where family records are kept." Sometimes Ned's knowledge of things was as surprising as his own.

Ben needed both hands to lift the huge Moroccan leather-bound family heirloom. "Of course! The family Bible. Good old Ned!"

The dog stretched out and yawned. "Good old Ned indeed, where'd you be without me?"

The boy placed the hefty tome upon the desk, smiling fondly at the big black dog. "Probably drowned off Cape Horn!"

It was a magnificent Bible, with a stained silver clasp holding it shut, faded gold-edged pages, and woven silk place-markers. Ben dusted off the cover with his sleeve, undid the clasp, and opened the ancient volume. On the inside cover was a hand-sketched angel, bearing a scroll written in gothic script.

"This Bible belongs to the Lord and the family of Winn. Blessed are those who trust in the Lord and live by His word."

Ben leafed carefully through the yellowed pages. Apart from beautiful illuminated verse headings and several colourful illustrations, there was nothing out of the ordinary. At the back of the book, he discovered a number of pages, some blank and others filled in by different hands over the centuries. Details recorded of births, deaths, and marriages provided an almost complete lineage of the Winns for several hundred years.

Ben read some of the details aloud.

"Listen to this, Ned. 'Edmond De Winn wedded to Evelyn Crowley. 1655. Lord deliver us from the plague of Black Death. 1665. A son, christened Charles in honour of our King. 1669. A daughter christened Eleanor.' It says here that Edmond fathered more daughters, Winefride, Charity, Gwendoline, and three others.

"Poor old Edmond, eh, Ned, a son and seven daughters. Quite a few mouths to feed." Ben closed the giant book. "This doesn't seem to be getting us anywhere."

The dog leapt up. Placing his front paws on the desk, he began frantically nosing at the Bible beneath Ben's hand. "What's the matter, boy?" Ben tried to push him away. "What'll Miz Winn say if you slobber all over her family Bible?"

But the dog persisted, sending out urgent thoughts. "The back of the book! I could see it from where I was lying. The back, Ben. Down inside the spine, something's there!"

Ben quickly shut the book and stood it on edge. He peered down the space between the spine and the pages. "You're right. It looks like a folded paper. Wait!" He took an ivory pair of chopsticks (one of the captain's souvenirs) and delicately fished the object out.

As Ben carefully unfolded the paper, the black dog looked on. "A piece of torn parchment, with two tiny holes burned in it. There's some wording on it. Read it, Ben, read it!"

The boy scanned the writing awhile. "It starts off strangely. Listen: 'Re, keep safe for the house of De Winn thy treasure.'"

Ned's tail wagged furiously. "Treasure! I think we're on the right track. But what does 're' mean?"

Ben continued staring at the scrap of parchment. "That's where the parchment was torn. 'Re' is probably the end two letters of a longer word. But well done to you for spotting this in the Bible's spine."

Ned's tail wagged. "Hah! Who said horses were man's best friend? What about us dogs, eh, shipmate?"

Ben put the parchment down. He leapt upon the big dog and wrestled him all over the floor, knowing this was his favourite sport, but the labrador got the better of Ben. Pinning him to the carpet, he began licking his face. "What other way can your poor hound serve you, O master?"

Ben giggled as the dog's tongue tickled his ear. "You can let me up, you great, sloppy hound!"

Though they searched high and low, there were no other clues to be found. It was late by the time Ben had tidied the room up and put everything back in its place. He folded the torn parchment and put it in his pocket. "Well, at least that's a start, though I don't know what the message means, or the two burnt holes in the paper. But it's something definite to begin with. Let's hope we can solve the problem before time runs out for Miz Winn and Chapelvale. Right, mate, bed for us, I'll just go to the bathroom and wash my face."

Ned looked indignantly at Ben. "But I just washed your face for you a moment ago, there's base ingratitude for you!"

The blue-eyed boy gave his dog a glance of mock severity. "One more word out of you and I'll wash your face for you, with soap and a scrubbing brush!"

SUNDAY MORNING, BEN ACCOMPANIED MIZ
Winn to church services, dressed in his new clothes. He felt
rather self-conscious in the new outfit, his unruly hair wetted
and brushed into a parting. The black labrador
had stayed home to keep Horatio company.
Mrs. Winn brought her walking stick, as it was
quite a walk to the church on top of the hill. At
the churchyard gate they met up with Alex and
Amy Somers, together with their parents. Mrs.
Winn knew the Somerses, and she stood and
chatted with them.

Alex caught Ben staring up at the spire,
looking rather nervous. "It's only a church
steeple, Ben, what are you looking for?"

There was a trace of perspiration on Ben's
forehead, and his face was slightly pale as he
answered. "The bell, has this church got a
bell?"

Mr. Braithwaite wandered close by, still in
his scholarly gown. He scratched his frizzy hair
as he peered over his glasses. "Er, what's that?
Oh, a bell y'say, hmmm? 'Fraid not, young er,
er, fellow. The, er, bell of St. Peter's church

was, er, donated to the cause by the clergy and parishioners during the, er, er, Napoleonic Wars. Yes, hmmm, indeed, to make armaments for the Duke of, er, Wellington's army. Bell metal, useful stuff, very good very good!"

The feeling of whirling waters, angel voices, and the *Flying Dutchman* out somewhere ploughing the misty main passed. Ben felt an immediate surge of relief. At least he did not have to worry about a church with a mute belltower. Amy tugged his sleeve to go inside, the service was starting.

St. Peter's, for all its size, was comparatively small inside. Beneath the arched wooden ceiling, supported by eight plain limestone columns, were two main aisles. There was an odour of lavender furniture polish on the benches, kneeling hassocks were of frayed chenille. Morning sunlight poured through the few well-preserved stained-glass windows, capturing myriad dust motes in slow swirls. Ben sat with his two friends whilst Reverend Mandel, a severe grey-haired man, delivered a sermon on the merits of charity to one's fellow creatures. Ben felt as if someone was watching him. He turned his head and took a quick glance at the pews behind. There was Wilf Smithers, with his mother and the girl from London. Obadiah Smithers was not given to attending church on Sunday, or any other day for that matter. Ben smiled at Wilf. Surprisingly, Wilf smiled back.

When the service was over, Mrs. Winn stopped to drop a coin in the box for the new bell fund. Wilf came up behind Ben and jammed a scrap of paper into Ben's pocket.

"Bet you won't be there!" he muttered in Ben's ear and moved away to join his mother and Maud Bowe at the lychgate outside, where a pony and cart were waiting to take them home.

Walking back downhill, Mr. Somers kindly assisted Mrs. Winn, offering her his arm. Ben walked ahead with his two friends, who saw him take the paper from his pocket and read what had been written on it. He laughed.

"Wilf slipped me this outside the church. Listen." Ben read out the badly written message: " 'You meet me this afternoon at four behind the liberry if your not scared. Do not bring your dog cos I only want to talk. I will be alone. If you do not come your a cowerd.

" 'Singed by W. Leader of the Grange Gang.' "

Ben sat down on the grassy slope, shaking his head and chuckling to himself. He passed the note to Amy, who read it again, smiling at the childish scrawl.

"Somebody ought to teach Wilf Smithers to spell *library* and *coward*. Oh, hahaha! He's put the letter *g* in the wrong place, instead of *signed,* it's *singed*. Written with a fiery pen, eh. Hahaha!" But his young friend did not find it the least bit funny.

"Of course you're not going. Are you, Ben?"

Summer breeze took the parting out of Ben's unruly hair, and he flicked it out of his eyes. "Why not?"

Alex had a number of reasons. He stated them all, anxiously. "Well, for a start, Wilf won't be alone. He'll have his gang hiding nearby. He doesn't just want to talk. You'll get beaten up, that's why he says not to bring Ned along. We know you aren't a coward, Ben, you don't have to go!"

Ben's strange blue eyes were smiling, but the younger boy could see something icy behind his careless merriment. It sounded in his voice as he stood up and continued walking. "Four o'clock, I'll be there. Wouldn't miss it for anything!"

"Then we'll be there, too!"

Ben turned to Amy. "I'd rather you left this to me, but if you really want to be there, you'd be best doing what Wilf's gang will do. Hide yourselves and keep an eye on my back. I'll shout if I need you, promise I will."

Amy's fists clenched at her sides. "We'll be there, won't we, Alex?"

Ben could see her brother's legs trembling as he replied, "You can count on us. We won't run off and leave you!"

Ben threw an arm about his shoulders and squeezed lightly. "Thanks, pal, I'll feel safer with a friend like you around. Thank you, too, Amy. Well, I'm off for lunch and a nice nap in a deck chair on the lawn. See you two at four. Oh, sorry, I won't see you because you'll be hiding, but I'll feel a lot better knowing you're there. 'Bye, pals!"

They watched him turn off to the house with Mrs. Winn on his arm. Alex gritted his teeth. "I won't run away this time, Amy, I'll stay and help Ben!"

Amy took the hand of her normally timid brother. "You never ran last time, Alex, you're getting braver by the day, just like Ben."

At midday Mrs. Winn took lunch on the lawn with Ben, Ned, and Horatio. It was a soft summer Sunday, and they had a pleasant time, basking in the quiet, sunny garden. Walking to and from church had tired the old lady out. Her eyes flickered as she watched two white butterflies circling, weaving inter- minable patterns around the lavender-blue blossoms of a bud- dleia bush. Bees droned lazily between dark crimson roses and purple-yellow pansies, the fragrance of flowers lay light upon the still early noontide. Within a short time she was lying back in her deck chair, sleeping peacefully.

Ben and Ned held a thoughtful conversation. "So then, ancient hound, what are your plans for the day?"

The big dog rolled luxuriously over on the grass. "Think I'll take a tour of the area with my feline friend."

Ben raised an eyebrow. "I take it you've finally got through to Horatio, then. A good talker, is he?"

Ned's ears flopped dolefully. "Not really. Sometimes he makes sense, but most of the time his thoughts are pure nonsense." He dabbed a paw at the cat's tail. "Isn't that right, pal?"

Horatio turned his staring golden eyes upon the dog.

Ben watched; it was obvious they were communicating. "What's he saying, Ned?"

The labrador shook his great head. "I'll translate word for word his exact thoughts at this moment. He's saying, 'Miaow miaow! Butt'fly, mouse, birdie, nice. Mowwwrrr! Winnie Winn give 'Ratio sardine an' milky milky tea, purrrr nice!'"

Ben chuckled. "Keep at him. I'm sure Horatio will improve."

The labrador stared forlornly at the cat. "Little savage, scoffing butterflies, mice, and birds. Ugh! What are you going to do for the rest of the day, Ben, sit out here and snooze?"

The boy rose quietly from his deck chair. "No, I'm off to do a bit of exploring by myself. . . . See you back here . . . shall we say about six?"

Ned waved a paw. "Six it is. Dinner will prob'ly be about seven. Mind how you go, Ben. Shout if you need me."

Ben walked briskly to the gate. "Righto, and you bark out loud if you want me for anything. See you later, mate."

CHAPELVALE VILLAGE SQUARE LAY DE-
serted and still in the summer afternoon. Ben was the only
one about. Crossing the square, he strolled up to the
 almshouse fence. Only the unruly lilac and
privet bushes held the rickety, sagging palings
upright. He stood at the gate, weighing the ancient building up. A poor jumble, its thick
hanging thatch, long overdue to be rethatched.

Ben unlooped a faded noose of cord that
kept the gate fastened, which creaked protestingly as he
opened it, and started down the weed-scarred gravel path.
A gruff voice cut the air with thunderous power.

"Out! Get out, you're trespassin'! Out, out!"

Ben stopped and held his arms out sideways. "Excuse me,
I was only—"

The voice from behind the almshouse door roared threat-
eningly. "Out, I said! I'll give you a count of three. I'm loading
my shotgun! Out, d'ye hear. . . . One! . . . Two!"

Ben ran then, clearing the gate with a leap. Behind him he
heard the click of shotgun hammers being cocked.

The voice called out in menace-laden tones. "Ye'll get
both barrels if ye come back! Be off now!"

Ben knew it was little use arguing with a double-barrelled

shotgun. Thrusting both hands deep in his pockets, he walked off across the square.

Dropping into the alley alongside Evans Tea Shoppe, the boy cut around the back of the stone buildings, circling the square furtively until he arrived in the shade of some hawthorn trees behind the almshouse. He stood still and silent there for several minutes, checking that his presence was unnoticed. Then, with a silent bound, he cleared the back wall, sinking down in a crouch amid the long grass and weeds. Three warped and weatherbeaten wooden shutters covered the almshouse's rear windows, with neither glass nor blinds behind them. Ben moved stealthily on all fours, over to the centre window. He found it was not difficult to spy inside through the ancient elmwood planks, which were riddled with knotholes and cracks.

A high, circular stained-glass window let in a pool of sunlight in faded hues. The rest of the illumination was provided by two storm lamps suspended from a crossbeam. A tall, heavyset, elderly man with a full grey beard, wearing bell-bottom pants and a close-fitting dark blue seaman's jersey, with a spotted red and white neckerchief, was seated at a table. Upon it was a welter of cardboard filing boxes and books, parchments and scrap paper. Around him, the interior appeared to be covered in dust and draped with cobwebs. The man was poring over a document on the table, leaning on one elbow, holding a pencil poised.

Suddenly he sat upright, moving a much-repaired pair of glasses from his face. He looked to the front door, as if he had heard a noise from outside. Rising slowly, he crept to the door and placed an ear against it. From his pocket he took a child's toy, a cheap green metal clicker in the shape of a frog, and taking a deep breath he bellowed out angrily, "I know you're still out there! Shift yourself quick! I never miss with this shotgun! Ye'll get a full blast through this door if ye don't move, I warn ye!" He clicked the tin frog twice. Ben wrinkled his face in amusement—it sounded just like a shotgun. The old fraud!

Satisfied the intruder had fled, the big man went back to his table, where he lit a small paraffin stove and placed a whistling kettle upon it. From a box under the table he brought forth a large enamel mug, brown cane sugar, and a can of condensed milk. Whilst doing this, he sang in a fine husky baritone. Ben recognized the song as an old sea shanty he was familiar with. He listened to the man sing:

> "I thought I heard the cap'n say,
> Go down you bloodred roses, go down!
> Tomorrow is our sailin' day,
> Go down you bloodred roses, go down!
> O you pinks and posers,
> Go down you bloodred roses, go down!"

The big fellow paused, scratching his beard thoughtfully, obviously having forgotten the rest of the words. With the danger of being shot no longer a threat, Ben could not resist supplying a verse to help the singer's memory. So he sang out through a knothole in a raucous voice.

> "And now we're wallopin' 'round Cape Horn,
> Go down you bloodred roses, go down!
> I wish t'God I'd ne'er been born,
> Go down you bloodred roses, go down!

O you pinks and posers,
Go down you bloodred roses, go down!"

The man began moving towards the shutter, a smile forming on his rough-hewn features as he took a turn with a verse.

"There's only one thing botherin' me,
Go down you bloodred roses, go down!"

He paused. Ben knew what to do, he sang out the rest.

"To leave behind Miss Liza Lee,
Go down you bloodred roses, go down!"

Then they both sang the last two lines lustily together.

"O you pinks and posers,
Go down you bloodred roses, go down!"

The old fellow banged a huge calloused hand against the
shutter, causing Ben to jump. He banged it again, laughing.
"Hohohoho! That weren't no Chapelvale bumpkin singin' a
good seafarin' shanty. They've all got one leg longer'n the
other from walkin' in plough furrows 'round here. Ahoy, mate,
what was the first ship ye sailed in?"

Ben shouted through a knothole, "The *Flying Dutchman,*
mate. What was yours?"

Placing his back against the shutters, the man slid down
into a sitting position, overcome with laughter.

"Hohoho, if I'm as big a liar as you, 'twas the *Golden Hind,*
with Sir Francis Drake as skipper. Hahaha!"

The boy laughed with him, shouting back a typical sea-farer's reply. "And did you bring your old mother back a par-rot from Cartagena?"

Bolts were withdrawn from the shutters, and Ben found himself staring into a pair of eyes as blue as his own. With a tattooed hand the man indicated a thick gold earring dangling from his right ear.

"Tell me, lad, why I'm wearin' this, 'tain't for fashion, is it?"

Ben shook his head. "No sir, that's in case they find your body washed up on a foreign shore, to pay for the burial."

The old fellow helped him through the window and shook his hand vigorously. "Jonathan Preston, Jon to my mates. Ship's carpenter, man an' boy, for fifty years. Served in both Royal and Merchant Navies with not a day's loss of pay on my discharge books."

"Ben Winn, sir, visiting the village for a while, stopping at my Aunt Winifred's house."

Jon produced another mug and wiped it clean. "Ho, then, better be watchin' me manners, seein' as you're the owner's nephew. Kettle's boilin', mate. Time for tea, eh!"

They sat together at the table, sipping hot sweet tea. Jon watched the boy thoughtfully. "Ye seem to have a fair maritime knowledge, m'boy. How d'ye come to know things only an old salt would know, eh?"

Ben had to resort to lies again, knowing the truth was too incredible for a normal person to believe. "Did a few trips along the coast, Jon. I read a lot, too. Ever since I first picked up a book, I always liked to read about sailors and the sea."

Jon's craggy face broke into a grin. "Well, now, 'tis the other way 'round with me, lad. Here's me been at sea nigh on fifty years and I like studyin' the land an' its history. It was Cap'n Winn who gave me a berth. When I gave up seafarin', he let me stay here, rent free. I'm a sort of caretaker, just keepin' an eye on the old place. After a while I got bored, so I took myself 'round to the library. Mr. Braithwaite got me interested in local history, I'm very keen on it now. Studying Chapelvale's past an' so on."

Ben cast an eye over the debris of papers and books on the table. "Aye, Jon, so I see. Perhaps you could give me a few pointers. I've become quite interested, too, since staying with my aunt."

The old carpenter's voice became suddenly grave. "So, you might have heard what's goin' on hereabouts, lad. If that barnacle Smithers an' his big-city cronies get their way, there won't be no village left to study. Rascals! They'll turn the place into a quarry an' a cement factory!"

Ben took a sip of his tea. "I know, Jon, it's a real shame, mate, but I'm doing what I can to help Aunt Winnie. Nobody else in Chapelvale seems to care. I don't think they're really aware of the situation. Either that or they're so worried that they push it all to the back of their minds and hope it'll go away."

Jon patted Ben's back approvingly. "Well, thank the stars there's someone else besides myself interested in helpin' the cap'n's wife. Y'are interested, aren't ye, boy?"

Ben did not need to reply, he merely stared straight into his new friend's eyes. Jon was taken aback at the intensity of the blue-eyed boy's gaze; it seemed to hold a world of knowledge and wisdom, so much so that the older man felt like a pupil in the presence of a teacher. Jon answered his own question.

"Right, I can see you are, Ben. Here, then, let me show ye what I've found out so far."

Rummaging through the boxes on the table, Jon found the one he wanted. It was made from sandalwood, the label stating that it had once held cigars, Burmah Cheroots. He opened it and took out what appeared to be a folded piece of thick, yellow paper.

"See this, 'tis real vellum, the kind of stuff that only very rich folk could afford to use. Want to know how old it is, lad, well, listen an' I'll read it to ye. Mr. Braithwaite translated it from Latin, the kind that churchfolk used long ago. Let me see, ah, here 'tis!"

From the cigar box he produced two pages, torn from a school exercise book. Squinting slightly, Jon read aloud. " 'Given in this year of grace, Thirteen Hundred and Forty-one, by the hand of Bishop Algernon Peveril, chaplain to his il-lustrious Majesty, Edward III, King of England. *To my good friend in God, Caran De Winn,* loyal servant to the King, Cap-tain and newly made Squire. Brother, I have marked the bounds of your land on a map. It will mark out the boundaries of the acres granted to you by our King, for your heroic services at the Battle of Sluys, which resulted in the defeat and capture of the French fleet. Chapelvale will be a fitting name for your property. I know you will receive good help from the honest folk thereabout to build the church we have planned. Friend Caran, make the name of Chapelvale and the Church of Saint Peter resound throughout the land. Thus will it add praise to the Lord, thanks to our King and grace to my true friend, Caran De Winn. I will send, under guard, a wagon to you, when winter's snows are cleared. It will contain the map, deeds, and title to your land, signed and sealed by the hand of our Monarch. There will also be gifts to grace the altar of our church, treasures that I give freely to you as a mark of my admiration and respect. Algernon Peveril, your friend at Court.'"

Jon looked rather proud of himself. "There now, lad, what d'ye make of that, eh?"

"That's marvellous, Jon. Where did you find the vellum?"

The carpenter pointed at the floor, which had been recently repaired. "Under some old floorboards I was fixin'. 'Twas in an old box, heavily sealed up with beeswax. A lucky discovery, eh, lad?"

Ben nodded. "Very lucky, mate, but will it stand up as proof of ownership? What happened to the King's signed deeds and the treasure? Did Caran receive them?"

Swilling tea around in his mug, Jon replied, "I don't know yet, Ben, I have been lookin' 'round for more clues. But 'tis difficult, I can tell ye. There was only one other thing in that box 'neath the floorboards, though it don't look very helpful. See what ye think."

Jon took the last scrap of paper from his cigar box. "Nought but an old torn piece o' thin paper, with two little holes burned in it an' a half line o' writin' on the bottom."

Jon noticed the boy's hands gripping the table edge, white-knuckled. "What's up, mate, are you all right?" Jonathan Preston's eyes grew wide as the boy slowly drew an identical scrap of paper from his pocket and unfolded it. "Great thunder, Ben, where did ye come by that?"

"In the spine of Cap'n Winn's family Bible!"

They stood staring at the two pieces of paper, fascinated. Ben flourished a hand over them. "You're the senior historian, Jon, put them together!"

Jon's big workworn hands trembled as he reunited the two

scraps. They fitted perfectly. The writing along the bottom of the piece now read:

> Lord, if it be thy will and pleasure,
> Keep safe for the house of De Winn thy treasure.

They stared at the writing for a long time, racking their brains at the significance of it. Jon stroked his beard. "Trouble is, it don't tell us what the treasure is or where to find it, though I'll wager whatever and wherever 'tis, the deeds will be with it, Ben. We'll seek it out together, mate, just you an' me, eh?"

Ben accepted the old man's sturdy handshake, adding, "Well, not quite just us two, friend, there's others interested. My two friends, Amy and Alex Somers. Then there's Aunt Winnie. I'll bet Mr. Braithwaite could be useful, too. Oh, and one other, my dog Ned, he's a good searcher. Actually it was he who really found that paper. You'll like him, Jon."

The old carpenter shook his head, chuckling. "I'm sure I will, shipmate, if he's anything like you! Alex and Amy Somers and old Braithwaite, your aunt, too? Looks like we've got quite a crew. You sure you don't want to bring the whole village along, Ben?"

The boy grinned. "Only if they want to come, Jon. I'm willing to take on any folk who'll try helping themselves, instead of sitting 'round hoping the problem'll disappear."

Jon took out a battered but reliable pocket watch and consulted it. "Nearly four, time for proper tea. D'you like corned beef sandwiches and some of Blodwen Evans's scones? I bought 'em yesterday, but they're still fairly fresh."

Ben remembered his four o'clock appointment. "I'd love

to stay to tea, mate, but I've got to go somewhere. Tell you what, I'll see you here tomorrow, say about eleven. Will it be all right if I bring my friends and my dog?"

Jon waved at Ben as he leapt up to the windowsill.

"Aye. See you in the mornin', then, partner!"

When Ben had gone, the old seaman sat looking at the two bits of paper. He had worked long and hard at trying to defeat Smithers and help his old cap'n's wife, without an ounce of success. However, he felt that with the arrival of the strange lad things were beginning to happen. Stroking his beard, he stared at the empty window space. It was as if the blue-eyed boy had been sent to aid him by some mysterious power.

CHAPELVALE VILLAGE SCHOOL WAS A SMALL, drab, greystone building with the year 1802 graven over the door. Very basic, merely a couple of rectangular rooms with a corridor between them, it was typical of most small village schools. The playground at its rear opened onto the back of the library, which had been built later and was slightly grander. The library had mullioned windows, behind which Mr. Braithwaite could be seen studying a catalogue at his desk. The school playground was hemmed by a low stone wall, with bushes growing over it. Wilf Smithers stood, apparently alone on the dusty playground.

From the far side of the schoolyard, Amy and Alex hid behind a gable of the adjoining library, watching him. All at once the village bully did a little hopskip, punching the air with both fists. A voice, obviously that of Regina Woodworthy, called out. "Give him the old one-two, Wilf!"

He turned to the thicket of lilacs growing over the far-side playground wall, hissing in a loud whisper. "Shuttup and keep your heads down!"

Alex blanched with fear as he murmured to his sister.,"That Wilf Smithers is a dirty liar, he was supposed to be here on his own!"

The girl was about to reply when Ben strolled by, not a foot from their hiding place. His lips hardly moved as he spoke quietly. "Don't worry, pals. You're here, too. Hush now!"

Wilf came across the playground towards his victim, hold-ing out his hand. As Ben shook it, the bully sneered. "Well well, didn't think you'd have the nerve to show up!" He tight-ened his grip like a vice and gave a short whistle. The Grange Gang clambered over the stone wall, surrounding Ben.

Smiling, Ben indicated them with a nod. "I see you've brought some help."

Regina poked a finger sharply into Ben's back. "It's you who's going to need the help, stupid!"

Keeping tight hold of his victim's hand, Wilf called out. "Any sign of that dog about?"

Tommo's squeaky voice reassured him. "Nah, it's all right, Wilf!"

Ben never blanched as Wilf applied more pressure to his hand. "Your note said you wanted to see me alone, just to talk."

Wilf's eyes grew mean and narrow. "Did it, now? Well, I told a little fib. I'm going to teach you a lesson, to keep your nose out of other people's business. That's if you've got any nose left when I'm done with you!"

Regina warned Wilf as the back library window opened. "Look out, it's old Braithee!"

Mr. Braithwaite had been studying in the library, notwith-standing the fact that it was Sunday. Time and tide did not count in the absentminded scholar's scheme of things. He looked over his glasses at the young people in the playground. "I say, er er, what's going on out there, er, not fighting I, er, hope! Not nice, er, fighting."

Regina called out in a little-girl voice. "Oh, no sir, we're only playing a game!"

The librarian-cum-schoolmaster scratched his bushy head. "Oh, er, very good, very good. Hmm, not nice, er, fighting!" He shut the window and went back to his studies.

Ben suddenly stood on Wilf's toe, did a neat twist, and, releasing his hand from the bully's grip, he stood grinning into the bigger boy's red face. "Hear that? It's not nice to fight, y'know!"

The sound of Wilf's teeth grinding together was audible as he leaped forward, swinging a fierce punch at his adversary's face. He struck air. Ben was out of his way, holding up both palms open wide, his voice soothing and reasonable.

"Steady on, friend, I don't want to fight you."

The gang were shouting out now, wildly excited.

"Knock his block off, Wilf!"

"Make his nose bleed!"

"Go on, Wilf, belt the little squirt one!"

Wilf charged like an enraged bull, swinging wildly with both fists. But each time, Ben either ducked or dodged nimbly aside.

From behind the gable wall, Alex almost sobbed with disappointment. "Ben won't stand and fight, he's scared!"

Amy began to feel the same way as her brother. She stood out in the open, fists clenched, willing Ben to land Wilf a blow each time the bully went staggering by. However, Ben kept up the same tactics, weaving around his attacker, still open-handed.

"I told you, Wilf, I don't want to fight you!"

Wilf, breathing heavily, gasped out, "That's 'cos you're a

coward. Come on, fight, you yellowbelly!"

This time he changed his assault, looping out a savage right. As Ben dodged it, Wilf kicked out just as Regina pushed Ben in the back, sending him onto the kick. It caught his shin. The kick did not injure Ben greatly; however, he decided it was unwise to leave his back uncovered.

Amy, with Alex behind her, came running towards the fray, shouting out, "Foul, foul! Keep your feet to yourself, Smithers!"

Not wanting them caught up in the fight, Ben backed off until he was up against the schoolhouse wall. Shoving aside Amy and Alex, Regina laughed gleefully. "Get 'round him quick! Hahaha, you've got him cornered, Wilf!"

She was right. Ben found himself against the wall with the others standing around in a half-circle. Wilf was right in front of him—Ben could not go left, right, or back. Leaping forward, Wilf aimed a swinging right at his face. Ben ducked, and there was a meaty thud, followed by an agonized scream. Amy went white, she could not see what had gone on.

Wilf Smithers came howling and screeching out of the melee, holding his right elbow in his left hand, his face the colour of a beetroot. As he stopped and did a dance of pain on the spot, his right hand flapped uselessly.

Mr. Braithwaite came hurrying into the yard, his dusty gown swirling about him as he called out to the dancing boy, "Er, er, what, er, seems to be the trouble, er, Smithers?"

Wilf had lost the power of intelligent speech and continued to scream and dance. Ben came forward, unhurt, calmly explaining. "We were playing a game, sir, and he punched the wall by accident. I think his hand is hurt. Are you all right, Wilf?"

Mr. Braithwaite showered dandruff around as he scratched his wiry mop furiously. "Hand, er, right, er, whatsername . . . Woodworthy. Go and get somebody, er, immediately. Yes, right away, er, I should think!"

Regina went dashing out of the schoolyard, straight into Mr. and Mrs. Evans, who were out for a stroll.

Blodwen Evans strode purposefully towards the speechless dancing boy, with her husband Dai trailing behind. She took charge of the situation, addressing Mr. Braithwaite. "Indeed to goodness, what's possessin' the lad?"

"Er, ah, er, hand I should, er, think, yes!"

She brushed Mr. Braithwaite aside, grabbed Wilf by his injured hand, and felt it. He gave out a last shriek and fainted. Blodwen Evans pursed her lips as she made a quick diagnosis. "Look, you, the lad's hand is broken! Dai, Mr. Braithwaite, you'll 'ave to help me carry him to the chemist. He's closed, but we'll rattle the door 'til he opens."

She seized the unconscious Wilf's feet, glaring at the librarian. "Don't lift him by the right hand, man, take his shoulders!" Between them they struggled out of the schoolyard, carrying their limp burden.

Regina turned on Ben immediately. "You're responsible for that. Couldn't fight him fair and square. Coward!"

Amy pushed herself between Regina and Ben. "Don't be silly, Wilf did that to himself!"

Regina took a swinging slap at Amy's face, but Ben's arm blocked it. He seemed to touch Regina at a point between ear and neck. Instantly she rose on tiptoe as he kept up the pressure with a slightly bent forefinger. Amy was amazed—the girl was standing rock-still, with her chin tilted upward and an expression of silent anguish on her face.

Ben's voice was soft, but with a hint of steel in it. "Listen to me, Regina, I've got you by a nerve point—painful, isn't it? I don't like hurting anybody, so save yourself some pain and say that we must not fight and I'll let you go."

The big girl's jaw was clenched so tight that all she could manage was something that sounded like "Gnn, ee nust nok kite!" Ben released her and she dashed off, sobbing, with the rest of the Grange Gang trailing behind sullenly.

Alex was lost in admiration. "Where did you learn to do that, Ben? You could've licked Wilf with one finger. Show me how you did it, go on, Ben!"

The flaxen-haired boy thrust his hands into his pockets, ignoring his friend. "Oh no, pal, you'd be going about paralysing anyone who came near you. What's the use of fighting, kicking, and punching another person just to prove your point? It only ends up with both of you getting hurt and solving nothing. Come on, I'm due back for dinner soon, have to get cleaned up. Don't want to disappoint Miz Winn."

They parted at the corner of the lane and turned. The dark-haired girl watched Ben lope off towards Mrs. Winn's house. Alex looked at his older sister, puzzled. "So Ben isn't a coward?"

Amy shook her head, slowly. "Far from it!"

"Then why wouldn't he fight Wilf? He could have beaten him easily with those secret things he knows."

Ben had now gone out of sight around the bend in the lane.

Amy gave her brother a long look before she replied. "You know, there's a lot more to Ben than either of us imagine. He has a sort of air about him—confidence, that's it. He acts as if he can do a great deal of things. Of course he could have beaten Wilf. I think he didn't fight because he knew he could win, but he didn't have to prove it to himself. It must be good, to be like that. He didn't need us when he went to meet Wilf, but he let us come. He said he needed us. You know, Alex, I think he was trying to give us a bit of confidence in ourselves. D'you see what I mean?"

Alex squinted his eyes. "Hmm, not quite, but one thing I do know, though. Our friend Ben is like nobody I've ever met."

THE BIG, LOPING LABRADOR MET BEN ON the way up to the house. He sniffed Ben's hand. "Where've you been all afternoon, young master?"

The boy grinned as they ambled along together, exchanging thoughts. "You were sniffing to see if I'd had anything nice to eat while I was out. Well, I didn't. I've made friends with the man at the almshouse. His name is Jon, you'll like him. He's not a bit mad, like they'd said. I'll take you over to meet him tomorrow." Ben roughed the back of his dog's neck. "Our friend Wilf, I think he's hurt his hand, took a swipe at me and punched a brick wall."

Ned interrupted. "Huh, I know that."

Ben stopped. "How'd you know?"

The black labrador winked one eye. "Horatio took me on a guided tour of Chapelvale. We found the place where that Smithers man lives, that lad of his, too. It's a big new house in its own grounds, up past the railway station. I was sniffing about outside, when Dai Evans and another fellow, the chemist I think, brought young Wilf home to his parents. Hoho, he must have given that wall a right old whack! You should see the wads of bandage and the splint on his arm—he was the colour of sour milk. Anyhow, before I could stop him, that half-witted cat followed them into the house. I got as far as the driveway, when Mr. Smithers came roaring out with a garden rake, so I got out of the way fast. Well, I went around the back of the house to see if I could locate Horatio. Huh, there he was, being fed a saucer of milk by a nice girl called Hetty.

"Now, there's a girl I could take to. She stroked me a bit, said I was a nice fellow, which I am of course, and gave me a great gammon hambone, with lots of meat on it. Then she said she was finished working for the day and put on her hat and coat. She knew Horatio. I think he pops over there regular and lets Hetty feed him, the furry little fraud. Anyhow, she picked Horatio up and said she'd better get him back home. So I went along with them both. Huh, I notice she didn't offer to carry me!"

Ben tweaked Ned's tail. "I don't blame her. Where is she now?"

The dog shambled up the driveway to the house. "Inside with Winnie, you'd better go and meet her."

Hetty was a thin, angular woman, clad in a long bottle-green coat with an old fox-fur collar, lace-up kneeboots, and a worn green felt hat that had seen better days. She sat at the kitchen table with Mrs. Winn, a pot of tea and some sliced fruitcake between them as they chatted animatedly. Mrs. Winn introduced her to Ben.

"Ah, Ben, this is Hetty Sullivan, an old friend of mine. Her mother used to be maid here when I was not long married and my son Jim was young. Hetty is the maid up at the Smithers house now. She often calls in for tea and a chat on her way home. Come and sit with us."

The boy pulled up a chair, listening to Hetty's tales of woe as Mrs. Winn poured tea for him. Hetty was one of those people who always had a tale to tell, usually in the manner of a complaint.

"Smithers! Don't talk to me about that family! 'Hetty fetch this, Hetty do that.' I'm at their beck and call every second. I wish I could work for you, Miz Winn, like my old mum used to. I always liked this 'ouse."

Mrs. Winn poured more tea for Hetty, remarking wistfully, "I wish I could afford for you to work here, Hetty my dear, but I'm only a widow on a Royal Navy pension. I can understand you not liking to work for Smithers—I wouldn't fancy the job."

Hetty pursed her lips as she sipped her tea. "No more you wouldn't, marm! That Obadiah Smithers, nasty bossy man, always asking me t'leave the room, so he can talk business, if you please! Then there's the other young madam, Miss Maud Bowe, wants waitin' on 'and an' foot. Wants to get back to Lunnon, that's what she needs t'do. An' that young Master Wilfred, dirty towels, muddy bootmarks, bad manners. Cheeky wretch, you should see the mess he leaves the bathroom in every day. But his mother won't hear a word said agin him. No, she drifts about there, givin' her orders like she was a bloomin' duchess or somethin': 'I think we'll have the gammon for lunch, Hetty, boil those potatoes until they're floury, Hetty, you may pour the tea, Hetty.' Humph! An' her the daughter of a Yorkshire sack an' bag maker. Oh, I notice these things, y'know. There ain't many secrets in the Smithers 'ouse that Hetty Sullivan ain't over'eard!"

Ben nodded sympathetically. "You haven't had it easy

working for them, eh, Hetty?"

The maid primped at her lank, mousy hair. "I certainly 'ave not, Master Ben!"

Ben seemed very concerned at the maid's plight. "What'll you do for a job if Smithers carries out his plan and takes over the village for his cement business? Surely you'll be out of house and home, won't you, Hetty?"

She tapped the tabletop with a stick-like finger. "D'you know what Smithers said, 'e said I could live there, in the spare room, an' he'd deduct lodgin' out of me wages. There! What d'you think of that, eh?"

Ben played the gossipy maid like a fish on a line. "So it looks like he's got things well in hand. Does he talk much about the new venture?"

Hetty looked this way and that, as if others were listening in on the conversation, then put a hand to the side of her mouth and dropped her voice to a confidential half-whisper. "Just between me'n you, 'e never stops talkin' about it. Now, I'm not one for gossipin' an' repeatin' things, but you should've 'eard the argument Mr. Smithers an' Maud Bowe 'ad this mornin' over breakfast. It was fearful, I tell you, fearful!"

Mrs. Winn caught the nod from Ben, so she immediately took over his role, leaning forward to Hetty like a conspirator, whilst dismissing the boy. "Er, Ben, perhaps you'd better go and wash up for dinner." As Ben left the room, he heard Mrs. Winn murmuring to the maid, "Oh, poor Hetty, you look so upset. Tell me all about it, dear."

It was seven-thirty that evening. Hetty had departed, taking with her a jar of homemade blackberry jam and Mrs. Winn's condolences for the indignities she was forced to bear under the Smithers regime. Ben was sitting with Ned at his feet, Mrs. Winn with Horatio at hers, all replete after a Sunday dinner of Winnie's roast lamb and vegetables, followed by trifle with fresh cream. Ben waited, containing his curiosity until the old lady was ready to divulge what Hetty Sullivan had told her earlier. Mrs. Winn allowed Horatio to leap up onto her lap, and she stroked him as she related the maid's conversation.

"It's not good news, I'm afraid. Apparently Hetty heard every word. They were shouting and ranting at each other. Smithers is confident of the Chapelvale takeover and kept ignoring Maud's argument that something urgent be done about me. Apparently I'm the fly in their ointment. Smithers reckons the other villagers will fall into line; he can bully them with his legal jargon, compulsory purchase orders, and talk of big-money London investment companies. But he's finding it difficult to push me about—I'm the only one who is resisting him, you see!"

The strange boy's blue eyes showed their admiration of the plucky old lady, and he winked knowingly at her. "And you intend fighting Smithers and the Londoners every inch of the way. Good for you, marm!"

Horatio jumped down from Mrs. Winn's lap. She shook her head wearily. "I don't let others see it, but I'm a bit frightened really. I own this house and I can prove it, but the rest? Oh dear, it's all a bit up in the air. Captain Winn knew more about it than me. What a pity he's not here to help. The almshouse is a big building—it takes up an entire corner of the village square. It was always regarded as belonging to the

Winn family, all the village land, too. I just took it for granted. Nobody ever asked me to produce title deeds, or confirmation of ownership. Not until Smithers and his London acquaintances came along. If I want to carry on the fight, I need proper proof of ownership!"

Ben interrupted her. "What else did Hetty tell you she overheard?"

The old lady fiddled with her worn wedding ring. "Well, Maud Bowe told Smithers that they would lose the contract if they don't have me moved out and the almshouse in their possession by the due date. Smithers blustered a bit, but wasn't quite sure how to deal with the problem. Then Maud said that she had friends in London who could take care of me."

Ben looked questioningly at her. "Friends?"

The old lady looked worried as she continued. "Aye, friends she called them. But Smithers knew what she was talking about. He said that he'd have nothing to do with Maud's plan, said he was a man with a respectable family and high standing in the village, and that he didn't want paid bullies coming here from London!"

This was an unexpected turn of events, though Ben was not surprised at the things big-city business firms would come up with in achieving their aims. He tried not to let his concern show. "Oh, and what are these so-called big-city friends supposed to do?"

The old lady fussed with her apron strings. "Frighten me out of my house, Maud said. Smithers told her that if it came to light, he'd deny all knowledge of the whole thing. But she replied that it was only the same thing he had been trying to do through his bullying son and the gang he has around him.

That seemed to shut Smithers up."

Ben had a question to ask. "When are these 'big-city friends' supposed to arrive in Chapelvale, Miz Winn?"

She shrugged. "Hetty never said, but she did mention that the minute Wilf arrived home this afternoon, Maud went up to her room to write a letter."

Ben pondered this for a moment. "Suppose it takes a letter two days to get to London from here. Give it another day for these people to get themselves organized, and say the better part of a day for them to travel up here. Four days. Say sometime next Thursday, late afternoon."

Mrs. Winn rose and started clearing dishes from the table. "What are we going to do, Ben?"

Gazing out of the window at the glorious summer evening, Ben patted his dog's head. "Leave this to us, Winnie!"

WHEN JONATHAN PRESTON
took down the shutters from the almshouse
back windows, morning sunlight flooded in. It

24 was nice to have a bit of light and
fresh air in the old place, he thought, taking the
lamps down from the beam and extinguishing
them. A piece of floorboard timber, weighted
down by two bricks, stood on the table; he lifted
them to one side. The old ship's carpenter
smiled with satisfaction at the two pieces of paper he had rejoined skilfully with fish glue and rice paper as a backing. He
held it up to the light, looking at the four small holes, murmuring to himself. "Good as new, writing's all joined up
proper now.

"'Lord, if it be thy will and pleasure,
Keep safe for the house of De Winn thy treasure.'"

He gazed at the paper awhile, then put it down, massaging
the corners of his eyes with finger and thumb. "Wish I knew
what those four little holes mean!"
He was putting the kettle on for tea and cutting some
bread and cheese, when Ben's face showed at the window.

"Morning, mate. Is it all right to come in? I've brought my friends along."

Jon straightened up, one hand on the small of his back. "Bring 'em in, lad, by all means!"

Amy and Ned climbed through the windowspace with Ben. Alex followed behind, a touch hesitant. When they were introduced, the old seaman cut up the cheese rinds with his clasp knife, feeding them to the black labrador and scratching vigorously behind the dog's ears. "This dog o' yours, Ben, he's a fine animal. Aren't you, boy?"

Ned gazed adoringly at the old carpenter, passing a thought to Ben. "What a nice old cove. He certainly knows how to treat a dog. Mmmmmm! Carry on, sir, more to the left, ah, that's it. Best ear scratcher I've met in many a year. Mm-mmmm!"

Ben nudged the dog with his foot. "Move over a bit, Ned, you're beating me to death with that tail of yours!" He pointed to the rejoined paper on the table. "You've done a good job there, old friend. Found any more clues or bits of information?"

Jon shook his head. "Nothing, lad, though I was just going to give this place a good clean up to see what I might come across. Would you and your pals like t'help me?"

Amy rolled up her sleeves. "Right, tell us what to do!"

Sweeping the floor was out of the question. It raised too much dust, but there was lots of old timber needed stacking outside. Ben and Amy passed it out through the window, and Alex and Jon stacked it up against the outside wall. They worked right through until midday, when they stopped to have a small lunch of the old seaman's bread and cheese and a cup of tea. All four sat on the window-ledge, surrounded by dust motes, which swirled in the air like tiny golden specks. Jon appeared well satisfied with the job they had done thus far.

"Looks a lot better, don't it. Now that old floorboard plankin' is out of the way, I'll be able to move my table into the corner."

The younger boy had lost his initial shyness about Jon and pointed to the table. "Look at that table's far leg. You'll either have to fix it or find another one."

Jon stared at the leg in question, which up until then had been hidden behind a stack of wood. "Aye, so I will, mate—there's a piece of it missin', see. 'Tis balanced on that tin biscuit box. Must've been like that since I arrived here an' I've never noticed it. Let me see, now."

The old man took the two bricks he had used as weights. Standing on edge atop of one another they were the depth of the tin. "Ben, Alex, hold that table up an' I'll wedge these under."

It was a heavy table, and the two boys gasped as they held it up. Amy pushed the tin out of the way whilst Jon stuck the bricks in position. "All right, you two, let it down easy, careful now!"

Jon tested the table, it was solid and unmoving. "That's shipshape! Let's take a look at that rusty, old tin box, Amy."

Amy placed the box on the table. "Feels like there's stuff inside!"

Jon traced the lip of the tin lid. "Rusted tight, hah! Villier's Afternoon Tea Wafers. Some years since I set eyes on them. Only one way to find out what's inside, mates!" Jon had a useful-looking can opener on his clasp knife. He punched it through the corroded metal and began vigorously working it along the edge. The tin was not as weak as it first appeared to be, and the old seaman's opener caused a shrieking noise that made the three young people wince. He stopped only when he had cut down three edges. "Papers!"

Covering his palm with the sleeve edge of his jersey, he wrenched the flap of tin back and shook out the contents onto the table. Immediately the four began sorting through the papers. They were yellowed with age. Amy studied one.

"Old back-issues of the *Chapelvale Chronicle*! Look at this one, it's dated 1783. 'Pitt the Younger becomes British Prime Minister.' 'American Independence to be recognized.' 'Monsieur Montgolfier is to fly in a balloon.' I'll bet Mr. Braithwaite would be interested in these."

Jon piled them in a stack. He seemed disappointed. "Well, they're of little use to anyone else. Come on, lass, let's take them over to him."

Being a historian, Mr. Braithwaite was delighted with the find. So eager was he to have the papers that he made a grab at them, knocked them off the library desk, and sent them in a cascade across the parquet floor. "Er, oh dear, er, I do beg your pardon, Mr. Preston. Very, er, clumsy of me, I'm sure!"

But the old carpenter was not listening, he was holding up a square of material which had fallen out from between the folds of one edition of the *Chronicle*. "Look what I've found."

Alex recognized the thing instantly. "That's a needlework sampler, like children used to embroider their alphabets on. What does it say?"

Amy knelt by Jon and read aloud the bit she could understand. " 'Evelyn De Winn. 1673.' Ben, it was sewn by one of Winnie's family!" The embroidered writing was extremely neat, showing what a clever needlewoman Evelyn De Winn had been, though it was hard to make out the rest of the letters, as a lot of them were strangely archaic, each letter *S* being shaped like an *f.*

Mr. Braithwaite was suddenly transformed from a bumbling librarian into a scholar of Old English text. He took up pen and paper excitedly. "Give it here, I'll translate for you. Amelia, sit there and write this down, please!"

There were no "ers," "ahs," or other hesitations from Mr. Braithwaite as he dictated in a clear, slow voice to her:

> "Take the Commandments paces west,
> away from the bless'd naming place,
> to where the heavenly twins stand ever
> gazing at Sol's dying face.
> Turn as a third Gospelmaker would
> to the house named for the rock,
> 'twixt here and there you must stop to drink,
> your first reward to unlock."

Mr. Braithwaite scratched his fuzzy mane. "Hmm, sixteen-seventy, a time of persecution for British Catholics and nonconformists. That was when the almshouse ceased to be St. Peter's and the new church was built on the hilltop. They called it the Chapelvale Church, though secretly it was still known to the local Catholics as St. Peter's, hence its present name."

Jon indicated the sampler. "Thankee, sir, you can keep this for your library archives, we'll make do with Amy's translation."

The librarian was once again his former self. "Er, quite, er, that is, thank you, Mr., er, yes, very good!"

BACK AT THE ALMSHOUSE ALL TIDYING UP was forgotten as they sat around the big oblong table and studied the poem from the sampler and Amy read out the first line slowly. " 'Take the Commandments paces west.' "

25

Jon shrugged his shoulders. "What's a Commandments pace?"

Ben had guessed, but he let Alex answer. "Must mean ten paces, because . . . there's ten Commandments!"

"True, true." The old man nodded approvingly.

Ben winked at Alex. "Well done, pal."

" 'Away from the bless'd naming place,' " Amy went on.

Alex looked disappointed. "That's not so easy."

Amy reasoned, "Whatever a bless'd naming place is, we've got to take ten paces away from it. Naming place, naming place. Any ideas, Ben?"

Ben looked stumped. "Naming place, let me see. . . . Does it mean the name of a place, or a name like mine and yours, Amy, Alex, Jon—"

The old ship's carpenter interrupted. "I remember when I was young, I hated my full title, Jonathan. Though my ma used to say, 'Jonathan you were christened and Jonathan you shall stay.' You can't change your christening name!"

Ned had settled down for his afternoon nap beneath the table, when Ben disturbed him by banging on the table as he gritted out in frustration, "The bless'd naming place, where is it?"

Recognition hit Alex like a slap in the face. "Christening! Naming place! It's where they baptize babies!"

Amy whooped delightedly and hugged him. "What a clever brother I've got, he's a genius!"

Crimson-faced, Alex shrugged off his sister's embrace. "Where was the naming place here, Jon, d'you know?"

Ned flashed his master a thought. "Right under this table, I think. Feels as if this bumpy chunk of stone's the base of something bigger that was broken off." The labrador shuffled lazily out to find another napping spot, remarking, "Of course, I might be wrong, but it's worth a try."

Ben mentally answered his friend's idea. "Thanks, pal. Now let's see if I can discover it without giving away our secret."

Jon was stroking his beard, looking this way and that.

"Hmm, baptismal font, every church has one, though I've never thought of a font being in this old place. Hmmm."

Ben patted Ned as he lumbered by. He spoke aloud to the dog, so his three friends could hear.

"What's the matter, old boy, not comfy enough under there? Let's take a look." Dropping on all fours, he crawled under the table. "Hahah!"

At the sound of Ben's exclamation, Amy crouched and

stared under the table at him. "Something there?"

"I think so, it's a sort of raised square bit with a broken part sticking out the middle. Will that be it, Jon?"

The old ship's carpenter nodded to Alex. "It may be. It may be. Let's move this table. You take one side. Lass, take care of the two bricks under the leg. Stay there, Ben!"

The table was moved, the boy stayed on all fours by the remnants of the baptismal font, looking up at Amy for approval. Instead, it was the labrador who received her hug.

"Good old Ned, it was due to you we found it, good boy!"

If a dog could ever smirk, Ned did. He flicked his tail towards his master. "Sorry about that, pal, but credit where it's due, y'know. Nothing like a hug from a pretty girl, eh!"

But Ben was more intent on solving the mystery than bantering with Ned. He watched Jon trace the graven lettering around the limestone base with his clasp knife blade, reading aloud. " 'In nomine Patris, et filius, et spiritus sanctus.' In the name of the Father, the Son, and the Holy Spirit—I remember that from Sunday Mass when I was a lad. This is it. This stub is probably the column of the font basin. How did the rhyme read, boy?"

"Take the Commandments paces west,
away from the bless'd naming place."

Alex walked over and stood by the font base. "Ten paces west from here. Anyone got a compass?" He met Jon's slightly disapproving stare blankly. "How're we supposed to know which way west is?"

The old ship's carpenter smiled. "I can tell you've never been to sea. Show him, lad."

Ben faced the open rear windows, warm with afternoon sunlight. "West's where the sun sets, over there."

Alex began measuring out ten paces solemnly in the right direction. Amy sat down on the floor beside her strange friend, and whispered to him. "Jon said that as if you'd been to sea. Have you, Ben?"

He tried to shrug off the question. "The sea? Oh, for just a little bit, nothing much really."

She stared curiously into his clouded blue eyes. It started to race through his mind again—how could he tell her: wind, waves, storm, the world of waters. A dumb boy and a half-starved dog, crouching in the galley of the *Flying Dutchman,* with a captain (Vanderdecken) roaring oaths at the heavens as he tried battling his way around Cape Horn in the teeth of winter gales. Murder on the high seas, an angel dropping to the deck, the numbing shock of being plunged into an icy green maelstrom of ocean.

He was wrenched back to reality by Jon clapping a huge arm about his shoulders. "Are you all right, lad?"

The feeling ebbed. He shook himself. "Er, yes, mate, I'm fine. Bumped my head on that table when you moved it. I'll be all right, it's nothing."

His dog had caught Ben's thoughts. To distract Amy he leapt on her and began licking her face.

She tried laughingly to push him off. "Hahaha, what've I done to deserve all this? Get off me, you great silly dog!"

Ben shook a finger at her as he held Ned's collar. "Don't blame him, Amy, you started all the hugging off!"

Her brother called, "I'm about three feet from the window here. That's ten paces. What happens now?"

The old ship's carpenter took over. He paced out ten

steps, going past Alex to arrive one pace outside the open windows in the churchyard. "Your pace was shorter than the person who wrote the rhyme, mate. Mine is slightly longer, I think. But it's somewhere about here."

They joined him outside in the late afternoon. Amy brought the translation with her, she read the next part.

"To where the heavenly twins stand ever
gazing at Sol's dying face."

Alex winked at Jon. "That's got nothing to do with going to sea, I'll bet. Come on, mate, let's see you solve this one!" A real friendship was beginning to show between the hesitant boy and the old carpenter.

Jon ruffled Alex's hair as he looked around. "Give me a bit of time, matey, we'll crack it!"

The labrador sniggered as he passed Ben a thought. "The heavenly twins, that could be us!"

The boy struggled to hide a grin. "Heavenly? Not you, mate. Now stop fooling about and help us."

Amy sat on the windowsill. "Heavenly twins. . . . Maybe it's those two stars, you know, the sign of Gemini. They're always called the heavenly twins!"

Jon gazed up at the sky, thinking aloud. "Only trouble with that is, it's daylight. How could the heavenly twins watch Sol's dying face?"

The younger boy plucked a blade of grass and chewed on one end. "What's a Sol?"

Ben had heard the expression before, so he explained. "Sol is a name given to the sun. The sun sinks in the west, you've heard the expression: The dying sun sank into the west.

I've read it in books many a time."

Amy nodded. "Ben's right. So what we're looking for are two things. Heavenly twins standing ever gazing at Sol's dying face." She walked out into the churchyard, grass rustling against her long skirt. Ben followed her. Together they stopped, about halfway across, and leaned on one of the many crooked moss-grown gravestones, staring at the back of the almshouse. Ben saw the twins straight away, but he waited a moment until Amy caught sight of them. She leapt upright, pointing. "There they are, underneath the middle window: the twins!"

Two gracefully fluted columns of limestone formed the window edges. Beneath them, as if supporting the columns with their wings, stood two carved stone angels, facing outwards, their hands joined in prayer, faces looking upwards to heaven. Amy's voice caused a prowling jackdaw to take flight as she shouted shrilly, "The heavenly twins standing ever gazing at Sol's dying face!"

Ned looked accusingly at his master, passing a thought. "You knew that, didn't you? Before Amy called out, you'd guessed where the angels were. I must say, though, having seen a real angel, those two don't bear much resemblance, huh!"

Ben raised his eyebrows. "Don't be hard on the stonemason, Ned, he'd probably never seen an angel."

" 'Turn as a third Gospelmaker would to the house named for the rock,' " Alex read out loud. "Now I'm really stumped. I don't know any Gospelmakers."

The old carpenter drew a silver watch from his pocket and consulted it. "Well, we can all go home and think about it. You'll be wanted for dinner soon. I say we meet back here tomorrow, same time?"

Alex grumbled a bit; he was certain they were on to something, but Jon was right. Ben and his dog stood with Amy on the other side of the wall, waiting while her brother bade his newfound friend good-bye. Alex held forth his hand.

"See you tomorrow morning, then, Jon. Don't worry, we'll solve it. We're doing something to save Mrs. Winn's village for her. Not like some of the dead and alive types around Chapelvale, eh, mate?"

Alex's hand vanished inside the old carpenter's huge grasp. Jon's eyes crinkled into a fond smile as he shook it. "Aye, mate, we won't go wrong with you helpin' us!"

Dinner had already been served at the Smithers house. Maud Bowe retired outside to the garden, where she sat, perusing the illustrated pages of a book entitled *Fashion Hints for the Lady about Town.* Though she gave the impression of enjoying her country stay, Maud was longing to be back among her friends in London. Young Wilf slouched out into the garden, a heavy bandage and splint on his right arm, which was resting in a sling. He scowled at Maud and slumped down into a cast-iron chair, drumming his heels hard against the legs. Maud glanced over the top of her book at him.

"Wilfred, do you have to make that din?"

He drummed his steel-tipped boot heels louder, staring defiantly at her. "Name's not Wilfred, it's Wilf!"

Closing the book, she stared primly at him. "All right, then. Will you cease that infernal noise, Wilf?"

He stopped, smiled maliciously, and started drumming again. "I can do what I like 'round here. I live here, you don't!"

"I'll tell your father!"

"Go and tell him, I don't care."

Maud massaged the side of her forehead daintily. The noise was really getting to her. Finally she stamped her foot.

"Why don't you go up to your room? I thought you were supposed to be injured. You should be in bed!"

Wilf was enjoying tormenting her and beat his heels faster. "Mother says I need fresh air. You go up to *your* room!"

Maud knew she had lost the battle of wills. Before she retired to her room, she stood over Wilf, hissing nastily, "Stupid village clod! Wilfred, Wilfred, Wilfred!"

Wilf continued drumming, grinning smugly at her.

"Miss Maudy toffee nose!"

She stalked off without another word, her thoughts racing. Maybe when her father's toughs came up from London, she could find a reason for one of them to give Wilf an accidental cuff across the ear. They were good at things like that.

When she had gone, Wilf produced pencil and paper from his sling and began laboriously writing, trying to use his left hand. It was useless, Regina would write for him. This time he would fix Ben for good, without violence or fighting. He sat waiting for his gang to visit.

DUSK WAS TAKING THE PLACE OF DAY-
light. Outside the lace-curtained windows, a nightingale's
melody was punctuated by an owlhoot, and dusty moths beat
their wings on the windowpanes, in an effort to
reach the interior light.

It was just before Mrs. Winn's bedtime. She
sat at the kitchen table with Ben, trying to help
him with the riddle. He had told her of the dis-
coveries that he, Amy, Alex, and Jon had made
so far. The old lady seemed tired and despondent. "Do you
really think any of this will help me and the village, Ben?
Time's growing shorter by the day now. This all sounds a bit
airy-fairy, compared to the way Smithers and his London firm
are forging ahead. I looked at one of those clearance notices
posted in the square. It's so official, so full of legal jargon. All
'wheretofore' and 'hereinafter' and 'clause B subsection D,' it
made my head spin. Oh, I wish we could come back at them
with something more solid instead of a few ideas based on
guesswork."

Ben saw the old lady was close to tears. She was plainly
scared and worried by the entire situation. He took her hand.
"Stop fretting, Miz Winn, everything will turn out for the best,
you'll see. Now come on, help me with this problem. 'Turn as

a third Gospelmaker would to the house named for the rock.'
Does that mean anything to you?"

Mrs. Winn went to warm some milk. "There were four
Gospelmakers: Matthew, Mark, Luke, and John. They're al-
ways referred to in that order, so Luke must be the third
Gospelmaker. Does that make any sense?"

Ben watched her spooning cocoa and sugar into a jug.
"Yes, yes. You're right! So which way would Luke turn, north,
south, east, west; left, right, backwards, or forward?"

The black labrador, who was lying with his chin on both
front paws, chuckled. "That's a question—which way would
Luke look. Luke look, get it?"

Ben looked sternly at the dog. "This is no time for jokes.
If you can't help, then take a nap."

Ned closed both eyes, thinking, "Luke looks left."

Ben answered the thought. "How d'you know that?"

The dog opened his eyes. "I can't explain it, but it sounds
right, doesn't it? Luke looks left."

Ben said it aloud. "Luke looks left. What d'you think, Miz
Winn?"

She paused from stirring warm milk into the mixture in
the jug. "Hmm, Luke looks left. . . . Of course, L is for left, R
is for right. Luke starts with L, so that must be it. Well done,
my boy!"

Ned snorted aloud and closed his eyes again. However, he
soon opened them again when the old lady filled his bowl with
hot cocoa. She poured warm milk for Horatio.

"He's never been fond of cocoa, so I give him warm milk."

Ned threw out a thought as he slurped cocoa noisily.
"Huh, foolish old feline!"

Mrs. Winn was far too tired to continue clue-solving. Ben

took her arm and walked her through to the downstairs room where she slept. When he returned to the kitchen, Ned was standing alert, watching the door. He communicated a thought to his master.

"Keep quiet, mate. There's somebody outside!"

The patter of receding footsteps sent Ben hurrying to the door. He opened it in time to see the fat form of Tommo, scurrying through the gateway. A note had been fixed to the door with a tack. After allowing Ned out to check the garden for other intruders, Ben took the note in and read it. Wilf's hand was useless for writing, he had dictated it to Regina, but her spelling and grammar were no better than his. Ben smiled as he perused the untidy pencil scrawl.

I carn't fight you cos my hand is dammiged, but I want to talk too you. Be outside Evans's shop tomorrow night, ten minnits before midnight.

　　　　W.S., Grange Gang Leader.

　　　　P.S. You better be their!

Ned trotted in from the garden, shaking his head. "No sign of anyone out there, Ben, what's in the note?"

The boy folded the paper and shoved it in his pocket. "Just another of Wilf's little games, tell you tomorrow. What say we go to bed now, eh, pal?"

The labrador wagged his tail lazily. "Good idea. Oh no, look who's at the window!"

It was Horatio. He had followed the dog outside and Ben, not knowing, shut the door on him. The cat stood tapping the windowpane and meowing plaintively. Ben let him in by the window, and Horatio cleared the sink in one smooth leap.

Landing lightly on the floor, he glared accusingly at Ned.

Ben chuckled. "What's he saying?"

Ned translated the cat's thoughts. "The usual gobbledy-gook: sardines, milk, butterflies, mice, and so on. Says he likes being out of a night, but prefers to finish his milk inside." The big dog drained his cocoa bowl.

"Sensible cat. Come on, Ned, bed for us. Good night, Horatio."

Ned followed his master upstairs, chuntering to himself. "Sensible cat, my paw! Great, foolish furball, more like it!"

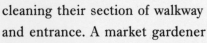

EARLY-MORNING SHOPPERS WERE drifting into Chapelvale village square, and shopkeepers splashed pails of water about, cleaning their section of walkway and entrance. A market gardener was delivering fresh vegetables and flowers to the greengrocers; the gardener's horse clopped its metal-shod hoofs against the cobblestones, causing sparks to fly.

Feeling slightly crestfallen, Ben arrived at the back of the almshouse only to find Alex and Amy already there with the old seaman. Furthermore, Amy had already solved the "Luke to the left" problem. Ben did not show his disappointment, telling himself that it was better for the villagers to help themselves anyway. He smiled at Amy.

"Clever bit of thinking that, L for Luke and L for left. I lay for ages trying to sort it out in bed last night—my mind was a blank. Good job you solved it, Amy."

Jon sat down on the window-ledge, stroking his beard. "Aye, our Amy's a bright girl, but it still don't solve much. Turn to the left yourself, Ben. What do you see?"

Ben did as Jon bade him, looking off to the left in a straight line. "Hmm, nothing much, just the usual countryside, trees, farmland, some fields, and the church on top of the hill."

Amy stood alongside him. "We're looking for the house named for the rock, though what that's supposed to be, goodness knows."

Alex had an idea. "Maybe there's a house or a cottage out there called Gibraltar; that's a rock. Sometimes people name their house after a place they've visited. Or a religious person might have named their house after the Rock of Ages, like in the hymn."

Ben nodded. "You could be right. Are there any places out there like that, named after a rock? Who'd know a thing like that?"

Jon stood up. "Mr. Braithwaite will know. Let's go and ask him."

As they were about to pull the heavy door of the almshouse shut behind them, a voice called out, "Now then, young 'uns, she's runnin' fine today!"

A cheery, ruddy-faced fellow, clad in dairyman's smock and gaiters, reined up a smartly varnished gig, pulled by a dun mare. Ben followed Amy and Alex as they ran to greet him.

"Good morning, Will." Amy patted the mare's flank. "Is Delia over her colic? She looks well!"

He eyed the mare fondly. "Ole Delia's bright as a button, thanks to your dad. I don't know what was in that medicine he gave her, but it certainly got rid of her colic. I've just finished my milk'n'eggs round, why don't you come up to the farm for a visit? Eileen'd be pleased to see you. Hi, Jon Preston, you ole hermit. Fancy a cup o' decent tea an' some scones up at my farm'ouse?"

Moments later they were in the gig, all sitting on empty

milk churns and egg crates, as Delia jogged spiritedly up the back lane towards the hill beyond.

Alex looked around. "Where's Ned?"

Ben shrugged. "Oh, that fellow, he's probably off exploring somewhere. Don't worry about the old boy, he'll find us when he wants to. Is it far to the farm?"

Alex gestured up ahead. "About halfway up the hill, it's called Hillside Farm. Will Drummond is our local dairy farmer. His family've had a place up there for centuries. My dad often tends his animals when they're ill. He says Will's a good man, you'll like him. Bet his mother knows if there's a place named after a rock hereabouts. She knows everything!"

Will's wife, Eileen, was a bustling lady with an ever-present smile. Holding an infant of just over two years on her forearm, she came out into the cobbled farmyard to meet them. "Look, liddle Willum, 'ere's daddy, an' friends with him, too. Come on, Delia my beauty, I got an apple for ye!"

Introductions were made all around. Ben and Alex helped the dairyman unload the empty churns and eggboxes before going in for tea.

Eileen Drummond's scones, served with clotted cream and strawberry jam, were a real treat. As they ate, Ben explained all they were doing in an effort to save Chapelvale but how time was running out. And how they couldn't figure out a house named for a rock.

It was cool and shady in the old, low-beamed farmhouse, with its whitewashed walls, tile floor, and little bull's-eye-paned windows. Will's mother, Sarah, sat installed in her wing chair by the fireplace, a Bible upon her knee, listening carefully until Ben finished talking. She was a bright, alert little woman, quick and bird-like in her actions.

Drawing a knitted black shawl close around her narrow shoulders, she shook her head disapprovingly at Jon and his three young friends and tapped the Bible meaningfully. "Place named after the rock?

"Hah, I can tell you haven't read your scriptures properly. But that's no surprise. Most folk these days don't seem to have the time to heed the word of the Lord!"

Will chided her gently. "Now now, Ma. Don't take on so. Just 'cos folks don't study scripture all the time, doesn't mean they ain't good people. Look at me, I don't read the Bible a lot, but I'm honest an' hardworking."

His mother gave him a hard stare. "Ye'd be a lot better if ye did, Will, an' your friends, too. They should know what the Lord said to his disciple. 'Thou art Peter, and upon this rock I will build my church'! 'Tis written here in the good book. So then, tell me, what's the name o' the church atop of this hill?"

Will blurted out, "St. Peter's!"

The old woman could not help looking slightly smug as she sat back, patting her Bible. "Tell me the rest of your puzzle."

Alex recited the lines from memory:

" ' 'Twixt here and there you must stop to drink, your first reward to unlock.' "

Eileen smote the table so hard that she almost upset her teapot. "I got it!"

Baby Willum thought it was a good game, and he began banging on the tabletop and giggling. Eileen passed him to his father. "Go to Daddy, there's a good lad. I got it, I solved your rhyme! Hillside Farm is 'alfway 'twixt the almshouse an' St. Peter's church. We're the only place 'round 'ere with a well!"

Will bounced the baby up and down on his knee. "Ain't yore mum the clever one, babe Willum!"

The old seaman leaned across the table, his scone and tea forgotten. "I never knew you had a well here."

Will allowed the baby to slide down and toddle across to Amy. "Been a well on this land as long as there's been a farm. Come on, I'll show it ye."

Across the farmyard from the milking shed was a separate stone building, used as a storehouse. Will lit a lantern and hung it from a centre beam. Sacks of potatoes, carrots, turnips, and root vegetables ranged around the walls. Cheeses lay on a wooden platform and hams hung from the rafters. In the centre stood the well, housed by a circular stone wall with a bucket and pulley.

Eileen leaned over the wall and shuddered. "Dark ole place 'tis, though the water's cold an' sweet."

Will wound the bucket down. They heard it splash into the water below. He hauled it up, filled to the brim. "Best water in the county, I reckon. It comes from an underground stream, purified by the limestone an' clear as a bell. What d'you reckon to look for down there?"

Jon stared down into the darkness. "The first reward."

Eileen chuckled. "No reward for you, Jon Preston, you're far too big 'n' heavy to fit into a water pail."

Immediately, Ben volunteered. "I'll go down!"

Armed with another smaller lantern, Ben sat astride the water pail. Jon and Will manned the pulley handle, the latter giving instructions. "There's some tools o' mine in the bucket if you need 'em. Go careful now, lad, and keep tight hold of that rope."

The pulley creaked as the two men lowered Ben down into the wellshaft. Amy stood by, holding little Willum's hand. "What's it like down there, Ben?"

The boy's voice echoed up out of the shaft. "Just an old circular wall, nothing much to see. I'll look at one side on the way down and the other side on the way up. Hold that, Will! My feet are touching water!"

Jon peered down at the light far below. The rope began straining and going from side to side. He called down, "Steady on, Ben. Don't bounce about so much!"

"I'm just turning around so I can see the other half of the wall." His voice echoed. "There, that's better, haul up slow now!"

Will and Jon bent their backs to the task. They had not given more than four full turns when Ben yelled, "Stop! Lower away a touch . . . a bit more. . . . There, that's it!"

Alex poked his head over. "What is it, Ben, what've you found?"

"One of the wall stones, bigger than the rest. Twice as large. It's not cemented in like the others . . . someone's jointed it in with lead. Wait a moment!"

There was a dull thudding of hammer and chisel, then Ben called up, "Aye, it's lead. Easy to get out, it's very old and perished. I can almost pull it out by hand."

A splashing sounded from below, followed by the boy's voice. "Sorry, Will, some of it has fallen into the water."

The young farmer leaned over the edge. "Don't you worry about that, boy, the stream'll wash it away. Let the stone go if you have to."

They could hear Ben grunting with exertion as he

manoeuvred the heavy stone, pushing it back and forth, using the chisel as a lever, reporting his progress as he went. "I've got it almost half out! Whew, it's a big 'un, but it's moving fairly well. Shall I try to get it into the bucket, Will?"

"No, the weight would be too much, lad. Let it go!"

This was followed by a booming splash, as Ben shouted out, "Well, that cooled me down. I'm soaked. Wait, I've got my arm in the hole where the stone was. There's something here!"

Little Willum joined in the cheering that broke out. Ben yelled above the din, "I've got it, haul away, me hearties, take me up. I've got it!"

Alex and Amy joined Will and Jon, helping to turn the handles.

Ben arrived, beaming over the wellshaft at them. "Let's get it out into the light for a proper look, pals!"

Eileen cleared the farmhouse table off, and they set the odd-looking object on it: a muddy lump, about twice the size of a normal house brick.

Ben prodded it. "Anyone fancy a guess at what it is?"

Eileen stopped little Willum trying to climb upon the table. "Dirty ole thing, what d'you reckon 'tis, Ma?" she asked.

Will's mother reached out a stick-like finger and scraped it across the lump, then brought it close to her face. "Hmm, won't know 'til we get all that tallow off it."

The younger boy looked baffled. "Tallow?"

She rubbed it between thumb and forefinger. "Aye, lad, wax made from animal fat. Tallow."

Jon took out his clasp knife. "You mean there's something inside that lump of tallow? Let's take a look. Good protection, wax is, a thing could stay forever encased in it."

Eileen stayed the seaman's hand. "Don't cut it, you might damage whatever it is inside. Let me melt it off."

The object was put in an old iron pot, which Will placed on the stone hearth, right against the fire bars. They stood around, watching it. Ben felt the room becoming oppressively hot. Smells of lamp oil and sea-damp clothing left to dry off came drifting back to his memory, the sway of deck planking beneath his feet, combined with the eternal sound of the restless sea.

"Oh, I can see a big golden ring!"

Amy's delighted shout cut through his thoughts, bringing him back to reality. Will's mother was waving her apron.

"Whew, take it out o' my kitchen, gold ring or no. It stinks!"

Will wrapped a cloth around his hand and carried the pot out by its handle. The iron vessel was quite hot and the wax was melting rapidly.

The boy was glad to be out in the fresh air. The soily sludge around the wax had dissolved and sunk. He could see the thing lying in the clear melted wax. It was not a ring; Amy had only glimpsed the rim.

It was a cup made from gold, an altar chalice!

The old seaman fished it out with two pieces of twig, then took the cloth from Will and carefully cleaned it off.

"Well, I never, look what a marvellous thing Saint Luke sent us!"

The chalice looked as new as the day it was made. Beautifully crafted in solid gold, covered in intricate carvings, with four pigeon-egg rubies set in its solid gold base.

Amy picked the chalice up reverently and held it high, letting the sunlight glint off the gold and rubies.

"The first reward, but what was it doing halfway down a wellshaft?"

Ben shrugged. "Who knows. I'd better go and get Miz Winn. She'll want to see this. It must be worth a great fortune."

Eileen came up with a good suggestion. "Let's make it a surprise for her. I'll make dinner for us all tonight, Ben. You tell Miz Winn she's invited. My Will can call at the house this evenin' to pick you both up. Ma ain't seen Winnie for ages, have you, Ma?"

Will's mother bustled back to the farmhouse, calling out, "I'd like to see Winnie. Better get the place cleaned up, though. Have to sprinkle some lilac water 'round, to get rid of that ole tallow smell."

Ned was waiting anxiously for Ben when he got back. Ben patted his friend's head. "Where've you been, mate? You missed cream tea and scones up at Drummond's farm. Oh, I've got something to tell you."

The black labrador allowed himself to be stroked as he passed on a thought. "I've got something to tell you first, Ben. I went up to Smithers's house and heard Wilf plotting with his gang. I was by the back hedge when I heard them talking on the lawn. Listen to this. They're terrified of Jon. Had some trouble with him. Call him the Mad Professor. But they don't know that you've met him. Wilf is going to dare you to go inside the almshouse at midnight. He reckons Jon will eat you alive, or whatever it is that Mad Professors do to whoever goes into their almshouses. Just thought you'd like to know."

Ben shook his head and grinned. "Then I'll just have to look sufficiently frightened when he dares me. Wait'll I tell Jon. Now, let me tell you what I found today. . . ."

MRS. WINN PUT ASIDE HER WORRIES
temporarily. She was delighted to be asked out to dinner
despite more signs having been tacked to every public
building in the village. She knew the

Drummond family well, and had not been up to
the farm since Captain Winn had passed away.
She became quite excited when Ben hinted that
an important clue had been found,
but even though she pressed him,
he would say no more. Whistling up his dog, Ben
went off down the driveway. He wanted to discuss the coming night's events with Jon. The old
lady watched the pair, suddenly glad that she had
taken in the boy from the sea and his black dog.
She had a feeling events were starting to move
along, things were about to happen. Mrs. Winn
allowed herself a brief shudder of anticipation.

The rest of her afternoon was spent rummaging out her
wardrobe for something pretty to wear at dinner.

The old lady was putting the finishing touches to her
hairpins when Will drove Delia to the gate. Alex and Amy were
with him. The labrador loped out and met Delia, decided immediately that they would be friends, and stayed by the horse's

side. The old seaman came striding jauntily up, his beard combed and a fresh red kerchief bound around his neck. He helped Mrs. Winn up into the gig and they were off.

The dinner was a success, thanks to Eileen and Will's mother: roast beef and potatoes with all the trimmings, followed by fresh strawberries and cream. Will and Jon cleared the table whilst the ladies sipped glasses of elderflower wine, which Amy and Alex's mother had sent along. Little Willum dozed off on the sofa, and Ben poured lemonade for his two young friends. Jon and the dairyman came in from the kitchen, carrying a glass of beer apiece.

After supper Will produced the chalice from behind his back and set it on the mantelpiece. It was filled with water and had six white roses in it. Mrs. Winn stared at it, enraptured. "Oh, it's so beautiful! Does it belong in your family, Sarah?"

Will's ma smiled. "No, it belongs in your family, Winnie!"

While Eileen and Will's ma excitedly related the tale of the discovery, Will showed something to the others.

"Miz Winn ain't the only one gettin' a surprise this evenin'. Look what I found when I was emptyin' the wax from that pot." He placed a flat piece of wood, about eight inches long by an inch wide, upon the table. It was dark, greasy, and well preserved from the tallow that had encased it.

Ben turned it over, running his thumbnail over the wood. "There's some carving on it—hard to make out, though."

Alex produced a pencil stub from his pocket. "Let me try."

They held the lamp close as he ran the pencil lead inside the carved grooves.

His sister studied the results. "It looks like the letter *U* carved alongside itself eight times, with some sort of stickleg creature at each end, very roughly drawn. Looks like two dogs to me."

The big labrador sniffed disdainfully and pawed at Ben's hand. "Dogs: indeed? If I were a dog and I looked like that, I'd drown myself. I'd say it looks more like two horses. You tell her, pal, go on, defend your friend the dog!" Ben did, and Will and Jon were inclined to agree with him.

At the other end of the table Mrs. Winn held the chalice lovingly. "Thank you, all of you, this is the most marvellous discovery. I don't want to sound ungrateful, but I wish that it had been something less beautiful and more practical, like the deeds to Chapelvale. That's what I really need."

The farmer's normally cheerful face darkened. "Aye, that rogue Smithers ain't even made us an offer for Hillside Farm yet. I wouldn't let him over the pasture fence. Still, if they started a quarry an' a factory, we'd be forced to leave. A man can't dairy farm with all kinds o' blastin' an' machinery chuggin' night 'n' day. My business'd be ruined. It ain't right, I tell you, it just ain't right!"

Eileen lifted the sleeping baby from the couch. "We know that, m'dear, but they got the law an' big-business friends in London, aye, an' plenty o' money, too. All we got is good intentions an' time that's gettin' shorter by the day."

The blue-eyed boy interrupted. "But we've got the golden chalice and this carved stick, which has got to be some kind of clue. We can't give up. Who knows, the next thing we turn up may be the deeds. With the value of that chalice and the deeds to the land, we'd soon have the upper hand!"

Jon stared hard at the stick, scratching his beard. "But

where do we look? There may be a clue to the carvings on this stick, but there's no words, no rhyme, no riddle. Maybe the carvings are describing someplace, eight letter *U*s and what we think is a horse . . . where's that?"

Will's ma spoke up. "Would a map of the area help ye?"

Ben felt a tremor of anticipation. "Have you got one?"

Without a word, Sarah Drummond went off to her bedroom. She returned with a framed picture. It was a child's picture of St. Peter's church on the hilltop, drawn in lead pencil and coloured neatly in with coloured wax crayons.

Will flushed to the roots of his hair. "Oh, Ma, you ain't goin' to show 'em that ole thing, I was but ten years old when I drew that in school."

She shook her head, reading out the writing across the top. "Master William Drummond. Aged nine years. Class 3a."

Ben studied it. "Pretty good for a nine-year-old, Will."

Will's ma slit the pasted backing strip with her fingernail. "Aye, Will drew it for me, I've always liked it. But that's not what I want to show you. Take a look at this." From behind her son's childhood artwork, Sarah slid out a paper, yellowed with age.

" 'Tis an ancient map of Chapelvale village an' its surroundings!" She unfolded two creases where the map had been folded under, one towards the top and the other towards the bottom of the map, commenting, "I can remember lookin' at this when I was a little girl, don't know who put it there, or where it came from, but, as you see, the map is bigger'n the frame. Whoever put it there had to fold the paper to make it fit. It's a very old map of hereabouts, but except for the railway station an' one or two other bits, Chapelvale ain't changed much, has it. Now then, missy, can you read the writin' on the parts that were folded under? My eyes ain't up to it."

Amy held the map up to the lamplight and read haltingly.
" 'E.D.W. Anno Domini . . . 1661'! That's what it says along the
top. The bottom bit has two lines of writing:

'Lord, if it be thy will and pleasure,
Keep safe for the house of De Winn thy treasure.'"

The old ship's carpenter's voice shook with excitement.
"Ben lad, those are the very words written on the two bits o'
paper *I* glued together. Here, look, I've got it with me!" He
took the repaired paper from his back pocket and read out the
lines triumphantly:

"'Lord, if it be thy will and pleasure,
Keep safe for the house of De Winn thy treasure.'

"Word for word, the same! Well, sink me!"

Ben found himself laughing at his friend's delight. "Don't
sink just yet, mate. Let's take a look at them together—the
writing seems the same. E.D.W. Ah, Edmund De Winn!"

Alex made a very sensible suggestion. "Your thin paper is
almost like tracing paper, Jon. Why don't you lay it on top of the
map and see if the writing matches up?"

Jon passed the thin paper to Amy. "My hand's beginning
to shake with excitement, you do it."

Brushing her dark hair aside, the girl placed the map flat
on the table. With careful precision, she laid the thin paper on
top, nudging it gently until the two lines of writing were exactly on top of each other.

"It matches almost perfectly, every dot and loop of Edmund De Winn's writing. Top and bottom, line for line!"

Alex placed his thumbs at the far side of both papers. "I'll hold them steady, anybody got a pencil?"

Being a carpenter, Jon invariably had a well-sharpened pencil stub behind his ear, which he produced. He winked at the boy. "Aha! I see your plan, shipmate. You want me to mark the map through the four holes in the tissue paper. Hold her steady, now."

As the old seaman painstakingly marked the map through the four holes in the thin paper, Ben caught a thought from the labrador.

"Look at Winnie. There's a picture of hope, you can see she really believes things are starting to happen."

Ben returned the thought. "Aye, and it's not just her. Look at Will and Ma. Look at us all. I'm glad the angel sent us here, pal. Smithers and his London gang don't know it yet, but I think they'll find these folk aren't too easy to ride roughshod over any more."

Will removed the thin paper from its position. They gathered around the table to view the pencil-dotted map as he tapped a finger on the first mark he recognized. "Look 'ere, this is our farm, an' the well, too! Haha, we've already solved one bit o' the puzzle, right, friends? Which is the next 'un? Come on, young feller. I'm beginnin' to like this!"

His ma clapped her hands together and rubbed them gleefully. "Me, too. Never thought I'd be part of a treasure hunt!"

Alex tapped the flat stick against his hand, staring at the map. "Hmm, we've solved the first saint's problem: that's Luke. So let's write Luke over the dot where this farmhouse is."

Jon nodded in admiration. "Well said, lad! So that leaves Matthew, Mark, an' John. I think they'll be in a clockwise position, stands to reason, don't it?"

The astute old lady's eyes twinkled as she took the pencil, licking the point briefly. " 'Matthew, Mark, Luke, and John, Bless the Bed that I Lie On.' Clockwise, eh, then this is the way it should go." She wrote lightly above the other three dots thus:

They went back to pondering the problem. Will stood silent, his arms folded, when suddenly his voice cut the silence.

"St. John, that's the next one we should look at if we're goin' clockwise. Though I'm just thinkin', that next mark is right where the railway station stands now."

His wife peered closely at the mark belonging to St. John. "When I went t' school ole Mr. Braithwaite told us that's about where the blacksmith once 'ad his stables."

Now the meaning of the marks upon the stick dawned upon Ben. He took the flat piece of wood from Alex. "Of course! Two horses and lots of letter *U*s, I'll bet the *U*s are meant to be horseshoes!"

Mrs. Winn squeezed Ben's hand. "Marvellous, I wish I was as quick-thinking as you! But I've just had an awful thought. Supposing they built the railway station right over the stables, what then?"

Eileen frowned. "Let's hope not. Don't you go frettin' just yet, m'dear. We'll go an' see Mr. Braithwaite, he'll know if anybody does!"

The old lady sighed. "You're right, we'll just have to wait and see. Thank you for the lovely dinner, Eileen, you, too, Sarah. Oh dear, it's getting late, we'd best get back home."

Mrs. Winn had the chalice wrapped in a clean teacloth that she intended leaving with Mr. Mackay the lawyer, for safe-keeping. They all climbed into the cart, and Will delivered them to their homes.

Ben had already laid his plans for the midnight encounter with Wilf Smithers. As Will was helping Mrs. Winn from the gig, Ben winked at Amy, Alex, and Jon, his voice dropping to a whisper. "See you later."

It was still only ten o'clock when Ben assisted Mrs. Winn to her room. She thanked him. "What an exciting evening, Ben, let's hope there's good news for us in the morning. Don't stay up too late, now, and lock up before you go to bed. Oh dear, I'm exhausted!"

BEN SAT AT THE KITCHEN TABLE, THE BIG,
black labrador at his feet, each immersed in his own thoughts.
Horatio sat with his tail curled about both front paws, watch-ing a moth beating against the outer windowpane, trying vainly to reach the lamplight. It had
been ten minutes since the hall clock chimed
half-past eleven.

Ben blinked and rubbed his eyes. "Come
on, Ned, time to go." He took the kitchen key
from its hook and quietly opened the door to the rear of the
house.

Horatio followed them out, purring. The big labrador
passed the cat a thought. "You can't come with us."

The cat replied mentally. "Prrrr, 'Ratio go catch butterflies."

The big moth that had been beating itself against the window flew into the kitchen and began circling the lamp. The
dog turned the cat around with a sweep of his paw, commenting, "Look, there's a moth, they're fatter than butterflies, go
and catch him. Bet you can't!"

Horatio curled his tail disdainfully. "Miaow, 'Ratio catch
butterflies, prrrr, mop be easier to catch, you watch!" He ran
back indoors. Leaping on the table, he began dabbing his paw
at the moth. "Rrrowwrrr, soon catch mopfly!"

The big dog nodded. "That's the stuff, Horatio. You catch the mopfly and have a midnight snack. See you later. Hmph, mopfly indeed—you'll soon have me as dotty as y'self!"

Ben locked the kitchen door, staring curiously at his friend. "What was all that about?"

Ned passed him a despairing glance. "Mopflies. You wouldn't understand. Come on, our friends'll be waiting."

Amid the dark night shadows Wilf Smithers and his gang stood in the alley alongside Evans Tea Shoppe.

Regina took out a fob watch, which she had received for her birthday, and consulted it. "Nearly ten minutes to midnight, he should be here by now."

A thin, nervous-looking boy named Archie gnawed his thumbnail. "I don't think he's comin', hadn't we better go home? My mum and dad don't know I sneaked out."

Wilf grabbed him by the earlobe, tugging him up onto his toes. "Scared stiff, that's your trouble, Archie. Well go on, then, run back home quick. But you won't be in this gang any more if you do!"

Tommo pulled a face at Archie. "Beat it back home. Who needs you, you skinny little worm!"

Wilf let go of Archie and turned his contempt on the fat boy. "Who asked you, puddenface, you look twice as scared as he does!"

"Oh, I don't know, he probably looks about one and a half times as scared as poor Archie, right, Tommo?"

Wilf almost jumped with fright as the blue-eyed boy emerged from the shadows. He recovered himself quickly and snarled. "How did you get here?"

As the black labrador and Amy and Alex materialized out of the darkness, Ben smiled. "Same way you did, of course. How's the hand, still sore?"

Wilf smiled thinly back at his foe. "Forget my hand. You're here because you cheated me at that fight. But you won't dodge your way out of this one. I'll bet that you're a snivelling coward, and too scared to take a dare, aren't you?"

Ben shrugged. "Why should I take a dare?"

Regina called out scornfully from behind Wilf. " 'Cos if you don't, then we'll all know you're a coward!"

Alex answered her, "Ben's no coward!"

She sneered at him. "Oh shuttup, Alexandra!"

Amy blazed at the bigger girl, "And you shuttup, you great bully!"

Ben placed himself between them. "No need for all this name-calling. I'll take your dare, Wilf, providing it's not something stupid, like jumping off the church roof and landing on my head, or punching the school wall with my bare hand."

There were one or two sniggers from the gang. Wilf silenced them with a glare before turning back. "It's nothing like that. There's nothing daft about this dare, so, will you take it?"

Ben flicked the hair from his eyes. "Go on then, what is it?"

Wilf took the fob watch from Regina and glanced at it. "Two minutes to go. Right on the stroke of midnight, you will go into the almshouse where the Mad Professor lives. Alone. We'll wait outside to see that you do. Well, will you do it?" The boy appeared to hesitate and backed off slightly.

Wilf grinned wolfishly. "Hah, you're scared!"

Ben sounded unsure of himself. "No I'm not, I, er, I just have my reasons for not wanting to go into the almshouse."

Regina pointed her finger at him. "Coward! Coward!"

Alex placed himself in front of his friend. He looked pale and his knees were shaking as he spoke in a voice barely above a whisper. "Leave him alone, Ben's already proved he's no coward. I'll take the dare from him, I'll do it."

Wilf stared at him scornfully. "You? Hahaha, I can hear your knees knocking like clappers. D'you mean to tell me you're taking a dare to go into that place?"

The young boy clenched his fists until the knuckles showed white. He swallowed hard and nodded his head.

Wilf curled both hands like claws, advancing on Alex, eyes wide, his voice in a mock horrified tone. "Who knows what you'll find inside that old almshouse, little boy. Spiders, cobwebs, rats, ancient ghosts . . . and the madman!"

A few of the gang giggled and shuddered with nervous anticipation. Somebody even gave a hollow ghostly whoop. Wilf silenced them with a glare before turning back to his victim.

"Ah yes, the great, bearded madman. He's got a big shotgun, you know. But I don't suppose he'd use it on a little shrimp like you. Oh no, I'll bet he's got butcher's knives and hooks and a hangman's noose, all ready for young boys called Alex who come knocking on his door at midnight, when it's pitch dark!"

Ben grasped his friend's arm, there was a note of frightened pleading in his voice. "Don't do it, Alex, he dared me. . . . I'll go!"

But Wilf had different ideas, he pulled the towheaded lad away from his young companion. The bully was enjoying tormenting Alex. "Oh, no you don't, you've already proved yourself a coward by refusing the dare. I'm going to let him go and get murdered. He wants to take on your dare, don't you, Alexandra?"

Amy was about to stand up in her brother's defence, when
Ben warned her off with a glance and Alex replied.

"I'll go. But if I do, are you willing to take on a dare in return? That's fair enough, isn't it? Dare for dare?"

A ready murmur of agreement came from the gang: It
sounded good enough to them. Wilf was their leader, he was a
big, strong lad, nobody had ever questioned his courage.

Wilf realized he would lose face if he refused in front of his
own gang. Fancy backing down from a mousy little runt like
Alex Somers! Wilf sneered. "All right then, but like your pal
said, provided it's nothing stupid, I'll take your dare. What is
it, jellylegs?"

There was laughter and approval from the Grange Gang.
Wilf swelled his chest and grinned to show them he was fear-
less.

The younger boy drew in a deep breath, as if gathering his
courage. "The dare is this. If I'm in the almshouse more than
two minutes, you've got to come in and get me out."

Regina spoke out scornfully. "Huh, anything you can do,
Wilf can do as well. If you're not scared, he certainly isn't!"

More murmurs of approval arose from the gang: They had
every confidence in their leader. Unfortunately Wilf did not
share their belief. He found himself wishing he had not
started the whole business of silly dares.

Ben interrupted his thoughts. "It's almost midnight.
Shouldn't we all get over to the almshouse?"

Regina cast him a wilting glance. "We? You and your dog
can do what you like. Coward!"

The labrador shot his master a thought. "Shall I nip her
ankle?"

The boy patted his faithful friend. "No need to, things are

working out quite nicely, pal. Alex is a great actor."

They crouched to one side of the rickety iron gate behind a lilac that grew over the fence. Regina looked at her watch. "It's turned twelve. Get moving, you!"

The young boy opened the gate and crept hesitantly towards the door of the almshouse. There was a titter from the gang as Regina called out in a loud whisper, "Go on, he won't eat you, I don't think!"

Reaching the almshouse door, Alex paused, then, raising his hand, he knocked faintly twice.

The door flew open and there was Jon, looking like something out of a nightmare. He had a blanket wrapped about his shoulders like a flowing cloak, flour on his face, lampblack underneath his eyes, and two Brazil nuts hanging down from his upper lip like fangs. Laughing madly, he grabbed Alex and pulled him inside, slamming the door shut. The effect was startling. Led by Wilf and Regina, the Grange Gang fled screaming across the square. Ned went around the back like a dark streak, cutting off their way through Evans Tea Shoppe's alley by blocking off the far end. Ben and Amy came dashing across the square in the gang's wake, effectively penning them in the narrow alley. Ben tipped Amy the wink. "You tackle Wilf. Leave Regina to me!"

Amy pushed her way through the melee of milling gang members and found Wilf standing paralysed in front of a snarling Ned. She grabbed the big boy by his shirtfront and shook him. "Get back to the almshouse and help my brother! You were the one who thought all this up and dared him. Come on, I'm going to see that you carry out your end of the dare!" She began to drag Wilf away from the wall that he was huddled against.

Everyone saw it: Wilf Smithers collapsed to the ground, clutching his bandaged hand and blubbering like a baby. "Waahahaah! I'm sick, my hand's hurting, let go of me, please, I want to go home. Waaaaahh!"

Regina had been scrambling her way to the back of the gang, intent on escaping into the square, when Ben grabbed her hand. "What about you going to help Alex? You were the one calling all the names. Why don't you take the dare for Wilf?"

She broke out in tears. "It wasn't anything to do with me! It was all Wilf's idea, he said we should do it!"

Ben called to the others. "Amy and I are going back to the almshouse. You lot run and get some help. Fetch a policeman, quick!"

The mention of police involvement sent them all stumbling past the big black labrador and off into the darkness, crying.

"My dad doesn't even know I'm out!"

"I'm not going to any police station!"

"Nothing t'do with us, it was Wilf!"

Ned let them go. Amy planted her shoe firmly against Wilf's bottom and shoved him on his way. "Get out of my sight, coward!"

Ben released Regina, and she shot off, sobbing. In a trice the alley was deserted, save for Amy, Ben, and his dog. The sound of bolts being withdrawn from Evans's side door caused Ned to melt back into the shadows. A light went on, throwing a golden shaft across the alley. Blodwen Evans's huge nightgowned figure appeared in the open doorway. She was holding a hooked window-blind pole and holding on to her mobcap, squinting at Ben.

"Indeed to goodness, what's all the row out here, boyo, eh?"

Ben flicked at his tousled hair and smiled disarmingly. "Sorry about the noise, Miz Evans. My dog's got loose and I was out calling for him. I don't suppose you've seen him?"

A gruff bark from nearby sent the boy running off, followed by Amy, who was calling, "Here, Ned! Good dog! Here, boy!"

Mrs. Evans shook her head as she closed the door. "I 'opes they get him, I need my sleep!"

THE OLD SHIP'S CARPENTER AND ALEX

36 had cocoa made for Ben, Amy, and Ned as they entered the almshouse through the back window. They related what had happened in the alley, the younger boy and Jon roaring with laughter at Amy's impression of Wilf sobbing and wanting to go home, hugging his injured hand.

Ben sipped his cocoa and winked at Alex.

"Wait'll they find out tomorrow that you faced the Mad Professor and lived to tell the tale. I don't think the Grange Gang or Wilf will ever bother you again, Alex. Or you, Amy. It was great to see how you went at the bully and had him bawling in front of his own gang. They'll respect you both from now on."

Alex put his empty mug down. "But only because of you, Ben."

The blue-eyed boy patted Alex heartily on the back. "Nonsense, mate, all I did was suggest a thing or two. The rest was you, having confidence in yourself. Isn't that right, Ned?"

The dog nodded. Jon looked over the rim of his cocoa mug at him. "I suppose that was his collar itching him again, eh, Ben?"

The strange boy's eyes twinkled. "You supposed right, mate."

Alex was beginning to feel sleepy; he blinked. "Supposed what?"

The black labrador leaped to the window frame, followed by Ben, who chuckled. "Supposed to meet at the library first thing in the morning, so we can have a word with Mr. Braithwaite. G'night, pals. Jon, will you see Amy and Alex get home all right?"

Ben and Ned vanished into the night like twin shadows.

Amy stared at the empty window space. "There's something rather odd about Ben. It's almost as if he and Ned are magic. What do you think, Jon?"

The ex-ship's carpenter wiped the last of the lampblack off with a damp rag. "Ben's no more magic than you, me, or Alex. He's just good, aye, and clever. He's certainly taught me a thing or two, as old as I am. Come on, mates, I'll walk you as far as your house."

"Not quite as far," Alex replied. "Leave us at the end of the lane, we've got to sneak in by the pantry window."

Jon's craggy face broke into a smile. "See, you're learning fast, pal!"

At breakfast next morning Hetty the maid brought the post into the dining room. She placed it next to Obadiah Smithers's plate, bobbed a brief curtsy, and left.

Mrs. Smithers cast a worried glance at Wilf's empty chair. "Poor Wilfred, perhaps he's stayed in bed because he's still feeling poorly. I'll tell Hetty to take him a tray up."

"No, you won't, madam!" Smithers slit an envelope

vigorously with his egg-stained breakfast knife. "Let the young whelp stay abed until he's hungry enough to get himself down here and take his place at table. Confounded fool, punchin' a wall of all things, losing to a lad half his size. Oh, I've heard all about it from Reggie Woodworthy, Regina told him. Can't hold my head up in the village! Man with a great, strappin' son who doesn't know the difference between the other fellow's nose and a schoolyard wall. Huh!"

Maud Bowe helped herself to a boiled egg and tapped the top daintily with her spoon, remarking caustically, "About what anyone could expect from that silly oaf."

Smithers slammed the letter down on his side plate, cracking it in the process. He glared at Maud.

"Keep your opinions to y'self, missie. It's not your place to criticize my family while you're a guest in my house!"

Sensing another verbal battle, Mrs. Smithers withdrew from the room quietly. She would take Wilfred a tray herself.

Maud thrust her chin out defiantly at the older man. "Sir, an oaf is an oaf, in any circumstances, more so when he is a bad-mannered oaf. That is my opinion, like it or not!"

Smithers, pretending not to hear, sorted a letter from the small pile of mail and tossed it across the table. "This is for you, young lady, from your father by the writing."

She took a nail file from her pocket and slit the letter neatly open, her eyes blazing at Smithers. "Sir, I give you your proper title. My name is Maud, you may address me as Maud, Miss Maud, or Miss Bowe. I resent being called missie or young lady. I trust you will refrain from such expressions in future!"

Smithers pretended to read his letter; he tapped it with his knife. "From the county planning office, final approval of com-

pulsory purchase of Chapelvale lands two days from today.
Providing, of course, that no majority property holder turns up
with deeds to more than one section. Huh, even old Mrs. Winn
can't argue with that, she can only prove the ownership of her
own house. She has no papers for that almshouse ruin, or any
other land. I've made sure of that, got a friend in the official
search office, y'know. Look, there's a formal notice with this
letter, to be posted in the square. I'll remove the old one an'
put this one up, eh. How's that for progress? Well, what's your
father got to say?"

Maud folded the letter carefully and placed it on the table.
"He says that the four men I asked for should be up by the
evening train tomorrow. He has paid them expenses and
money for the train tickets—"

Smithers's explosion cut her short. "Well, I'm damned if
I'd pay 'em a bent penny, missie. I've already told you what I
think of your proposal, sending toughs and blaggards up from
London. What'll happen if they're found to be connected to
this venture? I'll be ruined, and so would your father and his
fancy London partners. Then where'll we all be, eh? Answer
me that, m'dear!"

Maud's normally sallow pallor grew ashen with temper.
"I'll tell you . . . Smithers! You'd be sitting out here at the end
of some rural backwater with your fiddling little business.
This is a big venture, that's why you're in with a proper London company, and doing quite well out of it, too. My father's
company often uses the methods he needs—legal or not—
that's the way you get things done in this modern age. And
don't look so self-righteous—you had children trying to get
things done for you, that oaf you call a son and his gang. What
were you paying them, eh, sweeties, pennies?

"Well, that's all changed, you're in the game now for better or worse. It'll be worse if we listen to your piffling ideas, but better all 'round if you leave it to experts. That old lady Winn, she'll be shifted sooner than you think and for good, thanks to my suggestion to my father, so stop acting like a silly oaf, though the habit seems to run in your family!" Maud's ankle-length taffeta dress rustled stiffly as she swept out of her chair and vacated the room.

Smithers sat open-mouthed at the girl's impertinence, his heavy features flushing dark red. He gave vent to his ire with a bellow that would have done a stricken water buffalo credit, sending crockery and cutlery flying as his outstretched arms flailed across the table.

Sitting up in bed, Wilf heard the roar and the ensuing crash. He started with fright, upsetting his breakfast tray. A glass of milk, toast, lemon curd, and two soft-boiled eggs spilled into his lap. He sobbed, floundering about in the mess, his mind running riot. Had his father found out about last night, his second foolish scheme gone astray? It wasn't his fault if the Somers boy had gone and got himself murdered by the Mad Professor. Had the police found out yet, would they come around asking questions? Regina and the gang wouldn't take the blame, they'd lay it on him, their leader. Then what? Court, imprisonment . . . ? Regardless of the breakfast mess, Wilf pulled the coverlet over his head, wishing fervently that it would all go away. Tears, egg, milk, and lemon curd mingled on his face. He jumped as a timid knock sounded on the door.

"Finished with your tray, Master Wilfred?" It was only Hetty.

A muffled scream broke from beneath the stained counterpane. "Go 'waaaaaay!"

MRS. WINN'S LAWYER, MR. MACKAY, WAS A
man of small stature, exceedingly neat in appearance. Dressed
in knife-creased pin-striped trousering, an eight-button black
vest (complete with silver watch and chain), a

crisp white shirt, with starched wing-tip collar
and a dark blue stock with a modest peridot
stickpin, he sported spring-clipped pince-nez,
hanging around his neck on a black silk
ribbon. A snowy peak of white linen handker-
chief showed from the top pocket of his black fustian tailcoat.
Mr. Mackay had a centre parting in his dyed black hair and a
small, precisely trimmed moustache. He shaved twice daily
and had about him an aroma of macassar pomade. The con-
sensus of village opinion had marked him as a dry little stick
of a man, his movements quick and bird-like, his speech
clipped and precise, peppered with legal jargon. Now Mr.
Mackay sat looking at the chalice on his desk. He had heard
the story of its discovery from the old lady. Taking the pince-
nez spectacles from his nose, he let them dangle by their black
ribbon.

He stared around at the faces of Will and Eileen
Drummond, Mrs. Winn, the old ship's carpenter, Amy and
Alex Somers, and Ben. "I take it, madam, that you require

information regarding the location of the old stable and smithy from Mr. Braithwaite? Then so be it. You boys, run and fetch Braithwaite here. However, I think that I may be of some help in that direction—I acted on behalf of the Railway Company in conveying the land for the station and retained a copy of the paperwork for my own files."

Ben and Alex left the lawyer's office with the big, black dog in their wake.

Talking out of the corner of his mouth, Ben murmured to Alex, "See, over in Evans's alley, there's some of the Grange Gang. They're watching the almshouse, probably to see if your mangled body gets flung out the door. They haven't spotted us yet. Why not give them a wave?"

Alex strode off towards the alley. "I'll do better than that, Ben, I'll pop over and have a word with them."

Alex shouted, "Hello there, you lot! Hang on a moment, I want to see you!"

They fled like startled deer.

Ben shrugged. "That's odd, don't they like speaking to the ghost of a murdered boy?" The two friends laughed uproariously.

They brought Mr. Braithwaite back to Mr. Mackay's office, where the librarian stood scratching his wiry mane, dandruff sprinkling like tiny snowflakes on the shoulders of his black scholar's gown. "I, er, can't stop very, hmmmmm, long. Library, er, business, I'm afraid . . ." His voice trailed off as he sighted the chalice on the desk. Ignoring everybody around him, he picked the chalice up with great reverence. No hesitancy showed in his voice as he spoke.

"Calix magnificus! Magnificus magnificus! Byzantine tenth century. Crafted by the skilled goldsmiths and lapidaries of a bygone age. What a perfectly beautiful specimen. These pigeon-egg rubies, jewels beyond price. This tracery and engraving, exotic, fabulous! Who came by such a remarkable chalice as this? Where was it discovered? Oh, tell me!"

The grizzled old seaman related the tale in full. Omitting no detail, he brought Mr. Braithwaite up to strength on even the latest development. The old scholar scratched his frizzy head. The initial gusto of seeing the chalice was wearing off, and he returned to his customary self.

"Hmm, very good, very good! So I take it, you, er, er, wish to know the, ah, exact location of the, er, ancient stables and, er, blacksmith's forge, er, as it were?"

Mr. Mackay held up a sheaf of legal-looking documents. "They're not far from the station, according to my records, sir!"

Mr. Braithwaite raised his bushy eyebrows, staring at Mr. Mackay's small, dapper figure as if seeing him for the first time. "Not so, sir! I, er, that is, my, er, researches show, the, ah, smithy, stood on the, er, er, precise spot where the station was built, hmmm, yes indeed!"

Mr. Mackay was not one to bandy words. Drawing himself up to his sparse height, he spread the documents on his desk, tapping a neatly manicured finger on a map diagram. "Then look for yourself, sir. My records are undeniable!"

Mr. Braithwaite pored over Mr. Mackay's map, showering it with dandruff as he scratched his hair in bemusement. "Well I never, well I never, my, er, calculations were wrong, it, er, seems. I defer to your technical knowledge, sir. I, er, must consult you more often, in my, er, historical location studies. If I, er, may make so bold as to, er, suggest such a thing."

"Of course you may, sir!" replied Mackay in his clipped,

precise manner. He rolled the papers back into a scroll.

Mrs. Winn liked her lawyer, despite his somewhat pompous attitude, and could see his interest was aroused by the search. "Would you care to take a look at the site, Mr. Mackay? We'd be glad of your expert opinion."

A faint smile appeared on the lawyer's face. "An intriguing invitation, marm. I accept!"

The old lady turned to Mr. Braithwaite. "We'd value your help if you'd like to come, too, sir."

Scratching his head and pointing to himself, the old scholar grinned like a schoolboy. "Who . . . er, me? Oh, I say, rather, lead on, er, good lady, lead on, er, please do!"

It was a curious team that trooped out of the solicitor's office, heading towards Chapelvale Station. Obadiah Smithers and his wife, Clarissa, had emerged from their carriage in the village square, she intent on shopping and he intending to go to Mr. Mackay's office. Seeing the lawyer piling into Will Drummond's cart with the others, Smithers hastened across to him, waving the latest compulsory purchase notice, whilst holding on to his top hat.

"Hold up there, Mackay. Where the deuce d'you think you're going? I was just about to consult you!"

Mr. Mackay did not like Smithers. He considered the fellow an overbearing bully, and he stared officiously down from the gig at him. "Consult me without a prior appointment, sir? I'm afraid it's out of the question. I've got other business!"

Smithers waved the order. "But what about this, it arrived in this morning's mail. I want it to be pinned up in the square."

Mr. Mackay glared at Smithers over the top of his pince-nez. "Then fix it up yourself, sir, you look capable enough. There's a nail and a post for the purpose. You can either leave the present order up, or tear it down to make room for the new one. As you can see, I have other matters to attend, I bid you good day. Drive on, please, Mr. Drummond!"

Smithers was left standing red-faced and at a loss for words as the gig pulled off smartly. Mrs. Winn and Eileen stifled laughter with their kerchiefs. Not so with the other occupants of the dairy cart, they guffawed aloud.

"Well, that put him in his place, eh. Hahahaha!"

"Aye, did you see the face on him, like a beetroot!"

"Look, he's still standing there waving his silly paper. Hahaha!"

Mr. Mackay did not join in the merriment. Polishing his pince-nez, he blinked sternly at his travelling companions. "I would have liked to see the contents of that order. I fear it will be no laughing matter for Chapelvale, or you, Miz Winn. We must take a look at it on our return!"

They took the road past the station and over the level crossing. Ned passed a thought to his master as he allowed Amy to stroke him. "Whatever we're looking for, bet I'm the one who finds it. By the way, what exactly are we looking for?"

The boy answered, "I don't know, Ned. It's a large, over-grown area near the station we'll have to cover probably. With an old, carved piece of stick as our only clue. We'll need the help of a good sniffer."

Will halted Delia at Mr. Mackay's command, on what appeared to be a piece of common land, about twenty yards away from the railway tracks. Jon and Will spread the old map from the farmhouse cottage alongside the railway property map that

Mr. Mackay and Mr. Braithwaite were studying. Eileen, who had left her baby at home with Will's ma, sat in the gig watching the two boys, while Amy and the black labrador ranged out across the gorse-covered area. Mr. Mackay pointed to a corner of his boundary map.

"You see, here is the boundary line of the railway property. It ends ten feet away, where Will halted the gig on that bit of disused path. So this is all common land."

Mr. Braithwaite looked from one map to the other. "Hmmm, this has got to be the, er, place, very good! See the, er, tree, in the same place on both, er, maps, yes."

Jon pointed to the only tree left standing, on the far side of the common. "What, do you mean that one?"

Mr. Mackay shook his head doubtfully. "Your map is dated 1661. Surely that scruffy old tree hasn't been there that long?"

Braithwaite was glad to prove himself, not only as a history scholar but as a botanist. "I, er, must take issue with you on that, sir. Er. Let us take a look at this, hmm, tree."

They trooped over to where Ben and his friends were standing beneath the tree. It was a twisted and venerable old specimen with a huge, untidy crown of thin leaves that sported red berries. The trunk, a gnarled column, was very thick, seeming to consist of several thinner trunks welded together by age.

Jon instinctively knew what it was. "This is a yew, there's two growin' back o' the almshouse."

Mr. Braithwaite became very schoolmasterish, wagging a finger at the young people as he lectured them. "Quite right. *Taxus baccata,* the common English yew, specimens have been recorded of up to one thousand years old. The branches of this old tree may have provided the wood for English longbows to fight the French at the Battle of Agincourt. Jon, hand me that carved piece of wood and your clasp knife, please."

Mr. Braithwaite scraped away at the uncarved side of the wooden stick until clean wood showed, then he shaved a small section of bark from the trunk to reveal the wood beneath.

"Both common English yew, you see!"

Will smacked his open palm against the tree. "All sounds very good so far, but what're we lookin' for and where do we search?"

Amy placed both hands on her hips. "Around this tree, I suppose."

Ben sprang and grabbed a spreading limb. "Or maybe up in the tree!" He climbed into the branches.

The others started to search around the base of the yew. Alex soon got tired of the hunt below and with Ben's help climbed up into the boughs, too. The dog looked up, communicating with his master. "If you fall and break a leg, don't come running to me!"

After more than a half hour of scanning the trunk and the ground around it, Mrs. Winn gave up and went to sit in the gig with Eileen.

Will straightened up, holding his back. "Ain't so easy as it first looked. See anything up there, Ben?"

Ben clambered down. "Nothing, Will. As you said, it would help if we knew what we were looking for."

Being shorter than Ben, Alex found descending a bit difficult, but he made his way to the other side of the tree and found a low branch. Edging onto it, he hung there by both hands, facing the trunk.

The seaman stood beneath, reaching up with both hands. "Come on, mate, let go an' I'll catch ye."

But Alex hung on to the branch, his face towards the trunk, shouting, "I found it! Here it is!"

Ben shot back up the tree like a monkey. Making his way across to Alex, he leaned downward, peering at what looked like tiny knots sticking from the bark. He gave a joyous whoop. "It's the same pattern as the stick. Well done!"

Will shouted across to his wife. "Eileen, drive the gig over here, beneath this tree!"

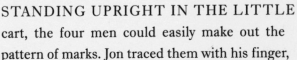

STANDING UPRIGHT IN THE LITTLE
cart, the four men could easily make out the
pattern of marks. Jon traced them with his finger,

then touched the point of his clasp knife to one.
"Metal! They're old horseshoe nails driven into
the trunk. The bark has grown over them, but
the pattern remains."

Mr. Mackay dusted dead grass from his
trouser knees fussily. "But with one difference,
sir, there's an arrow shape pointing down. That must mean we
have to dig down at the yew base, directly where the arrow
indicates."

The dairyman backed Delia away from the spot.
Grabbing a spade, Will began cutting away the top grass.
"Right about here!" The old ship's carpenter spat on his
hands and grabbed another spade from the gig.

But Eileen had different ideas. "I think 'tis a waste o' time
diggin' there, Will. Surely the girth o' the tree has growed bigger since sixteen hundred an' whatever. If you were lookin' for
somethin' buried 'twould be right under that trunk now! Don't
waste your energy. You either, Jon Preston."

Will threw his spade down dispiritedly. "You're right,
m'love."

Ben watched Ned go off with small, dainty paces, sniffing hard at the ground. He sent a thought to the dog.

"What are you doing, mate?"

The big, black dog did not answer for a while, but kept sniffing and going forward. When he stopped, he sat down a short distance off. "Tell them the arrow is probably pointing not down, but out from the tree, to somewhere around here."

Ben stared at the labrador. "You could be right, but why there, why not further out?"

Ned nosed the grass, turning up a soggy, moss-covered length of board and sniffling. "Because this is where the old smithy once stood!"

The boy turned to his friends. "Suppose the arrow is pointing not down, but out. Would that be about where Ned's sitting?"

Braithwaite was studying the piece of lath and its carving. "Hmm, about the length of a horse, eight horseshoes, and one more horse's length. What, er, d'you think, Mr. Mackay?"

The solicitor focused on the stick with his glasses. "You could have something there, sir. At least we've got a horse to test your theory with!"

Taking the gig to one side, Will unharnessed Delia. Lifting one of her back hoofs, he measured it with a yew twig, which he snapped off, then backed Delia up, until her tail was touching the yew trunk.

"Jon, take this twig. 'Tis a shoe's width. Mark off eight lengths from where my mare's front hoof is now."

The seaman did as Will bade. When he had marked off eight lengths, he stuck the twig in the ground. "Right here, Will." The dairyman brought his horse forward and stood Delia, with her tail hanging down, exactly over the twig.

The black labrador looked up and licked Delia's muzzle, which was directly above him, then looked over to where Ben stood, passing a thought to his master. "Told you I'd sniff it out, didn't I!"

Eileen chuckled. "That good dog o' yours, Ben, he looks as if he's gotten more sense than the lot of us put t'gether!"

Jon and Will started digging on the spot.

Eileen harnessed Delia back into the gig shafts. "Come on, Winnie, we'll go back to Hillside Farm an' get lunch ready for the diggin' gang."

Ben and Amy helped Mrs. Winn up into the gig. She waved to them as Delia trotted away and called hopefully, "Bring whatever you find straight up to the farm."

The old mariner and the dairyman dug a square hole, straight down about two feet. Clank! Will's spade struck something as he was shoring the side of the earth straight. "We were diggin' slightly astray, Jon. I think the dog was sittin' in the wrong spot!"

Ned sniffed. "Dearie me, showed you the place, didn't I?"

Ben heard the thought and agreed with his dog. "Aye, can't expect a poor old canine to be accurate to the inch, can we? Pay no heed, Ned. I thought you did splendidly!"

They dug down again, directly over the place where Will's spade had struck an object. After several minutes of hard digging a sandstone building block was uncovered. Between them the two men lifted it out. Alex cleaned it up with his hand until the letters *E.D.W.* appeared visible. Ben ran his finger over the letters. "Same as on your map, Will! And the same as that name in the back of Winnie's family Bible! Edmond De Winn, the one who had one son and seven daughters!"

Further speculation from Ben was cut short. The old seaman bent and began tugging with both hands at an object embedded beneath where the stone had lain. "Here's something, mates, an old chest!"

Will helped him pull the chest out. It was iron-bound, rotting, and fused hard to the soil around it. Once they got it out, a few smart jabs with Jon's spade soon caved it in, and it broke open. Braithwaite fell on his knees and lifted out the contents. Wrapped in sheepskin and heavily coated with solidified tallow, it was still fairly obvious from its shape that the thing was a cross.

High-noon sunlight streamed into the farmhouse kitchen. Will's ma shaded her eyes against it, peering out across the yard. "Here they come, Winnie. Put the kettle on to boil again, Eileen."

Little Willum toddled out, holding Winnie's hand. "Dad-deeeee!"

The dairyman swung his son up onto his broad shoulders. "I hope you ain't ate all our lunch, Willum, I'm starvin'!"

But food was out of the question once Eileen spotted the bundle.

"You found it, good men!"

Amy took little Willum from his father. "What about me?"

Will's ma wiped flour from both hands upon her apron. "An' you, too, m'dear, good work. Now, let's see what you got, my meat an' potato pie'll be ready directly."

Ben placed the bundle on the table. "D'you think we'll need more hot water to melt the tallow, Jon?"

Taking out his ever-useful clasp knife, the ex-ship's carpenter set to work, slicing through the greased string around the tallowed hide. "With any luck it'll just peel off."

Mr. Braithwaite was permitted to undo it. Finding an edge of the skin, he drew it back, exposing gold. In less than a minute he had stripped sheepskin and tallow away completely.

It was a crucifix, complete with a tiny monstrance chamber for displaying the host. The top and ends of both arms had pigeon-egg rubies set into the metal, identical to the ones on the chalice. At its base a marvellously graven gold bird supported the cross on semi-spread wings, its talons gripping a half-orb of solid gold. The old scholar's hands trembled as he held the object. He gazed at the embossed figure of Christ upon it, surmounted by the letters *INRI*. "Crucifixus anticus! *Wrought by the same Byzantine hand that fashioned the chalice.* Do you realize, we are the first ones to behold it since the seventeenth century!"

Jon and Ben were inspecting the tallow-bound sheepskin minutely when Will's ma wrinkled her nose in disdain. "What're you messin' with that ole sheep 'ide for?"

The strange boy replied without looking up. "For the next clue, but it doesn't seem to be here. Can you find anything, Jon?"

The carpenter's strong, tattooed hands delved through the tallowed skin. "Nothing, lad. The chest was empty once we took the cross out. I was hopin' we'd find something in this wrapping, but no."

Alex sat at the table, his chin cupped in both hands, downcast. "We've missed the next clue somewhere."

The black Lab's tail swished to and fro as he raised his eyes to Ben. "Tell them it's carved on the bottom of that half-dome the bird is standing on, I can see it from here. So could you if you were lying on the floor. Good job old Braithwaite held the cross up. What would you do without me, eh, mate?"

Ben sat down on the floor by the labrador and patted him fondly. "You're the best dog in the world, Ned. Excuse me while I break the good news to them."

Ben squinted up at the underside of the crucifix, then raised his voice in excitement. "Look, there's carving underneath that dome the bird is standing on. I can see it!"

Mr. Braithwaite harrumphed. "Bird, young man? That's the eagle of St. John the Evangelist you're talking about. Let's see!" He turned the cross upside down. With Mr. Mackay leaning over his shoulder, checking, he read aloud.

> " 'Twould seem at the wicked's fate
> that bell ne'er made a sound,
> yet the death knell tolled aloud
> for those who danced around.
> The carrion crow doth perch above,
> light bearers 'neath the ground."

Mrs. Winn looked around. "Well, what do you make of that?"

The lawyer meticulously copied the words onto a piece of paper, before taking charge of the cross.

"I'd better get this locked away in my office safe with all dispatch. Will, could you run me down there in your gig, please?"

"You 'ave some lunch first, sir," Eileen chimed in. "Then my Will can drop you all off."

Over hot meat and potato pie, Mr. Braithwaite made out another copy of the words for his own use. "Hmm, very good, very good. Must, er, get back to the, er, library, of course.

I'll, ah, er, study this and let you know my findings, yes, very good!"

Amy made more copies in her fine, neat hand and distributed them to everybody, keeping one for herself and her brother. After lunch it was decided that they would spend the rest of the day each trying to solve the riddle. They had the time.

Will delivered Mrs. Winn to her house first. Ben stayed in the gig, alighting in the village square with the others. Mr. Mackay read the notice tacked to the board on the post not far from his office. He turned to them, his face grave. "Two days from today the clearances start. That means Smithers and his partners will be here with the county official and the bailiffs. Payments will be made to the evacuating tenants, the land will be cleared, and, unfortunately, Chapelvale will cease to exist as a village community and become a limestone quarry and a cement factory. Those are the facts, my friends."

Ben's blue eyes grew hard. "Not if we can help it!"

SMITHERS TAPPED LIGHTLY ON MAUD Bowe's bedroom door, and he called out as gently as his gruff, demanding voice would allow. "Are you in there, Miss Bowe, I'd like a word with you in the sitting room, if possible."

33

Maud opened the door a crack and was confronted by Smithers's rather worried-looking face. "I think you owe me an apology first, for the way you insulted me this morning, Mr. Smithers."

It galled him to do it, but there was no other way. "Well, er, I was a bit, hasty shall we say. Forgive me, I'm a gruff fellow sometimes. Comes of doin' business among men all the time. I shouldn't have raised my voice to you, young lady. I mean, Miss Bowe."

She stared at him, enjoying her moment of triumph, then shut the door in his face. "I'll be down presently."

Obadiah Smithers drew in a deep breath, clenched his fists, and strode purposefully along the corridor to his son's room. Flinging the door wide, he marched in without a word and dragged the coverlet off Wilf, who lay huddled, still covered in breakfast mess. Smithers curled his lip in disgust as his son sniffed and sobbed.

"It wasn't me, he went in there on his own, I had nothing to do with it, honestly, I never!"

His father towered over him, ignoring his pleas.

"Enough, sir, no more lies! I saw Regina's father in the village this morning. He caught her sneaking in, long after midnight. So you can stop your snivelling lies. I know exactly what went on around the old almshouse last night!"

Wilf cowered on the bed, his face ashen. "Regina's the liar, it was her who got Alex murdered, not me. I swear!"

His father's voice was like thunder. "What nonsense is this, eh? Murder indeed, I saw the very boy you're talking of, the animal vet's young son. He was alive and well, sitting in a dairy cart with his friends. So you can stop your lying about murder!"

Wilf was temporarily lost for words. He sat open-mouthed as reality flooded in on him. Alex was alive, there would be no policemen calling on him. No judges, court, or prison.

His father ranted on furiously. "A disappointment to me, that's what you've been, lad, a thorough disappointment! Letting y'self get beaten by a boy half your size, then thinking up stupid murder plots. Still, I blame m'self in ways—you're not half the young fellow I was at your age, no backbone! Molly-coddled, that's what you've been, spoiled rotten! But all that stops right here and now, sir, d'you hear me? No more being waited on by a maid an' hiding behind y'mother's skirts. Oh no, m'lad, it's boarding school for you. They'll straighten you out, an' no mistake!"

Wilf had only heard the latter part of his father's tirade. He leapt out of bed, a look of horror on his face. "B-boarding school?"

His father took him by the arm and shoved him in the direction of the bathroom. "Aye, boarding school. There's a good one up in Scotland, so I'm told. I'll make the arrangements today. Now, get in there an' clean that mess off y'self. Then you can tidy your room up an' pack your trunk. I'm not havin' the good name o' Smithers scoffed at by village bumpkins. No use appealin' to your mother. My decision's final, sir. Final!"

Slamming the bathroom door on his son's stunned face, Smithers went downstairs and out onto the back lawn, where he took a deep breath of the summer air and straightened his starched collar. Maud Bowe was sitting primly, reading another of her young ladies' etiquette books, not a hair out of place and not a sign of a flush upon her cheeks. She shut the book decisively, folding her hands on the cover. "You wanted a word with me, sir. Well?"

Clasping both hands behind his back, Smithers circled her chair several times, finishing up facing her.

"Those, er, associates you're bringing up from London, Miss Bowe."

Completely composed, she stared levelly at him. "Yes?"

He dropped his eyes and lowered his voice.

"Let them come and do what they've got to do. But no mistakes or failures. I want them in and out of Chapelvale as quick as possible. Understood?"

Maud could not help revelling in her victory. "Jackman Donning and Bowe are an established London company—we don't deal in failures and mistakes. Like some I could mention . . ."

Blood mounted to Smithers's cheeks, and he struggled to

control himself. Turning on his heel, he made for the house, replying as he went, "I'll leave it up to you . . . my dear!"

A black cat appeared out of the hedgerow. Purring, it rubbed its flank against Maud's fine-grained, calf-button boots. She shooed it off with a swipe of her book. "Shoo, cat!"

Horatio prowled slowly back through the small gap in the hedge. "Miaow! 'Ratio go home now, Winnie got milk, sardines, purr!"

The black labrador rose slowly from his hiding place in the shade of some lilacs. "Come on, then, me old furbag, I've heard enough for today. Sardines, ugh, nasty, slimy little fishes, don't know how you can eat the things!"

Mrs. Winn was taking her afternoon nap in the sitting room. Ben sat outside on the sunny lawn. He unfolded the copy of the poem Amy had given him and began studying it.

> 'Twould seem at the wicked's fate
> that bell ne'er made a sound,
> yet the death knell tolled aloud
> for those who danced around.
> The carrion crow doth perch above,
> light bearers 'neath the ground.

Sweat suddenly beaded on his forehead, he felt cold despite the warm summer day. The bell ne'er made a sound . . . carrion crow. . . . Visions and images of death floated about in his mind. Villainous faces marked by evil appeared unbidden, the sounds of seawaves roared in his ears. Long, long ago, Vanderdecken, Petros, Scraggs, Jamil, he saw them all, leering, cursing. But others were there, mingled with the crew of the *Flying Dutchman*. Older, half shadowed, their features showing the wickedness of evil men the world over. Closing his eyes tight, Ben fell back upon the grass, shuddering, feeling the earth move like a rolling ship's deck.

Warm breath and a damp tongue against his cheek brought Ben back from his dreadful trance. "Now then, pal, are you all right?"

Something smooth and silky brushed his hand, and Ben sat up, glad to be back in the normal world. Ned was sitting next to him, he caught sight of Horatio vanishing into the house. Immediately Ben felt better. He hugged the big dog's neck.

"I'm all right now you're here, you old rogue. It just happened, I was reading the poem from the base of the cross, when this awful feeling came over me."

The labrador nodded. "*Flying Dutchman* again, eh?"

Ben ran his fingers through his tousled blond hair.

"Yes, it was Vanderdecken and the others, but there were strange faces there, too, frightening ones I'd never seen before. Good job you came and snapped me out of it. I think it was due to reading that poem."

A bee was taking an interest in Ned's nose, and he swatted at it with his paw. "Then don't read the poem, leave it to the others to solve. They're a pretty brainy lot, 'specially old Mackay and Braithwaite, real knowledge pots those two. Besides, we'll have other things to worry about tomorrow. Bet you'd forgotten about those rough types due to come up from London?"

Ben smote his forehead with an open palm. "Of course, the four men Miss Wot'sername said were arriving Thursday!

I've been so busy contending with riddles and dealing with Wilf and his gang, they completely slipped my mind. Have you found out any more about the situation, Ned?"

The black labrador winked. "Oh yes indeed, I spent a very profitable hour at the back of Smithers's lawn. You should have heard the racket. Mr. Smithers must have lungs of leather. By the way, isn't it time for tea? Come on, I'll tell you later, we've got the rest of the day. At least you won't have to worry about young Wilf any more."

Ben followed Ned inside. "What d'you mean about Wilf?"

Ned helped himself to a drink of water from his dish.

"Tell you later, come on, get the kettle on, slice the seed cake. Where's my old lady?"

Ben spread a clean cloth over the table. "Asleep in the sitting room, we'll surprise her with a nice afternoon tea when she wakes. Ned, will you tell Horatio to keep from under my feet?"

Ned shook his head. "No use telling him anything, unless it's about sardines!"

BY NINE O'CLOCK ON THURSDAY MORNING the sun was almost as hot as noon—it was a record summer. Jonathan Preston sat at his workbench, a pencil behind one ear. He stared at the poem and blinked.  Stroking his beard, the old ship's carpenter took a sip of tea and bit into a bacon sandwich. Hearing the noise of young people coming in through the back window, he spoke without turning around.

"Aye aye, mates, sun's been up since six, so have I. What time d'you call this to be rollin' up on deck?"

Tearing the crust and bacon rind from his sandwich, he fed it to the black dog who'd gotten to the table before his companions. "Like my breakfast better'n your own, eh, feller!"

Amy perched on the edge of the workbench, where she saw the poem. "Have you solved it yet, Jon? St. Matthew's message?"

The old seaman smiled slyly. "No, not yet. Have any of you?"

Both boys shook their heads. Jon watched Amy drumming her heels against the bench. "Now then, pretty maid, d'you know something you ain't telling us? How did you find out it was St. Matthew's message?"

Her brother sounded rather injured. "Yes, how did you? You never said anything to me!"

Ben gave her a mock severe look. "Nor me!"

The girl plucked the pencil from behind Jon's ear and wagged it at them. "That's because you were asleep, my dear brother, and how could I tell you, Ben, you weren't even there. So I thought I'd keep it a secret 'til we were all together. Now watch this."

She drew two lines between the words of the first line of the writing on Jon's copy:

'Twould see/m at the w/icked's fate.

"Now, spell out the letters between the two lines, Jon."

He did as she told him. "M–a–t–t–h–e–w. Matthew! Very clever, Amy, I been staring at this for hours, but I never saw that. How did you come to notice it?"

Amy shrugged airily. "It's called an inclusion—we did it as a word game in school last term. You look for words among words."

The blue-eyed boy nodded admiringly. "Well done, pal!"

Amy jumped down from the bench. "Not so well, Ben, I couldn't fathom out any more of the puzzle. Could you?"

"No, I had other things to think about, which I'll tell you later. I bet Mr. Braithwaite's managed to solve it."

Jon tossed the last of his sandwich to Ned. "I went over there earlier, but he didn't seem to be in the library. Maybe he's arrived by now—let's go and see."

Exiting the almshouse by the front door, they saw the gig with Delia standing patiently in the shafts outside Mr. Mackay's office. Amy ran across to stroke the mare.

"What's Will doing in Mr. Mackay's office this early?"

The door opened partially, and Eileen popped her head around it. "I was about to go 'n' see if you were up an' about, my dears. Come on in, we're all here!"

Mr. Braithwaite, Mr. Mackay, and Will were gathered around the desk, and the lawyer greeted the newcomers. "Good morning, friends. Mrs. Drummond was about to go and see if she could locate you. I arrived here early to look up some old survey maps and see if I could throw any light upon our search.

"Mr. Braithwaite and the Drummonds have been helping me. I think we're close to a solution, that's why I was sending for you. By the way, did any of you manage to solve the thing?"

Jon spread his copy on the desk. "Amy did, she figured it was the first Gospelmaker, St. Matthew, whose treasure we're after. But that's as far as any of us got. Look at this first line."

The librarian inspected the line of words, scratching away at his frizzy hair. "St. Matthew, eh. Well well, good, er, heavens, a simple inclusion. Hmm, and none of us, er, er, noticed it. Very good, Amy, yes, very good, very good!"

Amy could not conceal her impatience. "Mr. Mackay, you said that you were close to a solution. What have you discovered?"

The dapper little solicitor coughed importantly. "First we thought we were looking for a bell—does not the second line say 'that bell ne'er made a sound'? But if we look at the next line we see that the bell in this case is a mere figure of speech, 'yet the death knell tolled aloud.' This death knell means in reality that something is finished. For instance, we could say, if Caran De Winn's title deeds to Chapelvale are not found, that signals the death knell for the entire village, you see? However, the rhyme does not speak of a place, but of people, 'yet the death knell tolled aloud for those who danced around.' ' "

Will could not stop himself from blurting out. "Wait! I remember my ole granddad singin' a song when I was a little boy, something about a villain who ended up dancing around 'neath a gallows tree! Sorry for buttin' in on you, sir."

Mr. Mackay merely smiled over the top of his nose glasses. "Quite all right, sir. Mr. Braithwaite, would you like to tell them our conclusion?"

Mr. Braithwaite clasped the edges of his scholar's gown. "Indeed, thank you, Mr., er, hmmm. We also have come to that same gallows tree. We put emphasis on the word 'those,' er, yes, 'for those who danced around.' This, er, would lead us to believe that more than one, er, person, miscreant, or whatever, was hung at this gallows place. . . ."

Recognition suddenly dawned on Ben. "So we're looking for that place of execution; what d'you think, Jon?"

"Right, mate!" the old carpenter agreed. "Places of execution, or gallows trees, as they were called, and they always had those 'orrible birds nearby, like in the next-to-last line, 'the carrion crow doth perch above.' But what about the final line, 'light bearers 'neath the ground'?"

A quiver of eagerness entered Eileen's voice. "That's what we'll find out by diggin' on the exact spot. You got your little paper with the 'oles in it, Jon? We've got our map."

Between them they matched up the paper with the four holes to the ancient map from the farmhouse.

"It says *here*, 'prison'," Will murmured. "The likely spot for a gallows tree. But I don't know of any prison in Chapelvale, do you, Eileen?"

Will's wife shook her head. "Must've been knocked down

long since."

Mr. Mackay took out a large survey map and compared it to the old map, looking back and forth from one to the other. "I'd say the old prison was right about here!" He made a pencil mark on the survey map. "Right where the police station stands."

Ben and Alex were already making for the door. "Well, what are we waiting for?" the younger boy said.

THE POLICE STATION WAS A SMALL GREY-
stone building, sandwiched between two houses built at the
turn of the century. One house was for the station sergeant,
who often travelled to outlying communities,
the other for the station constable, who at-
tended to village matters and kept the station
house ledger up to date.

Constable Judmann was tending to the
rosebushes in his front garden; he was an
enthusiastic gardener, a big, beefy fellow close to middle age.
Seeing the two boys running ahead of the dairy cart, he wiped
his hands on a cloth and, donning a uniform jacket, he but-
toned it up from his ample stomach to a bull-like neck. Taking his helmet from the windowsill, he put it on and strode up
the garden path with suitable dignity. He nodded at Alex.

"G'mornin', young feller, an' wot can we do for you, eh?"

The gig pulled up and Mackay dismounted. "It's all right,
Constable, the boys are with us."

The policeman tipped a finger respectfully to his helmet
brim. He had always been slightly in awe of Mackay, feeling
that solicitors and lawyers were a cut above normal folk.

"Mr. Mackay, sir, wot brings you up 'ere, summat wrong?"

The lawyer straightened his black cravat. "No, no,

Constable. Everything's in order. I merely want to ask you a question."

The policeman's chest buttons almost popped as he stood erect, pulling in his stomach. "Question, sir? At y'service!"

"What happened to the original Chapelvale prison, which, according to my survey map, stood near this site?"

Constable Judmann jabbed a fat thumb over his shoulder to the greystone building. "Nothin' 'appened, sir. There 'tis. Of course, it's been a police station for long as anybody can recall. No need for a lockup prison 'ereabouts for many a long year now."

Mr. Mackay nodded solemnly. "But it was once a prison, and an execution ground, so I'm led to believe."

The constable brushed a finger over his handlebar moustache. "Sergeant Patterson says it was, sir, but that were long afore my time—or his, for that matter."

The lawyer looked from side to side with a quick, bird-like movement. "I wonder where the executions took place?"

Again the constable's thumb jabbed back over his shoulder. "Sergeant Patterson reckons it were in the yard, be'ind the station 'ouse. Says murderers were 'anged back there."

Eileen climbed from the gig, pulling her skirts up, and, smiling at the policeman, she stepped down. "You must be awful brave, Constable Judmann, livin' so close to a place where murderers were 'anged. I'd be far too afraid."

The constable's ruddy face turned a shade redder at the compliment, and his chest puffed out a bit further.

"There's nought there to worry about, marm, just a backyard with a plot o' garden. I sees it from my back bedroom window every day, tends the garden m'self. I like t'keep it tidy."

"I'll wager you do, Constable. D'you think we could take a look at it?"

The policeman appeared disconcerted at Eileen's request. "Oh, I don't know so much about that, Mrs. Drummond. That's official police property. The public ain't allowed in there. 'Twould be more'n my job's worth if Sergeant Patterson found I'd let folks go wanderin' willy-nilly 'round the station."

This announcement was followed by an awkward silence, which was broken by the arrival of the sergeant himself on his bicycle.

Patterson was a cheerful man in his mid-thirties, very tall and lean, with curly red hair and narrow sideburns. His voice carried the faint trace of a Scottish border accent, from Coldstream, the town of his birth. He touched his peak cap to the small assembly and smiled.

"Mornin' to ye, looks like another warm 'un today, eh!"

Sergeant Patterson nodded to the constable, his voice taking on a more serious tone. "Ah've just come from yon railway station. There's three truckloads o' machinery an' buildin' materials arrived there. They've been sent to Smithers, from Jackman an' Company of London. Aye, all shunted intae a sidin' for unloading an' cartin' tae the village square, where they plan on stackin' et! So ah told the stationmaster tae put a stop on the operation.

"Your man Smithers was there, too. Weel, ah soon put a flea up his nose! Told him he's not allowed tae unload a single nail until the morrow, when the court order comes intae force. Auld Smithers roared like a Heeland bull, so ah read him the riot act an' said that if he disobeyed the law, ah'd arrest him an' lock him up! Ah cannae take to the man, he's a pompous windbag, if ye'll pardon mah opinion, Mr. Mackay."

The lawyer nodded. "That is my observation of Smithers also, Sergeant."

Patterson parked his bicycle against the garden wall. "Mah thanks tae ye, sir. Constable, ah want ye tae go down tae the railway station an' stand guard over those wagons, d'ye ken? Oh, an' take a Prohibition of Movement order form. Pin it tae the delivery. Mind now, make sure et all stops right there!"

The constable saluted needlessly. "Right away, Sarn't. Leave it t'me! Permission to borrow your bike?"

Patterson looked as if he was trying to hide a smile. "Permission granted, Constable, carry on!"

They stood watching Constable Judmann wobble ponderously off down the lane. The sergeant chuckled.

"Will ye look at the man go! Och, he loves ridin' mah old bicycle. Weel now, an' what can I do for you good folk?"

Eileen answered. "We wanted to have a look at the old execution place, but the constable didn't seem too happy about it."

Will swelled out his chest and stomach, in a passable imitation of Judmann. "Invasion of police property, if I ain't mistaken, Sarn't. Sort of a peasant's revolt!"

The sergeant pretended to look grave. "Och, sounds serious tae me! Ye'd best all come in, ah'll put the kettle on for tea, an' we'll discuss the matter. Just hauld yer wheesht a moment!"

Patterson took an apple from his pocket and fed it to the mare, rubbing her muzzle affectionately. "Stay out o' this revolt, bonny lass. Mah gaol couldnae cope with ye!"

● ● ●

The walls inside the police station were covered thick with countless applications of whitewash on the top, and equally heavy layers of bitumen and tar on the bottom. All the woodwork had been painted dark blue many times over the years, some of it showing blisters around the blackleaded iron fireplace. A notice board by the window was crowded with official-looking posters, old and new. Patterson made tea, seating Mr. Braithwaite, Mr. Mackay, Will, and Eileen on tall stools at the charge office desk. Amy and her brother sat on a long bench with Jon and Ben.

Ned lay under the desk, gnawing a thick, gristly mutton bone, making his thoughts known to his master. "Good man, Sergeant Patterson, what d'you think, pal?"

Ben returned the thought, sipping tea from a brown pottery mug. "I don't know what it is, but I don't feel right in here. I'm starting to go cold and sweating at the same time."

The labrador crawled from under the desk, carrying his bone. "Hmm, you don't look too good. This is a creepy old place. Let's go outside and sit with Delia in the sun."

Amy saw the pair leave, she followed them out. "Are you all right, Ben? You look rather pale."

He leaned on the garden wall, taking a deep breath and letting it out slowly. "I'm all right now, thanks. There was something about the atmosphere in there. Don't know what it was, but I didn't like it."

She patted his hand. "There's no need to go back in if you don't want to. We'll stay out here and let the others talk to the sergeant.

"You're a strange one, Ben, not like anyone in the village, and certainly not like me or my brother. I hope you don't mind me asking, but where were you born? What other places have you lived in, before you came here?"

Avoiding the girl's face, he looked off into the distance. "I'd like to tell you, Amy . . . but . . ."

She watched her friend's fathomless blue eyes cloud over. It was like looking at a faraway sea when a storm broods over it. Without knowing why, a wave of pity for the strange boy swept through her mind. "Ben . . . I'm sorry."

When he turned and looked at her, his eyes were clear, and the colour had returned to his cheeks. Best of all, he was giving her the smile she had come to like so much.

"You've no cause to be sorry. You're my friend, that's what counts."

The old ship's carpenter provided most of the story, but Patterson let his gaze rove from Alex to Eileen, to Will, Mr. Braithwaite, and Mr. Mackay, as they put in their contributions to the intriguing narrative.

The sergeant sat gazing into the dregs of his mug before speaking. "Ah was posted tae this village four years ago, as ye know. 'Tis a grand wee place. Ah've come tae like it fine. But tomorrow modern progress is due tae move in here. Och, they cannae turn us out of the police station, 'tis Crown property ye ken. Though who in their right mind would want tae stay here, amid a dusty great quarry an' cement factory?

"Judmann's auld now, he'll take his pension an' move. As for me, och, I'll prob'ly put in for transfer tae another post. Though 'twill sair grieve me to go. Friends, if ah can help ye in any way, then ah will. D'ye want tae take a look 'round the auld hangin' ground out back, eh? Then be mah guest!"

Jon was like a big child on a Sunday school outing. He dashed out of the station, rubbing his large, tattooed hands together gleefully, calling to Amy and Ben, "Come on, mates, away boat's crew! We've got permission to search around the back—in fact, we've got the sergeant's blessing!"

His two young friends seemed glad, but not overimpressed. "You go, mate, we'll go around the outside of the building. See you there later."

The ex-ship's carpenter's craggy face showed concern. He ruffled the boy's tow-coloured hair. "D'you feel all right, son?"

Ben managed a cheery grin. "Never felt better, shipmate!"

The old seaman stared oddly at the pair for a moment. "Righto, see you two 'round there, eh. Hah, look at Ned, snoozin' away like an old grampus there!"

The black labrador was curled up in the gig, asleep under the shade of a seat. Amy wrinkled her nose sympathetically. "He's keeping Delia company, poor old boy. He must be tired in this heat—let him sleep."

IT WAS SHADY TO THE POINT OF BEING gloomy in the walled courtyard at the back of the police station. The wall enclosing the ancient execution site was over twelve feet high, totally covered by dark green clinging ivy, giving the impression it was built of vegetation and not limestone. It had a heavy timber door for access to the outside, the wood layered with countless coats of dark blue paint. Jon had to work vigorously on the rusty latch and bolts until the door creaked open to admit the two friends.

The feeling of dread Ben had experienced about the station returned, much stronger this time. He had an urge to run a mile from the drear, forbidding place. However, the presence of the girl at his side and the sight of Eileen, the policeman, and the rest of his companions was reassuring. Bracing himself, he strode in over the moss-grown cobbles. Sergeant Patterson was addressing the party.

"Ah'm afraid the history of this auld place is a mystery tae me. When ah first arrived here, I discovered that damp an' mildew had ruined the auld records. My orders were tae clean up the station, so ah made a grand wee bonfire o' the soggy documents. Och, ye should've seen Constable Judmann's face.

He never spoke tae me for a fortnight. Mr. Mackay, will ye read out yon poem again, sir?"

The lawyer donned his pince-nez and coughed officiously.

    " 'Twould seem at the wicked's fate
    that bell ne'er made a sound,
    yet the death knell tolled aloud
    for those who danced around.
    The carrion crow doth perch above,
    light bearers 'neath the ground."

Braithwaite shrugged apologetically. "So, er, as you see, Sergeant, we're searching for, hmmm, a gibbet. That is, er, a hanging place, as it were. Hmm, yes, very good."

Eileen shuddered, rubbing at her upper arms nervously. "Well, I don't see any sign of where they 'anged folk. Brrr! I feels it, though. Ma would, too, if she were 'ere!"

The dairyman nodded his agreement as he took stock of the courtyard.

An indefinable air of doom did seem to hang over the place. Snails and slugs had left their glistening silver trails over a border of smooth limestone blocks, which separated a garden area running around the walls on three sides. The soil was mainly clay, oozing damp. A few straggling shrubs were struggling to survive, overhung by a sickly laburnum and two purple rhododendrons. The whole atmosphere was hemmed in, dark and claustrophobic, eerie and silent.

The sergeant smiled wanly. "Nae much tae look at, is it? 'Twas over a hundred years since the last man was hanged here. Ah took a glance at the auld records before burnin' them. All written in curly, auld-fashioned script, an' very hard tae decipher. Here now, young Somers, d'ye ken how they used tae execute murderers?"

Alex shook his head dumbly, swallowing hard at the thought.

Patterson explained the process, his Scottish brogue severe as he told of the manner in which legal sentence was carried out. "Weel now, a magistrate, priest, sergeant, an' constable had tae be present, an' the auld hangman, o' course. Yon door, the one Jon opened, they let the public in through there tae watch—as an example of what happened tae criminals an' evildoers. Then the condemned man was brought out in chains, from the holdin' cell.

"Aye, 'twas a terrible ceremony. The shiverin' wretch was made tae stand on a box 'neath the gallows tree, while the hangman put the noose 'round his neck. That was when the magistrate read out the death sentence, then he stood aside for the priest tae pray with the condemned man. When the reverend was finished, they usually allowed the man tae say a word tae everyone watchin'. The doomed man'd tell them what a wicked fellow he'd been, an' how sorry he was tae suffer the penalty for his crimes. He'd then tell everyone tae live good lives an' profit from the sight of his punishment.

"When all that was over with, the magistrate tipped the hangman a nod, the executioner kicked the box from under the unfortunate wretch, an' the deed was done!"

Amy clapped both hands over her eyes as if she had witnessed it. "Ugh! It sounds so horrid and cruel!"

Eileen placed an arm about the girl's shoulders. "Indeed it was, my dear. From what I've read, it was quite primitive in small villages . . . they never died instantly. I suppose that's why the poem says they danced around. Sometimes it took as long as ten minutes before their legs stopped kicking. What a dreadful sight. I can't think why folks wanted to watch!"

Will clapped his hands, breaking the spell. "Enough of all this! Let's get searching, friends. Is there a gibbet, tree, or post around here? If there isn't, we're stumped!"

LOUD BARKING AND SCRATCHING ON THE yard door sent Jon hurrying to open it. The big, black labrador dashed in and straight across to his master. Nobody had noticed the towheaded boy not taking part in the discussion. He had quietly sat on the step of the station house. That was where he now slumped in a faint. The dog licked his master's face furiously, transmitting thoughts. "Ben, Ben, wake up, pal. Open your eyes. Oh, please!"

Jon sat down on the step and took the boy's head in his lap. Eileen bustled past and returned with a mug of cold water and a damp cloth, which she applied to the strange boy's forehead, while Jon patted his cheek lightly, murmuring, "Come on, me old shipmate."

Ben's eyelids fluttered, then he came around. Amy seized his hand and rubbed it. "Jon, get him out of here. It's this place that's caused him to faint, I know it is!"

Ben pointed to the corner of the garden, right by the angle of the wall. "No . . . wait . . . it's there!" Struggling from Jon's grasp, he made his way over to the corner, with the girl still holding his hand. He made a mark in the soil with his heel. "Here . . . dig here!"

Leaning on his dog and holding on to Amy, with Alex hovering anxiously behind, Ben allowed himself to be led outside.

Eileen followed out with the glass of water, and found them seated on the pathside by Delia.

"Good 'eavens, you poor lad. What 'appened in there?"

Ben took a sip of water and began feeling better. "I felt dreadful when I walked into the yard, so I sat on the step. Couldn't trust my legs to hold me up. It was while the sergeant was talking, all that stuff about how they used to hang murderers. I suddenly felt myself drawn to look at the corner of the garden. There was a dark shape there. I found I couldn't stop staring at it, and the longer I gazed, the clearer it became. . . ."

The younger boy shuddered and cried out shrilly, "What was it, Ben?"

"It was a man, dressed in tattered, olden-day clothes, chains around his hands and ankles. He was hovering about two feet from the ground, neck all on one side, his face horribly twisted, tongue sticking out. He was kicking as if he was dancing a silly jig. The man was looking straight at me. His hands kept twitching and pointing down to the ground beneath his feet . . . I've never seen anything so horrible. That must have been when I passed out."

He stroked Ned, leaning his head against the dog's neck. "Good old boy, you were the one who rescued me. I felt you coming to me, barking from far off."

Eileen clapped a hand to her cheek in wonderment. "You felt that, Ben? But how did the dog know?"

Before he could answer, Jon's voice rang clear over the

wall to where they were sitting. "We found it. Here 'tis, lad, we're comin' out!"

Will and Jon came running, waving their spades, followed by Mr. Mackay and Mr. Braithwaite, their clothing stained with soil and clay, bearing between them a bright green bucket. Sergeant Patterson was bent double, supporting the bottom lest it burst and fall. They flopped down on the grass with Ben, and he touched the object.

"What is it?"

Sergeant Patterson passed a forearm across his brow. "Och! 'Tis heavy, that's what it is. Auld bronze pail, either bronze or copper. See how green it is? Must've been very thick, because it's only gone through in one or two places. Ye'd be surprised at the weight of it!"

Amy chuckled. "Probably because it's filled with tallow."

Will lifted the pail and turned it upside down on the grass. "Well, we'll soon see. Loosen it off, Jon."

The old seaman began hitting it gently with the side of his spade, all around the sides. He tapped the pail's bottom sharply and lifted it off, just like a child making sandpies with a bucket at the seaside. The solid tallow wax was dark and dirty from soil and clay leaking into it.

Will spoke to the sergeant. "Have you got a big knife? Jon's old clasp knife ain't big enough to slice through this lot."

The sergeant hurried into the station house and was soon back with a large, fearsome-looking blade.

"Russian Crimean War bayonet, a souvenir brought back by Private Judmann. Ye should hear the tales he tells of how he came by it, a different one each time!"

The bayonet was more than adequate. In Jon's capable hands it sliced through the tallow, until he brought forth two slender objects with heavy, spreading bases, still caked with the stuff.

Mr. Mackay identified them immediately. " 'Light bearers 'neath the ground.' A pair of candlesticks!"

The three young friends searched through the shorn-off tallow, Mr. Braithwaite hovering anxiously around them.

"No, er, sign of any, er, further clues, scraps of, er, er, parchment and so forth?"

Amy looked up. "None, sir. Maybe the next clue is scratched on the bottom of the candlesticks, same as the cross."

Jon handed the candlesticks to the sergeant. "Put these in a basin of hot water. It'll clean 'em off, then we can take a proper look."

Mr. Braithwaite followed Sergeant Patterson into the station house, his dusty black scholar's gown flapping. "Very good, very good, go, er, careful now, Officer. Don't, er, drop them. Precious objects, yes, er, precious indeed!"

When cleaned up in soap and hot water, the candlesticks were things of great beauty, gold-fluted columns spreading to broad elegant bases, each of which was inset with three of the bloodred, pigeon-egg rubies, to complement the chalice and crucifix. Mr. Braithwaite was ecstatic, running his fingertips over the fine Byzantine tracery patterned onto the heavy gold pieces. However, when he looked at the bases of both candlesticks, they were smooth and untouched by any messages scratched on either one.

The only noise in the still midday air came from Delia's hoof as she struck it against the ground. The six sat staring at the treasure of St. Matthew glittering in the sun, the rubies shining as if they were afire.

Ben broke the silence by announcing to his crestfallen friends, "Listen, we can sit here all day looking at the candlesticks, but that won't get anything solved. We've worked too hard and long to let this thing defeat us!"

The dairyman farmer got up to strap Delia's nosebag on. "You're right, lad, but what's our next move?"

Mr. Mackay, who had been brushing clay from his clothing, rose smartly to his feet. "I suggest we go carefully back over all the evidence. Search the hole where we found the pail, inspect the pail, and sort through that tallow again. One of us will stay here and go over the candlesticks with a fine-tooth comb. If we're all agreeable, of course!"

Eileen took a pail from the gig to fill with water for Delia. "Good idea! Nothin' worth havin' is come by easy, I say. Ben, you take the candlesticks. Will, take Jon and the sergeant an' check that 'ole you dug. Mr. Braithwaite, Mr. Mackay, see if you can find any message in that old copper bucket. Alex, you 'n' me will rummage through that tallow again."

Amy pointed to herself. "What about me, Miz Drummond?"

"Oh, I'd forgot you, m'dear. Stay 'ere with Ben an' help with the candlesticks. Keep an eye on him in case he tries to faint again. Come on, you lot, stir your stumps!"

The labrador threw Ben a thought. "The lady forgot about me. I'll stay here, too, with you and Amy. Be with you in a moment, I'll just get a quick drink from my pal Delia's water bucket."

FIFTY MILES SOUTH OF THE POLICE STA-
tion a small boy was trudging along a country lane towards
the farmhouse where he lived. The boy, a small, sturdy lad of
about eight years, stopped to witness a strange
sight. Weaving from side to side and honking
furiously, a machine was coming towards him.
It was one of the new petroleum-driven motor-
cars, a bright green one, with its leather hood
down.

He scurried to one side, hugging the hedge as it rumbled
past him and ground to a halt with a screeching sound. There
were four men in the car. One of them, wearing a long duster
coat, gauntlets, and a cap with the peak backwards, climbed
from the vehicle. He had on a pair of light-brown-lensed
goggles, which he pushed up onto his cap as he approached
the boy. The lad shrank further into the hedge as the man
stooped and thrust his face forward.

"G'mornin', sonny boy. Is that there Chapelvale?"

The man pointed to a church spire in the
distance. The boy shook his head.

The man scratched his coarse, stub-
bled chin. "Oh, I see, well, wot's that
place called?"

The boy spoke a single word. "Church."

This seemed to exasperate the man. "I know it's a church, sonny, but wot's the name of the village where the church is, eh?"

The boy considered this for a moment. "It's not Chapelvale."

Another man emerged from the car, dressed in a suit of very loud green chequered material. He sported a pencil-thin moustache, his hair was plastered into a centre parting. He shouted out to his companion, "Come on, Gripper, the kid don't know nothin'. Let's get goin'!"

Gripper was about to shout back an answer, when a farmer appeared at the gateway of a farmhouse further up the road. He was a giant of a man, his sleeves rolled up to expose two brawny arms. Slamming the gate open, he marched aggressively up to the one called Gripper, whom he pointed a thick finger at.

"Hoi you! Gerraway from my lad an' leave 'im be!"

Gripper backed off hurriedly. "I don't mean the kid no 'arm. I was only askin' him where Chapelvale is."

The boy ran to his father and clung to his leg. The man ruffled his son's hair as he replied, "Chapelvale. 'Ow's Georgy supposed to know, eh, 'e's only a child!"

Gripper tried a friendly smile, it looked more like a leer. "Then p'raps you can tell me where Chapelvale is, eh, mate?"

The farmer did not like strangers. His big fists clenched. "No I can't, an' I'm not your mate. Now, get on your way, quick!"

Gripper drew himself up in a dignified manner and strode back to the motorcar, which was still running. He shouted back, "Stoopid big lump. Bet you'd 'ave trouble findin' your own be'ind with both hands!"

The farmer picked up a stone from the roadside. Gripper shoved his loudly garbed associate into the vehicle, leapt in after him, and accelerated off down the lane.

Gripper was the driver. The flashy one in the front with him was, aptly enough, named Flash. The two backseats were occupied by Chunk, a massive, unintelligent specimen who wore a suit three sizes too small and a pearl-grey bowler hat perched on his shaven skull; and Chaz, a small, weaselly type, dressed in a frock-tailed morning coat and pin-striped pants, a size too large. In lieu of a shirt or collar he wore a knotted scarf of once-white silk. He was perpetually sniggering at anything and everything, which was what he did as soon as they were out of stone-throwing range.

"Heeheehee, we're lost! I told yer, didn't I, Gripp. Heehee!"

Gripper clenched the brass steering wheel tight, keeping his eyes fixed on the road ahead. "Shut yer gob, Chaz, or I'll belt yer one 'round the 'ead, on me oath I will!"

But Chaz would not be silenced. "Why go onna train, 'e sez, let's keep the money an' steal a motorcar. Leave it to me, 'e sez, I'll find Chapelvale. When're yer gonna find it, Gripp, eh? Next week? Heeheehee!"

They all lurched to one side as Gripper threw the car around a hairpin bend, bumping off the high-banked grass verge. He snorted aloud in frustration. "Shut 'im up, willyer, Chunk; give the flamin' nuisance a smack fer me!"

Chunk took Chaz's scrawny neck in one huge paw, rendering him helpless. "Where d'ya want me to biff 'im, Gripp? In the eye?"

Chaz pleaded, "No no, 'e doesn't want yer to biff me anywhere!"

"Ho yes I do!" replied Gripper. "Biff 'im where y'like, Chunk."

In biffing people, Chunk always preferred the nose. Chaz had quite a big beaky nose, so Chunk biffed it enthusiastically. Chaz squealed and fell back in the seat, his nose bleeding profusely. He held the dirty silk scarf to it.

"Wot didjer do dat for? Be dose is broke!"

Chunk felt no sympathy or enmity towards Chaz. "I did it 'cos Gripper tole me to. Ain't that right, Gripp?"

Gripper carried on watching the road. "Right, Chunk, now per'aps 'e'll stop makin' smart remarks!"

Flash had noticed a milestone. "It said arf a mile to Church 'aven on that stone, Gripp. Must be wot that place is called."

They drove into the village of Church Haven and stopped outside the post office. Gripper went in to ask for directions; a kindly, old, silver-haired postmistress came out onto the street with him to explain things.

"Chapelvale, sir, my goodness but you are a long, long way from there. Where have you come from?"

Gripper was losing patience, but trying to stay polite. "London, marm, but which way is it to Chapelvale?"

The old lady shook her head wistfully. "I've never been to London, but I hear 'tis a wonderful city, St. Paul's Cathedral, Buckingham Palace. It must be so nice to live there. Do you ever see Her Majesty Queen Victoria?"

Flash leaned out of the car. "Lots o' times, me ole darlin'. We seen 'er only last week, didn't we, Gripp."

Gripper shot him a murderous glance, but he carried on. "Oh yes, we're special messengers for 'Er Majesty the Queen.

That's why we got ter get to Chapelvale. So could you tell us the way?"

The postmistress was only too willing to help royal couriers. "Most certainly—head straight down the High Street and take a left turn at the bottom, where you can't go any further. Then you'll be on the road to Great Sutley. You'll pass through there and on to Little Sutley, then Sutley-on-the-Marsh. Take a right there and make for Vetchley-on-the-Wold. Now, when you get there . . ."

Gripper got into the motorcar. "That'll do, we'll find it from there. Thanks, marm!"

She caught sight of Chaz in the backseat. "Oh dear, your poor friend's nose is bleeding. Has he been injured?"

Gripper pulled the motoring goggles over his eyes. "No, he's all right, marm. Sometimes 'e gets the nosebleeds with motorin', speed of the car, y'know. We been travelling at twenny-five miles an hour most o' the way."

She gasped at the thought. "Twenty-five miles an hour! It's a wonder you aren't all dead. Wait there, I'll get him a clean, damp cloth and a drink of water."

She scurried inside the post office. Gripper drove off with Chunk complaining from the backseat. "Why didn't ya wait, Gripp? I coulda done wiv a drink o' water."

They clattered off down the cobbled High Street in a cloud of exhaust fumes, arguing among themselves.

"Look, never mind the water, we can't 'ang about all day!"

"I'b bleedin' to death through be dose, you should ob waited an' let 'er see t'me."

"Shut yer mouf, Chaz, or I'll stop the motor an' give you annuder one. Where did she say to turn left, Flash, Little Sutford-on-the-Wold or Vetchley-in-the-Marsh?"

"I dunno, I thought you was lissenin' to 'er. Pass us one o' those sandwiches yore missus made, willyer, Chunk."

"She made those sangwiches fer me, not youse lot. Any'ow, I et am all. That's why I'm firsty for a drink o' water."

"Big fat greedy pig, didyer 'ear that, Gripp. 'E's scoffed all the sandwiches, the rotten ole lard barrel!"

"Sharrap, the three of youse! I'm tryin' t'think. Sharrap!"

"Are you finkin' why there's a fence acrosst the road, Gripp? Well, that's 'cos the lady tole yer to turn left an' you turned right. You'd better back the motor up."

"No I won't, 'cos I don't know 'ow to. You lot'll 'ave to get out an' push it backwards. Cummon, out, youse three!"

Whilst the others were searching, Ben and Amy took one of the candlesticks and began examining it minutely from sconce to base. They scanned the intricate engraving for any trace of hidden writing. Ned nudged the other candlestick with his nose. It fell over and rolled down the grass bank of the path-side. The labrador chased after it and grabbed it in his mouth by the top. Eileen was engrossed in searching through the lumps of tallow. Alex had lost interest, having already searched through it once, when he spotted the dog with the candlestick in his mouth. Scrambling forward, the younger boy grabbed the base of it and tried to tug it from Ned's jaws.

"Where are you going with that? Naughty fellow, give it to me. Let go, Ned!"

But the big labrador was not about to let go. He dug his front paws into the grass and tugged back, sending a thought out to Ben. "Huh, the nerve of the lad. Tell him to let go, mate. He's supposed to be messing with the tallow—these candlesticks are our job. Tell him, Ben!"

The boy turned his head to see what was going on, and saw Alex and Ned tugging the candlestick between them. All at once there was a pop, like a cork being pulled from a bottle, and the two fell back upon their bottoms—each holding a half of the candlestick!

Everybody came running at the sound of Ben and Alex shouting, "We've found it! We've found it!"

The big dog allowed Ben to relieve him of the top half, passing a highly indignant thought to his master. "You've found it? Well, of all the nerve, it was me who found it!"

The boy hugged the labrador's neck, returning the thought. "Of course you did, pal. When we get home, I'll make sure Winnie rewards you with the best feed you've ever had!"

The dog licked Ben's face. "Now you're talking, ship-mate!"

Mr. Mackay peered into the hollow cylinder of Ben's half-candlestick. "Ah yes, yes, yes, a small scroll of paper. I could get at it, if I had a pair of tweezers."

"Let me try, please." The lawyer handed the candlestick over to Amy. Her slim fingers and strong fingernails soon extracted the scroll. It was very thin, delicate paper, almost transparent. She gave it to the old seaman, who unrolled it carefully as the others looked on with bated breath.

Will leaned over Jon's shoulder and looked. His sigh of frustration was audible. "No message, just a lot of little lines."

Later, Sergeant Patterson made more tea for them as Mr. Braithwaite gazed at the thin paper lying on the charge-office desk. "Hmm, lines and a few dots. Spaced out in, er, rather a, er, peculiar way. Hmmm."

The lines and the dots seemed to have no connection.

The sergeant glanced at them as he passed out mugs of tea. "Very peculiar, ah'd say, what d'ye think, laddie?"

Ben stood with his eyes riveted on the paper. "I'd say we've got a real mystery on our hands this time!"

WILL'S MA TOOK LITTLE WILLUM TO VISIT
Mrs. Winn that afternoon. Not having heard from Ben or the
others, the anxious older woman was delighted to see them.

They had tea and hot, buttered crumpets.
Willum liked a dab of strawberry jam on his
crumpet and sat on the carpet, the picture of
happiness, his cheeks smeared with jam.
Catching sight of Horatio, he crawled off in hot
pursuit, attempting to get his sticky fingers on
the cat, calling, "Fussy ca', fussy ca'!"

Within minutes they had another visitor come calling.
Hetty Sullivan, the Smithers' maidservant. Mrs. Winn hastened to top up the teapot and toast more crumpets. Hetty
was a good sort—she rescued Horatio from little Willum's at-
tentions and put him out in the garden.

Willum protested aloud as she cleaned him up with a wet
flannel and towel. "Gaaah, wanna fussy ca'!"

The three ladies had just settled down to their tea when
Delia came clopping up the lane. Mrs. Winn threw up her
arms in mock despair. "Merciful heavens, it looks like open
house here today—there's a whole crew arriving!"

The servant girl could see the old lady was secretly
pleased to have so many callers on a Thursday afternoon. "You

stay there, Miz Winn, I'll see to them."

Mrs. Winn made a move to rise, then sat back down. "Thank you, Hetty, I'm afraid we've eaten all the crumpets. There's a Dundee cake and a currant loaf in the larder. Oh, and you'd best get the big teapot out!"

Wiping their muddy boots on the doormat, Ben and his friends trooped in. The open-faced farmer's wife swept little Willum up and hugged him. "You rascal, fancy findin' you 'ere!"

The older woman's cheeks were flushed to a rosy hue as she took Ben's hand. "So many people, lad! Well, did you have any luck?"

The boy winked at Amy. "Show her."

With a flourish the girl placed both the candlesticks on the table. "St. Matthew's treasure, the light bearers 'neath the ground!"

Mrs. Winn held up her hands, as if afraid to touch them. "Oh my! Oh goodness! They're absolutely beautiful!"

Mr. Braithwaite picked one up and rubbed a fingermark off with his sleeve. "Er, beautiful indeed, marm. Byzantine, er, er, workmanship, hmmm, a long-lost art, yes, er, very good!"

Mr. Mackay folded both hands beneath the tails of his coat and paced around before holding forth. "Unfortunately, madam, we have as yet been unable to find the deeds to your land. In my estimation we now have the three pieces sent up by Bishop Peveril from the court of King Edward the Third: a chalice, a cross, and a set of candlesticks to grace the altar of the church, which later became the almshouse. But it is the deeds that are vital to our cause. And we do not have them! Each piece has given us a clue, leading to the next one, from Luke to John and on to Matthew. But I regret to inform you

that the message we found with the candlesticks is very ob-
scure and far, far too cryptic for us to search further. Rather a
shame, seeing as the deadline is tomorrow morning." He
rolled out his prediction: "If the deeds are not found by then,
Chapelvale will be in the hands of the developers!"

The old woman put down her teacup. "Where did you find
the candlesticks?"

The younger boy answered. "Under the old police station
yard. Constable Judmann wasn't going to let us in, but
Sergeant Patterson allowed us to dig there. He even helped."

The Smithers' Hetty trundled in with a trolley, laden with
tea and cakes. "Sergeant Patterson, 'e's a nice bobby, where's
'e now?"

Alex took a wedge of Dundee cake. "Back up at the station.
There was a message coming in on the button machine. . . ."

"You mean the telegraph," his sister corrected him. "The
sergeant said he'd follow us up here after the message had arrived."

Will's ma was growing impatient. "Well, where's this ob-
scure clue? Don't we get to see it?"

"Here 'tis, Sarah, see what you make of it." The ship's
carpenter passed her the thin paper sheet.

Screwing her eyes up, Ma inspected it briefly before passing it to Mrs. Winn. "Lot o' lines an' dots, don't mean a thing
t'me!" she said as a knock at the door announced the
sergeant's arrival.

As Hetty served the young policeman tea, he took the
telegram from his tunic pocket. "Ah was on mah way tae check
on Judmann at the railway station, when auld Mr. Talbot called
me intae the post office an' gave me this telegraph, from the
postmistress at Church Haven, over fifty miles from here. It

says that early this mornin', four o' Queen Victoria's couriers passed through there. Seems the poor laddies were lost. Anyway, they drove off in a motorcar, without waitin' tae hear proper directions. Sounds odd tae me."

"D'you think it'll have anything to do with the village bein' turned into a quarry an' cement factory, Sergeant?"

Patterson folded the telegraph form, pondering the dairyman's question.

"Och, ah dinna think the Queen's even heard of our village. Tae mah knowledge, we've never had royal couriers visitin' Chapelvale. If any such thing were planned, London would contact the police station, not the local post office, an' ah've had no word at all from London, ye ken?" He tucked the telegram back in his pocket. "There's somethin' strange goin' on. Ah'm goin' back tae the village, tae look further intae this matter!"

"Could I come with you, Sergeant Patterson?" The blue-eyed boy had become alert at the mention of London.

Amy tapped the paper upon the table. "But what about solving this riddle?"

Ben made his excuses. "I won't be too long, Amy, Jon. There's something I've got to talk with the sergeant about. I'll bet with all the brains here you'll have the riddle beaten before I get back. Keep them at it, Mr. Braithwaite!"

The old scholar blinked, ruffling his arms in his sleeves, as Ben and his big, black dog accompanied the policeman out.

"Eh, er, keep them at it? Oh, er, yes, very good young, er!"

As the front door closed, Will's mother, more curious than ever, indicated the paper. "Where did you find this, Will?"

"Inside one of the candlesticks, Ma, why?"

"Which one?"

Eileen picked up a candlestick. "This one, I think."

Alex shook his head. "No, it was the other one. Ned's teeth made a slight scratch on that one. I noticed it when I put the two halves back together. See?" He pointed to the faint scratch on the other candlestick.

Mrs. Winn poured herself more tea. 'That's the one you found the paper in, eh, Jon?"

"Aye, that's the one, marm."

She took a sip of her tea. "Then why haven't you looked inside the other one? Doesn't it come apart?"

The good-natured farmer's wife laughed heartily. "Haha-haha! Good thinkin', Winnie, what a bunch o' puddin' 'eads we are!"

The ex-seaman and the dairyman took an end each, and they pulled, like two children with a Christmas cracker. The candlestick popped apart so easily that Will fell backwards and Jon bumped into Mr. Mackay.

Apologies were forgotten as they stared at the slim scroll of paper lying on the floor.

SERGEANT PATTERSON WAS AN EASY MAN to get on with. Ben explained to him how he had come by the information that Smithers's guest, Maud Bowe, was having four of her father's company thugs sent up from London to frighten Mrs. Winn into leaving her home.

The sergeant spoke without looking at Ben as they walked towards the village square. "Why didn't ye inform me of this before, lad?"

The boy thought hard before replying. "Well, I'd never met you before this morning. But when you got that telegraph message, and it mentioned four men coming up from London, I thought you'd better know about what I'd found out, so I'm telling you now."

The Scots sergeant nodded. "Aye, fair enough. I hope ye don't mind me askin', but how did ye plan on dealing with them? Always providing that what Hetty told Miz Winn was fact, and not just kitchenmaid's tittle-tattle."

Ben's blue eyes narrowed. "Oh, I'd think of something, one way or another."

The sergeant questioned him further. "Did ye tell any o' the others—Jon or Will, for instance?"

"No, you're the first one I've spoken to about it."

The policeman could not help admiring the boy's courage. "And ye were goin' tae handle it all on your own, eh?"

Ben stopped and stared at the bobby. "Me and Ned could do it!"

There was something about the pair, the manner in which the big, black dog stood by the boy and the determined light in the boy's blue eyes. Sergeant Patterson smiled. "Ah'd bet money that ye could. But there's three of us now, and ah'm the law. Ah was a constable for four years in the east end o' London. Ah think ye'd better let me give ye some assistance, son." He held out his hand. "All right with ye?"

The boy shook Patterson's hand. "Fine with me, Sarge. Righto, Ned?"

The black labrador held out his paw to the astonished sergeant, who shook it firmly and laughed. "Hahahah! Yon's a pretty intelligent dog!"

The dog flashed a passing thought to his master. "This young sergeant's fairly bright, too, eh, lad!"

The postmaster, Seth Talbot, had more news for them when they arrived at his office. "Message just come through from Drakehampton. I don't think those four men in the motor vehicle know who they are. Asked the postmistress there directions for Chapelvale, said they were racehorse buyers. Drove off and nearly knocked an old gent down who was crossing the road."

The sergeant turned to Ben. "Would ye like to go around tae the railway station sidings for me? Tell Constable Judmann ah can't relieve him yet and tae stay there. I'm going tae use the telegraph here. Get a description of our four friends and their motorcar from Drakehampton. Then ah'll contact headquarters in London and see what they know about them."

The constable was in his element. He stood holding on to the bicycle, in view of the "Prohibition of Movement" notice he had fixed to the railway trucks. Nothing but his sergeant's command would cause him to quit his post, he assured Ben, adding, "You tell the sarn't I'll stand 'ere all day an' all night, if needs be, lad!"

Sergeant Patterson was beaming when they returned to the post office. The labrador passed a thought to Ben. "I must look just like that when I get a big beef marrowbone!"

The boy could not hide a grin. "Aye, you do!"

Further thoughts were cut short by the sergeant, who met the two at the door. "Och, ye were right, lad! George Pearson, alias Gripper, Frederick Lloyd, alias Flash, Charles Hyland, alias Chaz, and Eric Wardle, alias Chunk. Driving a motorized vehicle, registration number BLH 98. Stolen from the front drive of Colonel Busby Hythe Simmonds of South Hampstead Crescent, London, yesterday evening!"

He strode from the post office, patting Ben's back and stroking the dog's head, a definite spring in his step. "Och aye, they've been guests at headquarters quite a few times. Felons, that's what they are, Ben. Known criminals!"

Ben had to trot to keep up with the sergeant's long strides. "What's the next move, then, Sarge?"

Patterson squared his shoulders. "Reception committee, lad. We've got tae give our London friends a warm welcome. Haha, if the constable knew he'd be sharpenin' his bayonet and cleaning up his auld army rifle. . . . Best leave him guarding the railway trucks, eh? Excitement, Ben, the very spice of life!"

"Ask him where we're off to now, pal?"

Ben caught the labrador's thought and asked the sergeant, "Where are we going now, Sarge?"

"Tae Miz Winn's house, o' course, ah want tae see if they've solved the candlestick riddle. Keep up there, partner!"

Relief flooded the boy as he marched jauntily alongside his competent friend. He had not really known what he was going to do about the London villains. Of course, he had put on a confident air when Winnie told him about them, but that was mainly for her benefit. Truth was he had acted just like a typical Chapelvale villager, pushing the matter to the back of his mind, hoping that it was all just Hetty's gossip. He counted himself very lucky that he had confided in Sergeant Patterson.

"Don't blame yourself too much, pal." The dog followed in Ben's tracks. "A boy and a dog are pretty thin odds against four full-grown rogues. Our policeman'll deal with 'em, look at the sergeant. He's actually looking forward to it."

Ben tugged Ned's tail. "Excuse me, pal, but d'you mind not cutting in on my thoughts?"

The labrador snapped playfully at Ben's ankle. "And what about my thoughts, pray? I was as worried as you about the issue. Thank goodness for the law, I say!"

They encountered a fairly pensive group in the Winn sitting room, studying a piece of paper that lay unfurled upon the table.

Ben looked hopefully to the seaman. "So you found something, is that it?"

"Aye, lad. That paper was rolled up inside the other

candlestick. What d'you make of it?"

The paper, for the most part, was blank, except for one corner, which had two rows of tiny cramped writing.

Ben read aloud. " 'Be of good heart, like a flame pure and true. May the light of St. Mark bring my words unto you. E.D.W.' "

The sergeant picked up the paper and inspected it. "Good, thick, quality stuff. Far more substantial than the thin slip in the other candlestick. Have ye tried matching them together in any way?"

Mr. Braithwaite placed the thin paper on the table. "We were just, er, about to do so, er, yes, quite so!"

Between them, Braithwaite and Mr. Mackay tried connecting both papers. Heeding every suggestion put forward by the rest, they placed the papers side by side, one over the other, semi-overlapping, and in every other possible combination that could be guessed at.

The result was absolutely nothing.

Will Drummond clenched both fists. Shutting his eyes tight, he called out in frustration, "St. Mark, are you listenin'? We're all of good heart! D'you think you could let us in on your secret, eh? Before 'tis too late for Chapelvale!"

Will's ma pursed her lips severely. "William Drummond! Don't you be so disrespectful to one o' the Lord's disciples, you won't get anythin' done like that!"

The blue-eyed boy felt pins and needles prickle his scalp, realizing the truth of her statement. He recalled another place and another time, long ago, when a man had ranted and called out against heaven. And he remembered the results of that day.

Eileen rescued little Willum, who was trying to sit on

Ned's back. "Ma's right, Will. Any'ow, I think there's too many cooks at the puddin' round 'ere. Ain't you got nothin' else to do, you menfolk?"

Sergeant Patterson had an idea. "Why don't you ladies and Mr. Braithwaite set your minds tae solving the puzzle. Ah'll take the men out into the kitchen—there's something Ah want tae speak tae them about."

Winnie exchanged a secret smile with her friend Hetty. "Agreed, Sergeant. Would you mind taking these dishes out with you when you go and washing them? We'll let you know when we want more tea."

The sergeant paused in the doorway. "Right ye are, marm. Ben, Alex, bring the dishes out. You're with the men now, ye ken!"

Amy handed her brother a cup and saucer. "Here you are, sir." Alex took them, giving her a stern glance. After all, he was classed as one of the men now.

In the gathering dusk, Gripper jammed on the brake, throwing the motorcar's occupants forward. "Flash, nip back 'n' see wot it sez on that signpost we just passed. Go on, move yerself!"

Flash blinked, rubbing his eyes. "Go easy, willyer, Gripp. I was jus' takin' forty winks there."

Gripper raised a threatening fist. "I'll forty winks yer. Get goin', yore supposed t'be the one keepin' watch."

Flash slouched off moodily back down the road. Gripper unfolded the sketch of Chapelvale, which had been supplied by Maud Bowe's father, squinting at it in the half-light.

"Can't be too far from the spot now, eh?"

He was answered by Chunk's stentorian snore from the backseat. Using the leather gauntlet he had removed, Gripper turned and belaboured the two sleepers vigorously. "Am I the only one wid 'is eyes open 'round 'ere? Wake up!"

The blows bounced off Chunk's stolid face, and he opened one eye. "Wot's the matter, are we there?"

Chaz snuffled, wiping a grimy sleeve across his upper lip and complaining as he inspected it. "Y'b started bee dose off bleedin' again. Wodjer doo dat for?"

Flash interrupted further complaints by climbing back into the front passenger seat. "It sez 'Adford. Any good?"

Gripper explored the sketch with a grimy finger, repeating, "Hmm, 'Adford, 'Adford, lemme see . . . Hahah! There 'tis!"

Up in the far corner of the drawing, a road leading out of Chapelvale was marked "Hadford Rd." Gripper realized that it was totally the wrong way to be approaching their destination. Hadford Road was at the north side of Chapelvale. Coming up from London, they should have entered by the south road, which ran parallel to the railway line. But he did not offer this information to the others.

Instead he announced proudly, "See, I wasn't lost. Told yer I knew the way, didn't I, eh?"

He continued driving, assuming that they agreed by their silence, until Flash spoke his thoughts over the chugging engine noise.

"But you said it was a four-hour drive. We been on the road since five this mornin'!"

Gripper had an explanation, as he always did. "Oh yerss, but lookit all the times we 'ad to stop. When that farmer was goin' t'chuck a rock, when those cows blocked the lane, when we turned inter that farmyard by mistake, when youse 'ad ter push the motor backwards, when we asked the post office lady the way. It all adds time ter the trip y'know, all adds time!"

Chunk sighed wistfully. "I liked the post office lady, she was gonna give me some water. Wish I 'ad a glass now."

Flash laughed mirthlessly. "Worrabout a glass o' beer, that's wot I need. An' a good plate o' steak 'n' kidney pie. I'm starved, I only 'ad a slice o' toast fer breakfist."

Chaz dabbed the scarf to his injured nose. "Yuh, bee too, I'b huggry, you nebber stopped for food, nod once!"

It was rapidly going dark. Gripper clenched his teeth as he bumped over a fallen branch lying in their path. "Sharrap about food, you lot! Eat, eat, that's all youse think about. One more word outta you, Chaz, an' I'll stop this motor an' give yer a knuckle sandwich. How'll that do yer, eh, eh?"

"Whoo!"

Gripper did not realize it was a nearby owl that had hooted. "You, that's who, Chaz. Now, shut yer gob!"

"Bud I nebber said nothig, Gripp."

Gripper nodded. "Just as well y'never, loose-lips. Aye aye, is that lights, up on that 'ill ahead?"

Chunk replied, "That'll be 'Adford, can we get summat to eat when we gets there?"

Gripper kept his eyes riveted on the road. "We could if we was stoppin' there, but we ain't. Mister Bowe's daughter'll be wonderin' where we've gotten to."

Flash pulled a face. "Oh, that one, liddle miss snotty nose. My daddy sez you got to do this, my daddy sez you gotta do that. An' she looks at yer like yer sumthin' she stepped in!"

Gripper sniffed. "She can look at us any way she wants to, as long as 'er daddy pays up. Five guineas apiece fer puttin' the frighteners on some old dame, just so she'll leave 'ome. Not bad money fer a small job like that!"

Chunk's stomach gurgled so loud it could be heard above the growl of the engine. He patted it sorrowfully. "Don't know about five guineas. I'd settle fer a paperful of fish an' chips right now, wiv salt an' vinegar on 'em."

"Can't you think of nothin' but yer stummick, y'great lump!"

A further abdominal gurgle almost drowned out Gripper's statement. Chunk gazed mournfully at the passing country-side. "Well, I can't 'elp it if me stummick's bigger'n yours, Gripp."

"Aye, if yer brains was as big as yer stummick, you'd be in charge o' the country, Chunk, doin' the prime minister out of a job. That's wot you'd be doin', mate!"

"Why, 'as the prime minister got a big stummick, Gripp?"

"The prime min . . . Jus' go back t'sleep, willyer, Chunk!"

Flash propped his feet up on the dashboard. "Kin I 'ave a snooze, too, Gripp?"

Gripper let go of the steering wheel with one hand. He gave Flash a numbing punch on his shin. "No, y'can't. You keep yer eyes open fer more signs!"

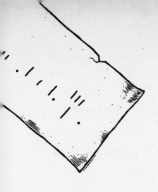

" 'BE OF GOOD HEART, LIKE A FLAME PURE and true, May the light of St. Mark bring my words unto you. E.D.W.' " Mr. Braithwaite and the ladies sat in the gathering gloom, staring at the paper as Amy read the rhyme for the third time.

Ben entered the room with a lighted taper. "Jon told me to bring some light to you before you ruin your eyesight staring at that paper."

Mrs. Winn had neither gas nor the new electric light, favouring the old ways, and kept four ornate oil lamps in her sitting room. The boy lit them all, one on the mantelpiece, two on the window-ledges back and front. He touched his taper to the wick of the largest lamp with its tall glass chimney and a cream-hued bowl. This lamp stood on the same table as the paper and gave off a wonderfully soft glow.

Ben chuckled. "Now you can see to think properly. Miz Winn, I'm going out with the men."

A worried frown creased the old lady's brow. "So that's what you were all discussing in the kitchen. I knew as soon as the sergeant read out the telegram about the four men coming here in the motorcar. Be careful, Ben, and do exactly as Sergeant Patterson tells you—they could be dangerous."

There was something in the blue eyes of the strange boy

from the sea that told the old lady he had faced danger many times. His hand felt reassuring as he touched her shoulder lightly. "We can take care of this, Jon, Will, Mr. Mackay, Alex, the sergeant, and myself. No need for you to worry.

"Don't open the door to anybody until you've looked through the window to see who's there. I'll leave Ned with you, just in case."

Little Willum had played himself out and lay on the sofa, surrounded by cushions. As his mother covered him with an old plaid travelling rug, Ned came to sit by her.

Eileen patted the big dog's head. "I'd like to see anyone try t'get past Ned if he didn't want 'em to come in. You go on, Ben. We're safe enough. Tell my Will not to forget Delia's nosebag an' water bucket."

Amy touched the boy's hand. "Be careful, Ben, and good luck!"

He paused at the door, tossing hair back from his keen blue eyes. "Good luck to you, too, pal. Don't worry, I'll keep my eye on Alex for you. Stay, boy!"

The black labrador winked at Ben. "All right, shipmate, I'm only coming to the door to see you off."

When they had departed, Mr. Braithwaite suddenly began pacing the room earnestly. Hetty whispered to her friend, "Lookit that ole buffer scratchin' away at 'imself, Winnie. The shoulders of that gown look as if 'e's been sprinklin' 'em with talcum powder!"

Mrs. Winn suppressed a smile. "Ssshh, he's deep in thought."

Mr. Braithwaite stopped, holding up a finger, like an orator about to deliver a speech. "Hmph! It, er, occurs to me, er, ladies, that we should, er, light a candle in one of those holders, as it were. Yes, very good, to see if the light of St. Mark brings any, uh, er . . . words to us. Yes?"

Mrs. Winn opened a drawer in the table. "It can't do any harm, I suppose, I keep some candles in here."

Mr. Braithwaite took a candle. Using his library key, he scraped the wax at its base until it fitted the socket of one golden candlestick. When he had lit it, the old scholar stood holding the candlestick in one hand and the paper in the other.

"Right, er, very good so far. Er, er, hmmmmmm."

He was at a loss what to do next. Will's ma, Sarah, came to his rescue, her voice mounting with excitement. "Give it to me now, I think I might know the answer!" She practically snatched both candlestick and paper.

The young girl watched curiously as Sarah held the paper over the flame. "Be careful, you might burn it!"

The old woman moved the paper back and forth across the flame confidently. "When I was a little girl, me 'n' my pals used t'send messages to each other, invisible notes. All you need is some white vinegar or lemon juice to write with, even an egg white'll do. See! I knew I was right, somethin's showin' on the paper. Here!"

Heat from the candle flame had caused markings to appear! They were rather faint, but still discernible.

The excited maidservant hugged the younger girl with a sob in her voice. "Oh, I 'ope it's somethin' that'll put a spoke in ole Smithers's wheel. What does it say, Mr. Braithwaite, sir? What does it say?"

Scanning the paper, the old scholar shook his head. "Er, nothing really, just shapes and, er, dots, so to speak!"

The women gathered around the table to view the odd markings.

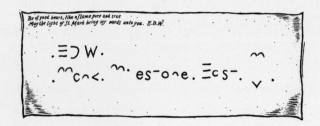

Hetty was both angry and disappointed. "I never learned to read or write, but that ain't no writin'. I can see that. An' it ain't nothin' a body could read, I'm sure!"

Will's ma glanced at Mr. Braithwaite. "What d'you think, sir?"

He stared at the markings blankly. "I, er, tend to agree with Miz, er, hmmm!"

Sarah turned her attention to Amy. "An' you, girl, what d'you make of it, eh?"

Amy picked up the thin sheet of paper with the lines and dots on it.

"I'd place this paper over that paper and see if it matches up."

The dairyman's wife clapped her hands. "So would I, m'dear, try it!"

Amy placed the thin paper over the thicker one, lining up the first dot over the one beneath.

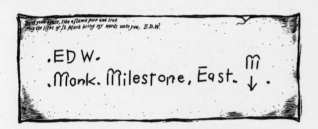

Mrs. Winn kissed Amy. "Thank you, you clever, pretty girl!"

The black labrador stood with his paws upon the table, passing a thought to Horatio, who had prowled in. "We mustn't forget to thank good old Edmund De Winn, too, eh?"

"Mrrrowr! Sardine, milk, waaiow! 'Ratio hungry!"

Ned stared down his nose at the cat. "Don't think too hard—you'll damage that amazing brain of yours!"

The librarian-schoolteacher flopped down in an armchair, shaking his head. "Thin paper over thick paper and join up the marks. Well, I, er, never. Hmmm, must be getting, er, er, old if I can't see that, er, ah yes . . . old."

WITH THEIR WINDOW BLINDS PULLED down, the village square shops looked as if they were sleeping. Dust had settled on the leaves of the hawthorn trees, without even the faintest breeze to stir it.

In the window of Mr. Mackay's office, the clock showed ten minutes after midnight. Dark clouds obscured a pale, crescent moon; the air was still and warm from the long summer's day.

A villainous-looking man, his matted beard showing beneath a battered slouch hat, sat holding the reins of a horse and gig in the shadows. He turned this way and that, watching every possible entrance to the village square.

Concealed in some bushes at the side of the Hadford Road, Ben and Alex were first to hear the distant chug of a motorcar. Without a word, side by side, they ran back to Chapelvale.

The villainous man looked up as the boys came panting up to him. "Did you see them?"

"No, but we heard the motorcar!"

"It's coming in on the Hadford Road, be here soon!"

The man nodded. "Good, boy, collect Mr. Mackay from Station Road. Alex, get Will from School Lane. Make your way up to the police station, see you there. Now go, an' remember, lads, keep out of sight!"

Gripper stopped the motor just short of the square. Flinging off his gauntlets and goggles, he rested his forehead against the steering wheel and sighed thankfully. "Chapelvale at last!"

Chunk sounded slightly doubtful. "You mean we're 'ere, Gripp? 'Ow d'yer know that?"

Flash shook his head in amazement at Chunk's ignorance.

" 'Cos we passed a sign on the road that said Chapelvale. But I suppose you was kippin' again."

Chunk straightened his bowler and stretched. "Nuffin' wrong wid sleepin', is there? It is night-time, y'know. I got pains in me guts wiv 'unger. Where d'we get sumthin' to eat? You promised us, Gripp."

Gripper massaged his temples with both hands. "Chunk, give it a rest, willyer. Forget yer stummick for a minute. Chaz, you ain't asleep, are yer?"

"Huh, 'ow cad I sleeb wid be dose bleedin' like a tap? You shuddena told hib to hid be, Gripp, id hurds!"

Gripper raised a single finger in warning. "One more word outta you, Chaz, just one more!"

Flash began tugging at Gripper's sleeve. "Gripp, Gripp!"

Gripper shook him off. "I'm 'ere. Y'don't 'ave to tear the coat off me. Wot is it?"

Flash pointed. "Some ole geezer sittin' watchin' us, wiv an 'orse an' cart. Over there, look!"

Gripper got out of the vehicle and nodded to his crew. "There's four of us an' one of 'im, let's see wot 'e wants."

The villainous-looking man, who was in reality the old

ship's carpenter wearing a disguise, stared down from his perch on the gig at the four toughs. His voice held a sneer. "So, yew got 'ere finally. Wot time d'yer call this t'be rollin' up fer the job, eh?"

"We got los . . . Oof!"

Flash had the wind knocked from him by Gripper's elbow. Gripper did his best tough stare and spat in the dust. "None of yer business, Granddad, we 'ad a few problems, that's all. Now, where's this old biddy's place? We'll do the job. Don't get yer whiskers in an uproar about that. Show us the way."

Jon shook his head pityingly, looking them up and down. "Company toughs, eh, huh! It's too late t'do anythin' tonight, Mr. Smithers an' Maud wants to see yer up at the 'ouse."

"Do they 'ave food up there, you know, eats?"

The old seaman winked at Chunk. "All yer likes, tons of it!"

"Ad hab dey got bandages an' thiggs, too?"

Jon chuckled wickedly. "Probl'y, but they mightn't 'ave enough to go 'round yore big 'ooter. Fell on it, didyer?"

Gripper fished a leather-bound cosh out of his pocket and began smacking it ominously in his palm. "Lissen, ole man. Yore too nosy fer yer own good, but I can soon fix that. Now, are y'takin' us up to the 'ouse, eh?"

Jon indicated the cart. "Cummon, 'op in. I'll take ye."

Gripper grabbed the back of Flash's coat as he began to mount the gig. "We got a motorcar, you get goin'. We'll foller yer."

Secreted with Ben and Alex in the rosebushes to one side of the police station door, Mr. Mackay, armed with Sergeant Patterson's long pacing stick, whispered hoarsely through the open charge-office window. "They're coming!"

Gripper stared suspiciously at the greystone building. "This don't look like no toff's big 'ouse!"

The shipman climbed down from the gig. " 'Cos it ain't, it's my 'ouse. Mr. Smithers don't want you lot t'be seen 'round 'is mansion. Well, are you big, brave 'ooligans goin' to sit out 'ere in yer motorcar all night?"

Gripper silenced the engine and got out, pointing a finger. "Watch who yer callin' 'ooligans, Granpop. Cummon, youse lot!" They swaggered up the path nonchalantly, letting Jon see that they were not the least bit afraid, while he followed them.

Gripper was about to raise the lion's-head knocker on the door when it was flung open and Sergeant Patterson pulled him inside. As he did, he roared, "Now!"

Will sprang forward and grabbed Chunk, charging from the rear, as Jon and Mr. Mackay bulled Chaz and Flash into the station with their two companions. The boys watched through the window as the sergeant locked the door.

Gripper was pale with shock and indignation. He immediately recognized the interior, having been in many police stations. "Wot's all this, then? We ain't done nothin' wrong. I'll see our lawyers about this!"

The sergeant towered over Gripper and folded his arms, smiling. "Colonel Busby Hythe Simmonds, ah presume."

Gripper sensed the policeman had made a mistaken identity. "You've got the wrong man, Sergeant. I ain't Colonel Bubsy Wots'isname, neither are me friends. Never 'eard of 'im afore!"

Patterson nodded understandingly. "Well, ah'm glad we've got that cleared up, sir. Perhaps you'd like tae tell me what ye are doing in possession of the colonel's motorcar, number BLH 98, which was stolen from outside his house at South

Hampstead Crescent in London last evening?"

Flash groaned. "Told yer we should've took the train, Gripp."

Gripper shot him a murderous glance, silencing him. He turned back to the sergeant. "You can't 'old us 'ere. We ain't committed no crimes, we found the motorcar, see."

The sergeant's voice still retained its pleasant tone. "Found it, sir, where, in Church Haven outside the post office?"

Chunk smiled in remembrance of the visit. "That's right, Sarge, where the ole lady nearly give me a drink o' water. I liked 'er!"

The two boys listened in through the open window, chuckling as the sergeant replied, "Och aye, ye'd be one of the four royal couriers, or is it one of the racehorse buyers who asked directions at Drakehampton post office. Which were you? Think!"

Chunk took off his bowler and scratched his shaven head. "Er, I fink the game's up, Gripp. 'E's nabbed us fair'n'square!"

Gripper stamped his boot down on Chunk's foot. "Sharrup, thick'ead. Don't say another word, none of youse!"

The sergeant sat at the charge-office desk, his pleasant mood evaporating suddenly as he rapped out, "Enough o' all this nonsense. George Pearson, Frederick Lloyd, Charles Hyland, and Eric Wardle. Ye are under arrest for the theft of a motor vehicle, pending further investigations revealing any other felonies. Ye'll be held in custody here until such times as ye appear before a magistrate. Have ye anything tae say t'the charges brought against ye?"

Flash whispered to Gripper, " 'E knows our proper names!

'Ow'd 'e find that out?"

Gripper ground his teeth together audibly. "Shut . . . up!"

Sergeant Patterson stared levelly at the four accused. "Ah said, have ye anything tae say t'the charges?"

Gripper glared sullenly back at him. "We wanna lawyer!"

Mr. Mackay looked them up and down with disdain. "I'm a lawyer, the only one in Chapelvale, but I don't deal in criminal law. Besides, I've quite enough clients at the moment, thank you. So, what are your plans, gentlemen, eh?"

Chaz's nose had stopped bleeding, and he sniffed carefully before blurting out, "The company we work for in London, Jackman Donnin' an' Bowe, 'll get a lawyer fer us, a real one from London, not some 'ayseed like that feller!"

Gripper groaned and, clenching both fists, he turned on Chaz. "You stoopid, loudmouthed squealer! I'll . . ."

Chaz skipped nimbly out of range, placing himself behind the formidable figure of Will Drummond.

"Keep 'im away from me! It was Gripper who pinched the motorcar, 'e's the on'y one of us wot can drive. I 'aven't done nothin', an' I'm not gonna be left carryin' the can fer miss snotty nose Maud Bowe an' 'er father's firm. No! Not fer any local bigwig who's in with 'em, either!"

It was at that moment when Constable Judmann pounded on the station door and the old seaman let him in. "I thought you were comin' to relieve me, Sarge. 'Ello, what've we got 'ere?"

Sergeant Patterson took hold of Chaz firmly. "Ah'll tell ye all about it later, Constable. Lock those three up in the holding cell, will ye. Ah'll keep this fellow here with me. Ah've got a feeling he wants tae tell me more." The sergeant relieved Mackay of his stick.

"Thanks for the help, gents. Time yon lads were in bed, though. Does your dad know you're out this late, Alex?"

The younger boy who stood framed by the open window with the blue-eyed boy replied, "It's all right, Sarge. Me and Amy told him we'd be stopping over with Ben at Miz Winn's tonight."

The sergeant winked at Ben. "Weel, you make sure they get straight off tae bed, and don't stay up late yourself!"

Ben grinned cheekily. "Bed? Not on a night like this. It's gone midnight, d'you realize? Today's Thursday, the dead-line day for Chapelvale. I'm going back to see if Miz Winn and our friends have cracked the riddle!"

The boys ran off, with Will, the shipman, and the lawyer in their wake, calling, "Hi, wait for us!"

43

WILL'S MA HAD TAKEN LITTLE
Willum to bed with her, in Winnie's room
on the ground floor. On the sofa formerly occupied by
little Willum, Mr. Braithwaite lay, wrapped in his
gown, overcome by slumber. Hetty took the plaid
travelling rug and covered him over with it.
"Good old feller, it was him who thought of
lightin' the candle. That got us started."

Mackay bobbed his head in a small bow.
"But I've no doubt he couldn't have got much further without
the help of you ladies, excellent work all 'round!"

Amy, Eileen, and Mrs. Winn were far too excited to con-
template sleep. They showed the results of their labours to the
menfolk, who told them of the capture of the London toughs.

The blue-eyed boy took a look at the writing, then at the
old map with the four dots upon it. "It's marked here as Eastpath, where's that?"

Eileen blushed in the lamplight. "Oh, 'tis a pretty little
lane. Will an' me used to walk there, when we was a-courtin'."

Mr. Mackay knew a bit more about the area. "Ah yes, Eastpath. Now, correct me if I'm wrong, Jon, but isn't that the old
stagecoach way, to the east of the village square?"

Jon confirmed the solicitor's words. "Aye, that's the

place," the old shipmate said. "Once the new road was built from Hadford, for the waggoners to use, the path fell into disrepair. Of course, that'd be nigh on a hundred years back. Eastpath will be so overgrown we'll have a right old job tryin' to locate a milestone."

Will shook his head. "Oh no we won't, friend. I recall trippin' over that stone an' sprainin' my ankle one evening as I was runnin'."

Amy chuckled. "Were you chasing after Eileen?"

Will's big, jolly wife gave Amy a nudge, almost knocking her over. "No, it were I who was chasin' after Will!"

Mr. Mackay coughed officiously to dispel any more talk of the romantic escapade. "Harrumph! Yes, well, we're going to need spades, lanterns, and so on. Shall we get started? Our time is short now."

The black labrador passed a thought to his master, who was sitting stroking him. "Pity the poor girl who ever tries to chase that dry old stick."

The gig was loaded up, ready to go. Ben stood at the door with Mrs. Winn. The old lady looked very tired, he hugged her affectionately. "You go back inside and have a nice nap, Miz Winn. Leave this to us. I promise we'll come back here with anything we find, straightaway!"

She kissed Ben's cheek. "I'll have breakfast ready for you."

The dog was obviously holding a mental conversation with Horatio. As they climbed into the gig, Ben eyed the labrador. "What was going on between you two, Ned?"

The black labrador laid his chin on Ben's lap. "I told him to keep an eye on things while we were gone."

The boy scratched the back of his dog's ear. "I suppose he gave you a lot of nonsense about sardines, butterflies, and mice. Poor old Horatio, he's got a bit of a one-track mind."

Ned shook his head. "No. Surprisingly, he said he'd watch over the house and if anything happened he'd track us down and let me know. I think that Horatio's finally come to his senses. Just in time—can't go around with a headful of sardines and butterflies all his life!"

Delia trotted dutifully through the darkened village, passing the almshouse and heading up the overgrown path. It became very dim, overshadowed by an archway of overhanging trees. Ben was imagining what it had been like all those years ago: stagecoaches laden with passengers and mail, carriages bearing merchants and gentry, carts laden with produce. All of them fearful to be travelling such a lonely and shaded path, where highwaymen and thieves might lurk. The strange boy glimpsed the crescent moon, struggling to cast its light through the leafy canopy. Unwittingly his mind wandered back to the *Flying Dutchman*, Vanderdecken, and his villainous crew—they would probably have revelled in the highwayman's trade.

Amy bumped against him as the gig lurched to a stop. "Don't go to sleep, Ben, I think we've arrived at the place!"

Three lanterns had been brought, the seaman lit them and gave one to each of his young friends. "Here y'are, mates. You're in charge of lightin' and the maps. Stay close to 'em, Mr. Mackay. Me an' Will can do the digging. Where is Will?"

Eileen had unharnessed Delia from the shafts, allowing her to rest and crop the grass. She pointed. "Over yonder, t'other side o' the path, with Hetty." She raised her voice. "You found it yet, Will?"

The dairyman called back to his wife. "No, not yet, my dear. Ouch!"

The maidservant Hetty could be heard giggling. "You found it now, Will. Tripped straight over it. Like as not sprained your ankle again!"

Will was thankful the darkness hid his furious blushes. "No harm done. Bring some light over here, you young 'uns!"

A massive ancient oak tree overshadowed the path at that point. Beneath the shade of its outstretched limbs a half-buried milestone had been standing for centuries. Ben held his lamp close to the stone. "This is it! Look. 'Chapelvale One Mile.' See, beneath the letter M of Mile, there's the arrow pointing downwards!"

The labrador passed him an observant thought. "Or is it supposed to point outward, like the one on the tree at the ruined smithy?"

Ben looked up at the lawyer. "What d'you think, sir, do we dig down, or is the arrow meant to point outward to another spot?"

Adjusting the glasses on his nose, the solicitor peered at the stone. "D'you know, I'm not too sure. What's your opinion, Jon?"

The old seaman put down the spades and pickaxe he had brought from the gig. "Who's to say, sir? There ain't no clues tellin' us what number o' paces we should tread if we were to dig in another place."

Hetty settled the argument by taking a penny from her apron pocket. "Trust to luck, sez I. Toss a coin. Tails, we digs down, 'eads, we digs somewheres outward from the arrow."

She spun the coin, Alex held the lantern over where it fell. "It's tails!"

MORNING SUNLIGHT FILTERED INTO THE
bedroom as Maud Bowe sat at the bedroom mirror, inserting
a last clip into her elaborate hairdo. The Smithers household

had grown peaceful and quiet since that young
horror Wilfred had departed for boarding
school, accompanied by his mother. Mrs.
Smithers would take up lodgings close to the
school, until her dear Wilfred was settled in, as
she put it.

Maud smiled at her reflection in the mirror. Today was
the last day she would have to spend in Chapelvale, dreadful
rural backwater!

"Hetty! Hetty! Where the blazes are you, I want my breakfast!"

Arriving downstairs, Maud found Mr. Smithers red-faced
and irate. "Ah, Miss Bowe, have you seen the maid, is she dusting upstairs?"

Maud swished by him on her way to the kitchen. "No,
she's not, though if she'd been anywhere within a mile of the
house, she'd have heard you bellowing, sir!"

Smithers followed her out, watching as she put the kettle
on and buttered a slice of brown bread. "What're you doing,
miss?"

Cutting the bread into triangles, she placed it on a plate. "Making my breakfast, obviously. It must be clear, even to you, that Hetty can't come for some reason."

Smithers waved his hands uselessly. "But the table isn't laid, my dress clothes haven't been brought out of the wardrobe. Nothing's been done—wineglasses, sherry decanters, side trays, and clean linen. Where are they? I'm supposed to be holding a reception this afternoon for the county planners, a magistrate, business associates arriving from all over to begin our plans!"

Maud spooned tea leaves into the pot. "Then you'll just have to change your arrangements. I'm not your maid of all work."

Smithers wiped sweat from his reddening brow. "Piece o' bread 'n' butter an' a cup of tea is no breakfast for a man to start a full day on, eh?" He blinked under Maud's frosty stare.

"Then cook something for yourself—this is my breakfast!"

Having made tea, Maud put it on a tray with the bread and butter and retired to the garden with it. A few moments passed before Smithers emerged, eating a thick slice of bread with strawberry jam slathered on it and holding a beer tankard filled with milk. He plonked himself moodily down next to her at the wrought-iron table.

"That maid, Hetty, she's sacked, finished, bag an' baggage!"

Maud curled her lip in disgust as milk spilled down Smithers's chin from the tankard. He wiped it off on his sleeve.

"What're you turnin' your nose up at, little miss high 'n' mighty? All very prim an' proper, aren't you, eh, eh? What happened to your bullyboys from London? Never turned up, did they? Well, whether or not, things'll go ahead today. You'll see, I've got it all organized on my own, without your help, missie!"

Maud was about to make a cutting reply when a carter, wearing a burlap apron, appeared at the gate and shouted, "Hoi! Mr. Smithers, we've 'ad the stuff that you 'ired brought over from 'Adford. Been waitin' in the village square since six-thirty. Wot d'yer want us t'do with it?"

Smithers yanked the oversized watch from his vest pocket. "Twenty past seven already, I'd better get movin'. Listen, you'd best get down t'the station at nine-ten an' meet the of-ficials. Don't be late, now, d'ye hear me?"

Maud shooed a sparrow away from her plate. "I'm hardly likely to be late meeting my own father."

Smithers stopped in his tracks. "Your father? You never said anything about him arrivin' today!"

Maud considered her lacquered nails carefully. "He'll be travelling up from London with some investors just to check on the amounts of money paid out to the villagers. They'll ar-rive on the eight-fifty. To meet up with the magistrate and county planners coming down on the nine-ten. I'll show them the way to the square—you'd best have things ready there."

Maud thought Obadiah Smithers looked about ready to take a fit. He stood scarlet-faced and quivering. "Check on the money? What's the matter, doesn't the man trust me?"

Maud was satisfied her nails were perfect. She replied coolly, "When it comes to business, my father trusts nobody!"

At eight-fifteen Blodwen Evans opened the front door of the Tea Shoppe and began sweeping over the step with a broom.

She stopped to view the activity in the square. Directly in front of the notice board post, two wagons had pulled up. Men were unloading a table, chairs, and what looked like a small marquee with an open front. Smithers was directing two other men to put up a large sign, painted on a plywood board. Shopkeeper Blodwen called to her husband, "Dai, look you, see what's 'appenin' out 'ere!"

Dai Evans emerged, wiping flour from his hands, and gave a long, mournful sigh. "Whoa! Look at that, now, will you. Our village square full of strangers. Read me that notice, will you, Blodwen, I ain't got my glasses with me."

Blodwen read it aloud slowly. " 'Progressive Development Company Limited. Payments made here for all land and properties within the Chapelvale area. All persons wishing to receive the stipulated compensation must be in possession of legal deeds to their land and property or payment cannot be made.' "

Blowing her nose loudly on her apron hem, Blodwen wiped her eyes. "There's sad for the village, Dai. I never thought I'd see this day!"

Dai put an arm about his wife. "There there, lovely, you make a cup of tea. I'll go an' look for the deeds to our shop."

Blodwen stood watching Smithers approaching, she called over her shoulder to Dai, "You'll find 'em in the blue hatbox on top of the wardrobe!"

Smithers had a spring to his step and a happy smile on his face. He touched his hat brim to Blodwen cheerfully. "Mornin', marm, another good summer's day, eh. Am I too early to order breakfast and a large pot of tea?"

Blodwen Evans drew herself up to her full height, which was considerable, and stared down from the front step of her shop. "Put one foot over this step, boyo, and I'll crack this broom over your skull!"

Smithers beat a hasty retreat back to the square, where he began finding fault and bullying the workmen. Blodwen held her aggressive pose for a moment, then sighed unhappily and leaned on the broom. Chapelvale, the little village she had come to love so much, was about to be destroyed. In a short time, the drapers, butchers, post office, general shop, and the ironmongers, those neat, small shops with their wares gaily displayed behind well-polished windows, would stand empty, waiting for demolition, their former owners gone off to other places.

Even the almshouse, with its tall, shady trees in the lane behind, would be trampled under the wheels of progress. Children dashing eagerly into her Tea Shoppe, pennies clutched in their hands for ice-cream cones, old ladies wanting to sit and chat over pots of India and China tea, with cakes or hot buttered scones. They would soon be little more than a memory to her. But such a beautiful memory. Blodwen Evans lifted an apron hem to her face and cried for the loss of the place she knew as home.

IN MR. MACKAY'S OFFICE WINDOW, THE CLOCK stood at half-past nine. A lot of people had gathered in the square at Chapelvale. It was, as Smithers had predicted, a  good summer's day, with hardly a breeze stirring and the sun beaming out of a cloudless blue sky. However, the square was still and silent, despite the large gathering of villagers.

Percival Bowe stood with his daughter Maud upon his arm. In subdued voices they made small talk with the magistrate, the county planning officer, and their lawyers. Principal shareholders, who had travelled up from London, stood apart, with the project engineers. They carried on a low-key conversation, every so often casting quick glances from under the marquee shade at the faces outside of the sad, puzzled, hostile villagers.

Smithers felt untidy and out of place, trying unsuccessfully to mingle with those in the marquee. He approached Mr. Bowe, rubbing his hands nervously. "The, er, Tea Shoppe is closed today, or I'd have sent for some refreshments." He wilted under the icy stares of Maud and her father. Wiping perspiration from under his collar with a grubby finger, Smithers shrugged apologetically. "I was goin' to have a reception up at the house, but, er, maid's day off y'know. Haha..."

Percival Bowe had a sonorous voice that any undertaker might have admired. "So I gather, sir. Not quite what I was led to expect from your letters. What time is it?"

Eager to please, Smithers fumbled out his oversized watch. "Nine-forty exactly, Percy... er, Mr. Bowe. Nine-forty, sir!"

Mr. Bowe touched the pearl stickpin he wore in his cravat. "Those bumpkins out there will stand all day, staring dumbly at us like a herd of cattle. Do you not think it might be wise to encourage them forward? I assume they will want payment for their properties today, as small as it is."

There was nobody about to do Smithers's shouting for him. Acutely embarrassed, he stood outside the marquee facing the villagers and cleared his throat, conscious of the carter and his men from Hadford chuckling behind his back. He held forth both hands like a politician at a meeting.

"Er, good morning, er, will you please listen t'me. I want you to form an orderly line, no pushin', er, haha. We will begin the payments to those who have their deeds or, er, appropriate papers with them!"

There was not a move from the villagers. They stood silent.

Smithers tried again, this time with the voice of reason. "Oh, come on now, it's for your own good. Form a line, right here where I'm standing. Come on, please. Anyone?"

Blodwen Evans's voice rang out from her bedroom

window. "For our own good, is it? You any relation to Judas? He sold the Lord for thirty pieces o' silver!"

The Hadford workmen guffawed aloud, one or two clapped.

Smithers glared up at the window before marching back into the marquee, where he confronted Bowe. "They're not movin'. Can't you do anything?"

Bowe looked over Smithers's shoulder at those outside. Men, women, children in hand, none moving. "Give it half an hour or so, then I'll send out one of my London lawyers to read them the official notice. Any of those bumpkins too stupid to understand it will just have to stand and wait out there until sundown. By then the bailiff will have arrived with his deputies, they'll hand out any unpaid monies and possess their houses and properties. By force, if necessary!"

Mr. Bowe turned away from Smithers. As he did, his eye caught a movement.

It was a two-wheeled dairy cart carrying four women and a baby. A young girl and a boy held the reins, leading the horse between them. Behind the cart strode four men, another boy, and a big black labrador. Slightly to one side of the odd cavalcade, a police sergeant marched, nodding amiably to the village folk.

Mr. Bowe gave an inward sigh of relief. At last some of these rustics were coming forward. He moved to the table in front of the marquee, calling to his colleagues.

"To your places, gentlemen, our first customers are here!"

Two lawyers, the magistrate, and an official with a bag containing a ledger and a wad of certified money orders, took their seats at the table. Maud Bowe tried to whisper

something to her father, but he ignored her. Putting on a smile
of false cordiality, Bowe addressed the group. "Well well, it's
nice to see decent folk acting sensibly. Hope you've brought
your deeds along with you, eh!"

Mackay ignored Maud's father and strode up to the table,
looking very dapper, from his clean-shaven face to his crisp
white shirt, freshly pressed trousers, and tailcoat. Placing a
leather satchel on the desk, he opened it and produced a long
and ancient-looking scroll, which he unrolled.

Looking over the top of his nose glasses, he inquired po-
litely, "Which one of you is the magistrate?"

The magistrate stared over the top of his spectacles. "I
am, sir, state your name and business."

Seething with impatience and excitement, the dapper
lawyer kept his feelings hidden as he announced in a voice
that could be heard all around the village square, "I, sir, am
Philip Teesdale Mackay, a solicitor and chartered member of
the legal profession. I represent Mrs. Winifred Winn, who re-
sides in Chapelvale. On her behalf, it is my duty to inform you
that said lady lays claim and title to the entire village, up to its
boundaries and all dwelling houses, places of business, and
land within the curtilage of such establishments!"

In the silence that followed, the drop of a pin could have
been heard. Then the magistrate spoke. "I trust you have
proof of this unusual claim, sir?"

Mr. Mackay's eyes never left the astounded official. With
a dramatic flourish he held out his right arm, palm open. Amy
and her brother stepped forward. Picking up the weighty
scroll, they unrolled it and placed it in the lawyer's well-
manicured hand. He grasped it firmly by its top. It was a huge
thing, real calfskin vellum, with several silk ribbons—blue,

gold, and purple—hanging from it. These were sealed with blobs of scarlet wax with gold medallions set into them.

The diminutive figure of the lawyer seemed to increase in stature. His voice boomed triumphantly forth, like a town crier.

" 'Be it known to all my subjects, nobles, vassals, and yeomanry. I do acknowledge the valiant deeds of my liege Captain Caran De Winn in the capture of the French fleet and our victory at Sluys. He served his sovereign and country right worthily, no man braver than he.

" 'Hereby I grant unto him freely the acres of our good English land, to be known hereonin as Chapelvale. Caran De Winn, his sons, daughters, and all who come after, bearing the name of Winn, will have squiredom over this place. Without let or hindrance, tax or tithing, for as long as any monarch shall rule our fair land. Let no man raise his voice or wrath against my edict. May the family of Winn serve God and England with loyalty, faith, and forbearance. Given by my hand on this Lammas Day in the year of Our Lord thirteen hundred and forty-one.

" 'By the grace of God. Edward III, King of England.' "

Ringing cheers and shouts of delight erupted throughout the village square. Hats flew in the air and the cobblestones echoed to the stamping of feet. People hugged and kissed one another indiscriminately; it was a scene of total jubilation. The black labrador dodged to safety beneath the gig as Ben was surrounded by his friends, Will and Jon shaking his hands, whilst Mrs. Winn and Amy seized him and kissed both his cheeks. Mr. Braithwaite pounded the boy's back, shouting, "We did it, boy. We did it!"

Catching his breath, Ben roared back. "No, it was

you who did it, friends. I only started the search, me and good old Ned."

The labrador sent a thought from beneath the gig. "Keep me out of this, mate. I don't want to be crushed, battered, and slobbered over!"

When the blue-eyed boy managed to break free, he saw Alex, with a crowd of other young people congratulating him. Among them was Regina Woodworthy and the former members of the Grange Gang. Amy clasped Ben's hand. "Look at my brother, the village hero, thanks to you, Ben."

The boy warded off an embrace from Eileen and little Willum, who had painted his face with a toffee apple somebody had given him.

"Don't be silly, pal. Look at Ned. He knows the safest place—under the cart. Come on, Amy!"

They scrambled beneath the gig, laughing at the sight of Blodwen Evans leaning out of the bedroom window, waving a Union Jack and a Welsh red dragon flag, and hooting.

"Put those deeds back in my hatbox, Dai, let's open the shop!"

Mr. Bowe's normally sallow face had taken on an ash-grey pallor as he turned his accusing gaze on Obadiah Smithers. "So, the old lady presents no problem, eh? Fool! I should never have listened to you and your harebrained schemes. Do you realize what this'll cost my company?"

Smithers collapsed onto a vacant chair, his eyes wide in disbelief. "I—I—I'm ruined!"

Bowe stood over him, jabbing a finger savagely into Smithers's arm to accentuate each word. "If you aren't, then

I'll make sure you are. You'll be glad to get a job selling matches on street corners when I'm done with you!"

Straightening up, Bowe offered an arm to his daughter. "Maud, I'll talk to you back in London. Come on, girl, or we'll miss the train!"

They turned to go and walked straight into the sergeant, whose voice was flat and official. "Mr. Percival Bowe and Miss Maud Bowe, ah'd like ye tae come up tae the station house with me."

Mr. Bowe, who tried stepping to one side, flinched as the strong arm of the law captured his shoulder.

Sergeant Patterson whispered confidentially in his ear. "Now now, sir, don't want tae show ourselves up tae all the folk around here, do we? You and the young lady come quietly, ah've got four of your employees in mah holding cell on a vehicle theft charge. They're making all sorts of accusations against Bowe and company. Ah'm sure it's all quite unsubstantiated, but ah'd just like ye tae take a stroll up there and we'll sort it all out."

Mr. Mackay folded the scroll and handed it to the old seaman. Mrs. Winn linked arms with the solicitor. "Well, seeing as all the business is done, let's go for lunch. Mrs. Evans has invited us all over to the Tea Shoppe for a celebration!" Waving her gloves, the old lady called out to her young friends. "Come on, you three, bring Ned, too. It's free ice-cream today!"

Mr. Mackay straightened his cravat. "Just a moment, marm." He turned to the magistrate. "Excuse me, sir, perhaps you'd like to join us."

Distancing himself from the company shareholders, the magistrate smiled his approval. "It would be a pleasure, sir!"

EVANS TEA SHOPPE PUT ON A WONDERFUL spread. Dai Evans pushed four tables close so the friends could sit together. Blodwen brought tray after tray of sandwiches, tea, cakes, and ice-cream, dismissing any offer of payment.

"Look, you, 'tis the least we can do for the folk who saved our village. Indeed to goodness, put that money away. Hoho, 'twas worth it just to see Obadiah Smithers's face. In the name of heavens, though, 'ow did you find those deeds?"

Mr. Braithwaite scratched his wiry mop. "Deeds, you say, marm, well er, hmm, 'fraid I can't, er, enlighten you, I was, er, er, asleep on Miz Winn's, er, sofa, yes. You tell her, er, er."

Amy put aside her ice-cream and explained.

"It's a long story, but we had a clue that led us to the old milestone on Eastpath. I never knew milestones were that big, there was only a small part showing above ground!"

Will confirmed her statement. "Aye, the one on Eastpath is a disused old millstone, a great, flat, round, granite wheel, with a hole through its middle. Well, me an' Jon had to dig it out, y'see. We dug a fair deep pit around that stone, though we had t' get out pretty quick, because it began to shift. We were no sooner out than the stone toppled. It blocked the hole completely! Good job young Ben had a bright idea."

The labrador passed a thought from beneath the table to his master. "Tut tut, *you* had a bright idea?"

The boy's blue eyes twinkled as he slid a ham sandwich to his dog. "Sorry about that, pal, but it wasn't your idea, either, as I recall. Didn't you say Delia suggested that we use her to move the stone?"

The big dog huffed a bit as he dealt with the sandwich. "Aye, but I was the only one who knew what she was thinking. A very intelligent mare she is. Take my word!"

The dairyman farmer allowed Amy to continue with the tale.

"We passed a rope through the hole in the stone and threw it over a thick branch of the oak tree growing nearby. Will harnessed the rope to Delia and she hoisted the stone clear. As the stone came up, we saw something sticking up out of the hole. I thought it was an oak root at first. Mr. Mackay, tell them what it was!"

Brushing a crumb from his vest, the dapper lawyer allowed himself the briefest of smiles. "Ahem! It was the arm-piece from a suit of armor. Mr. Braithwaite identified the object as being from about the mid-1300s. Who knows, it could probably have belonged to Caran De Winn. We took it back to Mrs. Winn's house. The entire armpiece was sealed with tar on the outside and tallow within. When Jon Preston cut it open, there was the deed, perfectly preserved. A most timely and fortunate discovery, sir. The document states not only the title to ownership, but on the back, it also has a map, marking the boundaries of lands granted to Caran De Winn quite clearly.

"So, you see, my friends, my client is the owner of quite a considerable area, of which Chapelvale village is merely the centre! Mark Milestone East, and an arrow pointing downwards, that was all the clue we had to go on. But our united efforts brought about its successful conclusion. Remarkable!"

The magistrate took Mrs. Winn's hand. "Remarkable indeed. Madam, may I be the first to congratulate you upon your elevation to the squirearchy. You are, through the help of your friends, a very fortunate lady!"

The old lady blushed, fidgeting with her ecru linen gloves. "Why, thank you, sir. My late husband, Captain Winn, always said that the price of true friends is above that of gold. I wish he had lived to see himself as Squire of Chapelvale. He loved our village dearly, even though a great deal of his life was spent away from it, at sea. When things get back to normal, I am going to do something he would have approved of. I will grant to all the people of Chapelvale that piece of land which their home stands upon, house, shop, business, or farm. I can do that now that I legally own all this land, can't I?"

The magistrate rose to leave. "You can indeed, marm!"

Dai Evans came hurrying in with a tray of drinks, elderberry wine, beer, and lemonade, which he began serving to the party.

"Wait, sir, join us in a toast to our new squiress!"

Smiling, the magistrate raised his glass. "I'm not sure squiress is right, but whatever it is, I'm sure Mrs. Winn will perform her duties admirably, with all of you as her friends!"

Will Drummond raised his glass. "Aye, that's the toast. Friends."

As the company clinked glasses they chorused together. "To friends!"

Celebrations at Evans Tea Shoppe, and throughout the village, went on into the mid-noon. Now every villager was his or her own landlord, owning the actual ground their house or business stood upon. The square resounded to the noise of happy folk who had occupied the marquee previously set up for those who had planned the destruction of Chapelvale. Amy Somers was watching Blodwen Evans coaxing her brother to take on yet another portion of ice-cream, when she noticed that Ben and his dog had slipped away during the merry-making.

She found them sitting in the alley together, enjoying a respite away from the bustle and noise indoors. The dark-haired girl sat next to Ben, her back against the wall, noting how he and the dog were looking at each other.

"You two are talking together, I can tell."

Ben shrugged. "We're just exchanging a few thoughts, feeling happy for Miz Winn and the village. Old Ned looks happy, doesn't he?"

Amy stroked beneath the black labrador's chin. "Yes, he looks very happy indeed. I'll just sit here and be happy with you both."

Mischief danced in Ben's blue eyes, as he sighed peace-fully. "All you need for real happiness is the sun on your face and a friend by your side."

The girl smiled fondly at him. "That's nice, but what about Ned?"

The strange boy smiled back at her. "Ned's the friend I was talking about."

She dived on him, pummelling away playfully. "Ooh, you rotter!"

Ben giggled helplessly. "Mercy please, I meant you, too!"

The dog threw a thought in. "Go on, m'girl, teach the cheeky young pup a lesson!"

ONE MONTH LATER

SUMMER ROLLED ON TOWARDS AUTUMN.

One morning after breakfast, Ben and his dog accompanied Winnie into the village on her weekly shopping trip.

 They sauntered into the square together, Ned slightly ahead, carrying the woven cane basket in his jaws. Ben stared at the ground, scuffing the dusty cobbles. Winnie watched him with some concern.

"What is it, Ben, you don't look too cheerful today. Do you feel ill, is that it?"

The quiet boy flicked his hair aside and managed a smile. "Oh, I'll brighten up, I suppose. Didn't sleep too well last night, that's all. I'm all right, really."

The old lady's hand caressed his cheek. "You're thinking of leaving, aren't you."

Ben took the basket from his dog's mouth and handed it to her. He could not explain the dreams that had been haunting him for the past two nights. Booming waves, hissing surf, creaking rigging, and the slap of wet sails against taut ropes. Vanderdecken's ranting voice and his mad eyes. In his dreams the angel's voice echoed clear again.

"When you hear the toll of a church bell, you must leave this place and travel on!"

The boy turned his clouded blue eyes away from the old lady. "You do your shopping, Miz Winn. I'll go over to the almshouse and see how the new project's coming along."

She watched him walking across the square with Ned trotting alongside. A boy and his dog. A sudden sadness descended on her, and she called after her strange friend.

"I'll see you at Evans Tea Shoppe for lunch, Ben."

Without turning, he waved his hand.

As Ben dropped his hand, his big, black dog licked it. "I know, you don't have to tell me, mate, we share the same dreams, remember?"

Ben scratched the dog's ear gently. "Aye, we've left a lot of places behind in our travels, but this village and the friends we've made here . . . I tell you, it's going to be hard to leave Chapelvale."

Looking up, he saw Alex waving to them from the almshouse door.

Almost everybody was there. Amy threw an arm around Ben's shoulder, leading him into the building. Sheaves of reconstruction blueprints were laid out on the table. Jon, Will, Mr. Braithwaite, and Mr. Mackay were studying them. Amy coughed, waving her hand at the dust that was floating about. She called to Regina and her friends. "Stop that sweeping for a moment, please. Could you start carrying those benches outside?"

Her brother wrinkled his nose. "Oh, all right, bossy boots. Come on, Regina, Tommo, let's take this big one between us."

The old seaman took a pencil from behind his ear and

made a minor adjustment to one of the blueprints. "There, we can extend the evening tea garden out into the old graveyard at the rear."

Ben raised his eyebrows. "Evening tea garden?"

The girl nodded. "Wonderful idea, isn't it? Dai and Blodwen Evans are employing Hetty Sullivan to run the tea garden five evenings a week, after the Tea Shoppe closes in the late afternoon. They'll be supplying her with the materials, of course. Hetty's delighted with her new job. Show him the other plans, Curator Preston."

The old ship's carpenter assumed a mock dignified attitude. "Ahem, that's my new title, y'know, Curator Preston, of the Preston-Braithwaite Collection. I'm going to be Caretaker Handyman, too. Good, isn't it, I never had that many high-flown titles in my sailin' days. Mrs. Winn wants the old almshouse to be part of our village life, not an old ruin mouldering away unused at the corner of the square. Apart from rethatching the roof, and the addition of a window or two, the outside'll look pretty much the same, nice an' quaint.

"But inside there'll be the collection, the cross, chalice, candlesticks, and deeds, all in display cases, together with the story of how Chapelvale was saved. We all get a mention in it, even good old Ned. Then there's the evenin' tea garden and an extra room inside for any village meetings, dances, young people's events. We're even gettin' a small library—Mr. Braithwaite will be in charge of that. A proper little village hall for everyone to use, eh, lad!"

The boy shook his friend's big, tattooed hand heartily. "Sounds wonderful, mate. When will all the rebuilding work start?"

Mr. Mackay interrupted. The dapper little lawyer was

positively beaming. "First thing Monday morning, m'boy! My friend the magistrate and I visited the firm of Jackman Donning and Bowe in London last week. We came to an amicable agreement with them. This morning I received by special post a cheque for a considerable amount. Together with the express wish that the name of Jackman Donning and Bowe never be associated with past events in Chapelvale and the hope that all will be forgotten."

Mr. Mackay actually performed a small dance of triumph as he pulled forth the cheque and waved it over his head. "Sufficient funds for our almshouse restoration fund. The workmen arrive with materials on Monday morning, eight o'clock sharp!"

Mr. Braithwaite looked up from a list of new books he was studying. "Quite, er, very good, very, er, er, good. Yes!"

Will Drummond picked a crowbar from a wheelbarrow of tools he had brought from the farmhouse. "Aye, lad, meanwhile 'tis our job to clear all the rubbish from this almshouse an' make it ready. Here y'are, Curator Preston, the crowbar you asked for, sir!"

Jon hefted the long curved iron, moving to the centre of the room.

His blue eyes twinkled as he winked at Ben.

"You can lend a hand later, shipmate, but first there's something I've got to do, just to satisfy my own curiosity."

The boy gave his friend a puzzled look. "Of course I'll help, but what's the crowbar for?"

The old seaman looked up at the ceiling. It was cracked, damp-stained, and bellied. "Ever since I first docked at this almshouse I've wondered what that big, ugly hump atop of the roof could be. I ain't going to let no team o' strange workmen find out afore I do. So cover your eyes an' mouths, everybody. There's goin' to be a load of old dust an' rubbish an' whitewash comin' down.

"Stand clear now, pals. Here goes!"

Whump! Bump! Thud!

A mess of dried rushes, twigs, old plaster, and limewash showered down. Ben and the others shielded their eyes and noses. Jon shaded both eyes with a hand as he battered furiously at the growing gap in the ceiling.

Crack! Whump! Thud! Whack!

He stopped a moment and stared into the huge, dark cavity he had made. "Push that table over here, quick!"

Suddenly Ben knew. He grabbed Ned's collar and hurried outside. The black labrador sensed it, too. They began running to get as far away from the almshouse as possible, both knowing that they would not outdistance the sound of inevitable fate.

The ground beneath Ben seemed to sway, like the deck of the *Flying Dutchman*, and cold sweat broke out on his face, like seaspray. The distant hiss of escaping steam from a train pulling into the station sounded as if it were the gales off the coast of Tierra del Fuego, so long ago, so far away.

"Leave this place, do not stay to watch your friends grow old and die one by one, while you are still young. You must go!" At the sound of the angel's voice, the dog increased his speed, pulling at his master's hand on his collar, dragging Ben along with him.

Jon stood on the table. He had not noticed Ben and his dog going; amid the curtain of dust and falling rubbish, neither had the others. Will climbed up alongside the old ship's carpenter, holding up a lighted lantern. "What is it?

What's up there, Jon?"

"It's a bell, Will! That's what the hump was, a little bell tower. Our new village centre will have a bell! Listen!" The old seaman swung the crowbar and struck the inside of the bell. *Booonnnnggggg!* The sound of the bell boomed out over Chapelvale.

As the brazen echoes reverberated far and near, a baby cried.

Eileen popped her head through the back window of the almshouse, looking none too pleased. "Stop that noise this instant! I just got little Willum nicely to sleep out 'ere, now you gone an' wakened 'im, poor mite."

The old man lowered the crowbar sheepishly, stating his excuse. "But, marm, that's the first time the bell's sounded in nigh on three hundred years!"

Eileen stood with her hands on her hips. "Oh is it now, well, let it be the last for the moment. Get down from that table, Will Drummond, an' you, too, Jon Preston. Standin' up there like two naughty children, covered in dust an' muck an' I don't know what. You should see yourselves!"

Will climbed from the table, dusting himself off. "Sorry, my love, you go an' have a nice cup o' tea at Evans, I'll get Willum back to sleep again."

Amy could not help smiling at the two big men, now friends. As Jon got off the table, she brushed whitewash flakes from his beard. "Go on, the pair of you, take Eileen over for tea and crumpets. I'll see to Willum."

Jon threw his arms about Will and Eileen. "Come on, you two, let's do as Amy says—my treat, though!"

They were halfway across the square when Jon noticed his friend's absence. "Wait, I'll go an' ask Ben if he an' Ned want t'come to the Tea Shoppe with us."

Eileen gave him a playful shove. "Go on with you, what does the lad want with old fogies like us? Ben's prob'ly lookin' after little Willum with Amy. Leave the young 'uns to themselves, you great fusspot!"

The farmer was in full agreement with his wife. "Aye, she's a pretty girl an' he's an 'andsome lad. Leave 'em be, mate."

An engine tooted and the stationmaster's whistle shrilled over at the railway station. Jon checked his old pocket watch. "There goes the ten-fifty, right on time."

Eileen patted a cloud of dust from the old carpenter's back. "I've never been on a train! Huh, progress they calls it. Noisy, great, smelly things. Trains are only for travellin' folk an' those in a hurry to leave home. I ain't in no rush t'go runnin' off. Chapelvale's my home!"

ONE WEEK LATER

SATURDAY ARRIVED AGAIN, MISTY AT FIRST, but soon clearing up to reveal a warm, soft day. Mrs. Winn had done her shopping, but there was so much of it that she

had paid the delivery boy to take it up to the house. Evans Tea Shoppe was pleasantly busy. She sat alone at the window, reading and rereading the precious letter she had received.

Blodwen Evans brought a pot of tea and Mrs. Winn's usual tea cake to the table. Winnie caught her trying to glance at the letter and covered it with her handbag. Pretending she had not been trying to pry, Blodwen looked through the window.

"Look you, 'ere's Amy an' Alex."

As the young people drew closer, Winnie tapped the windowpane with her worn gold wedding ring, beckoning them inside. "Bring ice-cream and lemonade for them, please, Blodwen."

The brother and sister seated themselves in the window corner. The old lady poured herself tea. "What are you two up to today, still helping Jon at the almshouse? He's not short of willing hands these days."

Alex settled himself back against the cushion. "We're going to help him build a new fence and gate for the front."

Mrs. Winn sliced her tea cake precisely into four and leaned closer to Amy, keeping her voice low. "I hope you're over the weeps and sniffles now. Come on, let's see a little smile?"

The girl tried a smile, which did not quite work. She looked down at the tablecloth. "We still haven't heard from him, Miz Winn."

Alex blinked several times and sniffed. "We liked Ben, and Ned, too—why did they have to go? It's not fair!"

There was silence. Alex looked away through the window as Winnie did her best to answer the question. "There's a lot in life that isn't fair, you'll find that out as you grow older. When Ben first came to me, he said that he could only stay awhile, I never pressed him about it. He was a bit of a mystery, I suppose as much to you as to me, a good boy, a real friend, but so strange. What made him leave so suddenly I'll never know—his rucksack and change of clothes are still in his room. Did he ever mention leaving to you?"

Amy dabbled her ice-cream spoon thoughtfully. "I remember the afternoon we met him outside the station. I asked him would he be staying in Chapelvale, he just said, I don't know, maybe. As if he was teasing, or just shrugging the question off. I could never tell with Ben. He had those sort of eyes, cloudy blue sometimes, bright, shining blue at other times. They could twinkle and smile, make you feel happy somehow. But often they would grow distant and mysterious, so you couldn't tell what was going on behind them."

Mrs. Winn watched Amy apply herself to the ice-cream. "I sensed the same thing. Perhaps not as much as you did, but I'm an old lady and you're about the same age as Ben, so you understand him better. What about you, Alex?"

Alex snorted on his lemonade. "Boys don't notice things like that about their pals, but I liked Ned's eyes. They were friendly, brown I think. I know this much about Ben, though. He made me feel brave . . . I'm not scared . . . not of bullies or anything these days. That's why I miss him so much, he could've taught me lots more if he'd stayed. I bet you miss him, too, Miz Winn?"

The old lady pursed her lips. "It's different when one's older. I tell myself I remember Ben fondly and I always will. You and I, this whole village, look at the mess we were in before he came. Ben changed all that by getting us to help each other. I think of him as my gift, loaned to me for a while, like a kind of good angel. But that sounds silly, doesn't it. Nobody could imagine a rough-and-ready angel with a great black dog lolloping round at his heels!"

At the thought of it, they all burst out laughing. Mrs. Winn touched the corners of her eyes with a handkerchief. "Oh dear, what a vision. But now, would you like to hear some good news? I received a letter today. This'll cheer you up. It certainly made me come alive again."

Amy touched the letter sticking out from beneath the handbag. "Is this it?"

The old lady beamed with pleasure. "It certainly is, would you like to read it out to Alex and me? Well, go on!"

Mrs. Winn's happiness was complete. She even let Blodwen Evans hover nearby to listen as her young friend read the letter. " 'Hello, Mum! It's your wandering son Jim putting pen to paper. Sorry I haven't written for a while, but here's some exciting news for you. My wife Lilian and I have been thinking lately of moving back to dear old England. We miss it a lot. Jamie and Rodney are growing into fine big sons. Would you believe, Jamie was fourteen last week and Rodney turned twelve in April.

" 'School is a bit makeshift in Ceylon, or should I say was, because we've taken them out of it and decided on coming home to get them a proper education. Most of all, they want to see their grandma and Chapelvale. How is the old place? I'm always telling Jamie and Rod about when I was a boy in the village. They're dying to see it. Well, we've got sufficient savings from my investments, and Lilian would like to purchase a house in Chapelvale. I'll turn my hand to some sort of new job (you know me, jack-of-all-trades, or should I say Jim, ha ha). We are at present aboard the steamship *Ocean Monarch*, travelling to England, expect to be there within ten days of you receiving my letter.

" 'Now, don't fuss, Mum. No need to come hurrying up to Liverpool docks to meet us. We'll make our own way to Chapelvale quite easily. I understand you've got a train line running to there now. You can meet us at the station. Got to close now, due at the captain's table for dinner. See you soon, love from your son Jim, Lilian, and the boys. X X X X

" 'P.S. Hope you know some nice young folks the boys can pal up with.' "

Alex clenched his fists, squinched his face up, and shuddered with delight. "Nice young folks like us, Miz Winn!"

Will slapped his hand down on the table. "Ahah, thought I'd find you here. Come on. You, too, Jon. We're just goin' 'round to your dad's, Alex. One of my cows, Buttercup, she's in calf. Eileen an' Ma are with 'er now. It's a bit early, but she's due today, Ma says. So, would you like to see one o' my baby calves bein' born?"

Amy and Alex chorused eagerly. "Yes, please, Will!"

Jon was already hurrying out to the cartful of young people.

"Last one in the gig doesn't get scones an' cream at the farm!"

Winnie stayed where she was, watching them pile in.

"Regina, did you save me a place?"

"Course I did. Hurry up, Alex!"

"Shove over, Tommo!"

"Amy, sit here by me!"

"Ahoy there, what about me?"

"You'll have to run behind, Jon. Hahaha!"

"Up here by me, Jon. Good job Delia's a big, strong gal!"

"I'm with ye, Will. Gee up, Delia!"

Winifred Winn sat watching the sunlight's lovely play through the fine haze of dust they had left as the gig sped from the village square. Dreams she had never dared to dream had come true. Yet in the midst of all her happiness she felt a tinge of sadness, picturing the towheaded lad and his dog a short while ago, crossing the square. He was wearing the new outfit she had bought for him, the black labrador trotted at his side faithfully. They halted halfway across the square. He flicked the blond hair from his eyes and stood there. Those blue eyes had never seemed so bright. Ned barked once, Ben raised his arm, shouting as he waved.

"Miz Winn!"

She half rose from her chair, the name forming on her lips.

"Ben . . ."

Then the dust settled and an old lady was left gazing at an empty village square.